CW00847367

THE SOUL BANK

ADAM ECCLES

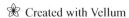 Created with Vellum

For Robin & Willow

About the Author

Adam Eccles is a sarcastic, cynical, tech-nerd hermit, living in the west of Ireland for the last couple of decades, or so.

www.AdamEcclesBooks.com

facebook.com/AdamEcclesWrites

twitter.com/AdamEcclesBooks

Chapter One

Excruciating, awkward, stressful and generally weird. Dinner parties…

Willingly inviting other humans into your home to consume nutrients and alcohol in your presence. Why do we do it?

Kirsty has been fussing in the kitchen all day, and I awoke to a text message containing a long list of chores to complete.

Why the upstairs en-suite shower needed to be scrubbed for a dinner party, I'll never understand. But that, among many other seemingly pointless tasks, has been my Saturday so far. The prize at the end of it; having to endure Kirsty's obnoxious friends all evening as they get louder and drunker. Fabulous.

The only saving grace is that my best mate, Dave, was allowed to be invited, as long as I took responsibility for him behaving himself.

That restriction is in place since one time Dave came over and perhaps partook of slightly too many beverages, and we found him asleep in the bathtub the next morning in nothing but his underpants. I say we, but it was Kirsty who found him and then screamed blue-murder. A bit over the top, if you ask me. I mean, who hasn't found themselves semi-naked in someone's tub after a heavy night? At least he hadn't puked or shat himself.

Taking responsibility for Dave is like trying to stop a speeding train with a rolled-up newspaper. It's an impossible and thankless task, but my secret ingredient in the mix is his current girlfriend, Michelle. They've only been going out a few weeks, so he might tone it down a bit for her benefit. Then again, he could go all out crazy and end up pissing in the plant pots. You just never know with Dave.

Laura and Nathan… They have their own brand of bad behaviour, but theirs is more socially acceptable, according to Kirsty, as they have money and status. Knob-heads, the both of them, if you ask me. Still, Laura is Kirsty's best mate from school days. What can you do?

Laura got with Nathan a couple of years ago now, and I've hated the twat since the first time I met him. An accountant, but all modern and edgy. Hair carefully messed up, jeans ripped in all the right places. Bright-red Tesla. Always vaping something fruity. By that, I mean banana or apples or forest-berries, not weed. Mind you, I'm pretty sure he's dabbled with some pharmaceutical powders in his time. There's something about him that sets me on edge. Gives me a shiver thinking about him.

Laura isn't too bad, I suppose. If you can get past her constant judgemental looks, which are likely the cause of Kirsty's panic and fluster all day. She's some kind of consultant for god knows what high-paying malarkey. I never paid attention.

· · ·

The menu tonight was carefully chosen; not too expensive, not too cheap. Artsy, but not fartsy. Kirsty is making something from a Jamie Oliver cookbook. Supplemented, of course, with several twenty-quid bottles of wine. Costing us a bloody fortune, this dinner.

Why do we do it? Well, I know why Kirsty does it. She says she enjoys the company, that we barely ever socialise and go out any more. She reckons a dinner is a grounding and wholesome thing, and that we need to get out of our shells and mingle. But mostly, I think she likes to show off at any excuse.

This particular dinner excuse is to discuss our impending group holiday with Laura and Nathan. Two weeks in Portugal with those knobs. I'm looking forward to that as much as a dog looks forward to the castration anaesthetic at the vet.

Why do I do it? As I plod into the kitchen and catch sight of Kirsty stirring a pot of something, done up in her party dress, heels and stockings, low cut and skin tight, I'm reminded of exactly why I do it; Kirsty.

She's bloody gorgeous, always was, always will be. Ten out of ten and way out of my league. We've been together for six years now, and I don't know how I managed it. So putting up with this dinner and holiday is a small price to pay. Well, the holiday wasn't a small price, I can tell you. But it's Kirsty's thirtieth birthday present, and she chose all of it and paid for half of it. I can't complain. No, I can and do, but she doesn't listen.

For my thirtieth, we went to the local Chinese and then watched some crap on Netflix.

"Smells good." I peer over her shoulder into the saucepan, catching a glance of her cleavage and a grope of her pert bum as I do.

"Oi, you. Keep your hands off the merchandise!" She laughs and passes me a teaspoon. "Taste this, will you?"

"What is it?"

"Marsala gravy for the duck."

"Very fancy." I take a spoonful and taste it. "Not bad, not bad at all. Maybe just a pinch more salt?"

"Salt isn't good for you, Andy."

"Tastes good, though."

"So does chocolate. Doesn't make it good for you."

"Whatever you say, my darling." I leave her to it with a casual look back at her delicious arse. "You know best."

"Too right!" She wiggles her behind a little for my benefit. "Put my playlist on, please."

I wander into the living room and flick on the stereo. Obviously, I'm not allowed to play my choice of music as it would be 'inappropriate' for the evening. 'Kirsty's Dinner Tunes' it is, then. I tap the iPad and mellow notes seep into the room.

I flop down on the couch and check my phone. All my chores are ticked off and done. I'm dressed, showered, cologned and ready for the onslaught. Might even have time for a sly can before they all show up to ease the stress.

A text message buzzes into my hand from Dave. 'Soz, mate. Gonna have to cancel dinner. Something has come up.'

Seriously?

I reply. 'What! You are meant to be my buffer here. What are you doing?'

A photo arrives, and I wish I hadn't asked. A blurry picture of his protruding middle finger, on top of what looks like… A pair of tits. Lovely. He's doing 'it' right now while he's texting. How romantic.

'Well, hurry and finish and get over here.'

Another photo arrives; a forest of empty and squashed Heineken cans on the coffee table, spilling onto the floor. A pair of knickers haphazardly draped across the cans. 'Never mind.' I sigh. Now I'll have to cover for the dickhead and listen to Kirsty's wrath and 'told you so'

I get up off my arse and go back to the kitchen.

"Need a hand?"

Kirsty scoffs at me. "Everything is taken care of now. Could have used your help earlier, though."

"I was scrubbing the shower and wiping the upstairs windows, for some reason."

"Hmm."

I can't tell the intention of that mumble, but I carry on, unfettered. "Bad news, I'm afraid."

She looks over at me, still stirring on the stove. "What?"

I motion with my phone. "Dave can't make it." She looks blank. "He got called into work at the last minute. Some support issue in Boston."

Kirsty raises an eyebrow but says nothing. She pauses for a moment, then looks at me dead on. "I hope you are hungry. There's two spare meals now."

Smooth, Andy. Smooth. I think she swallowed it and I get extra dinner.

"Bloody starving, as it goes."

"Good. You can have a night off the diet, then." She smiles. "I can't say I'm surprised, honestly, but you could have come up with a better lie."

"Hey?"

"I can read you like a book, Andy. Dave isn't doing support for Boston, is he?"

I turn away. "Umm, well, no. Not strictly speaking."

"What's he doing, then?"

"Banging Michelle." I assume it's Michelle, anyway. Hard to tell as I've never seen her tits before.

Kirsty tuts. "Why do you bother covering for him, Andy?"

I shrug. "He's my mate."

"Well, it'll just be us and Laura and Nathan, then." She smiles. "Nice and snug."

"Yeah." I sigh inside.

———

"I was just admiring your knockers." Nathan and Laura appear at the door, fifteen minutes early. I shoot a sideways look at Kirsty, who blushes a little, then switches to a scowl and looks up at Nathan expectantly. "On the door." He points to the brass door knockers, one above the other, rather than my girlfriend's ample and unsubtly exposed bosom. Crisis averted.

A flurry of hugs, triple-cheek-kisses and manly handshakes ensue, and Laura gushes over how fabulous Kirsty looks, downplaying the seven-hour stint she's no doubt been on at the salon before she arrived. The way she says it hints at sympathy, rather than awe. 'Wow, despite your minuscule income and plain looks, you've managed to look great!' I internally roll my eyes and try to be patient. The nuance seems to be lost on Kirsty, who returns the compliments.

"Where did you get them, if you don't mind me asking? The knockers." Nathan, towering at six-four, in a pink shirt and faded, ripped blue-jeans, stoops down to address me.

"Err, I'm not sure. They sort of came with the house." I raise an eyebrow.

"Strange that there's two of them."

"It is a bit, but maybe they had a BOGOF deal at the time?" Nathan looks blank. "Buy one, get one free."

"Ah, yes. Maybe." Sarcasm is apparently below Nathan's level.

"Come through to the living room," Kirsty ushers everyone in. "Andy, fetch some drinks if you please."

"Yes, Madam." I turn to Laura, "Would the lady prefer red or white?"

"Glass of white would be lovely, thanks, Andy."

"Nathan?" I turn to the jolly pink giant. No point in offering him a beer.

"Yes, white… Please." His pause duration before adding the 'please' feels like a kick to the stomach. A perfunctory addition, rather than a pleasantry. Glass with the chip in it for Nathan, coming right up.

I already know what Kirsty wants. She'll have exactly the same as her friends, so as not to draw attention and seem odd. I slope off to the kitchen, leaving them to mingle.

"There's only the four of us tonight, Dave and Michelle couldn't make it, I'm afraid. They called him away for a work thing." We sit down at the table to beautifully arranged starter plates of salad, and tiny spring rolls that Kirsty made from scratch this morning. Drizzled with something pungent, dark and tangy. I'm thankful she went with my excuse plan, but it's probably out of embarrassment rather than any loyalty to me or Dave.

"That's a shame." Laura looks at me with her sympathy grin.

"And why I don't work in support." Nathan pipes up, chuckling and slurping four quids' worth of wine in one gulp.

"Dave is the global escalation manager for IT systems, not really support."

"Well, you know, that kind of thing." He waves vaguely.

Yeah, can't wait to spend two weeks away with these people... I smile and pick up my glass. "Well, a toast to Kirsty for creating this wonderful spread. Looks amazing, babe."

Kirsty blushes and smiles. Laura and Nathan spring into action, wine at the ready. "Absolutely. Looks wonderful."

"Thank you. Well, tuck in everyone."

I'm permitted to scarf down my seconds, but only if I do it surreptitiously in the kitchen as I take empty plates back. Otherwise, it may seem crass, so Kirsty said. Whatever. I sneak a duck-leg and a spring roll and return with a fresh bottle of wine. None the wiser. To be honest, they probably didn't even notice I was gone from the table.

The discussion is around the best restaurants that no one knows about in Lisbon, discovered only by Laura on previous trips. I'm getting tired of hearing about it, and I wonder if our budget for meals is going to last more than three days into the holiday. I hadn't bargained for the extravaganza that Laura seems to be planning. I'll stick to the salad, I guess. Two weeks of rabbit food for me, and booze snuck into the hotel room from whatever passes for an offy out there.

The urge to pull my phone out and fart around on Reddit is almost overwhelming. I instinctively reach down to my pocket and have to stop myself many times. If Kirsty caught me browsing now, I'd get the silent treatment for days, and no chance of a ride for weeks. Best behaviour, Andy. Don't forget we're living in the moment.

I wouldn't be tempted to drift off if I was part of the conversation, but they've moved on to art and museums and this entire trip sounds like an expensive stint in Yawnsville. Lying around on a secluded beach, then browsing through dusty museums. If I wanted to be bored to death, I could stay at home and go to work.

Memories of our first trip, just me and Kirsty, come flooding back, and I feel a grin spread across my face. We'd only been seeing each other a few months, and it was a rare occasion that we got time to ourselves. I lived with my sister, temporarily, and Kirsty shared a flat with two other girls. A long weekend away together in Bruges was like having a taste of heaven. Granted, I mostly only saw the hotel room ceiling, but when we made it out of the room for mulled red wine and waffles, it was like being in a fairytale. The taste of snow as I kissed the flakes from Kirsty's nose was better than anything in Jamie Oliver's repertoire.

Good times, those. I remember we walked by a jeweller's shop, and I was that close to going in and buying her a ring, then and there. But my bank balance stopped me, and the moment never came up again since. I think about marriage occasionally, but Kirsty has never once mentioned it. I keep quiet because once you go down that road, there's only one logical conclusion. Babies. I'm not ready for that. I can't even adequately look after myself. Responsibility is for adults, isn't it? Not thirty-five-year-old kids.

· · ·

"You are very quiet, Andy." Laura, the droopy side of tipsy, reaches over the table and grabs my arm. "Are you looking forward to the trip?"

Stunned, I glance at Kirsty, but she's midst some animated discussion with Nathan. "Err. Yeah, course. Be a laugh."

"Anything particular you want to see or do?" I can't tell if she's flirting or just drunk and unaware. Her hand on my arm remains, a finger gently stroking up and down. Do I pull away now, or ignore it? The longer I don't make a move, the more awkward it will get.

What I'm mostly looking forward to is sleeping in every day and catching up on some reading. But I don't think that's what she wants to hear.

"I wonder if there are any gigs on? Some live music is always good."

"I'm sure we can find something to keep you entertained." Laura brushes back her hair and leans forward, granting me a view of her tanned cleavage. What's going on here?

I take the opportunity to pick up a wine bottle and offer her a top-up. Not that I think she needs more booze, but just to break contact.

"You trying to get me drunk, Andy?" She grins. "Go on then, but I won't be responsible for my actions."

I laugh, trying to defuse a potential bomb. "Right, yeah. No, just being polite."

Laura pushes her glass over to me with a subtle lick of her lips. Bloody hell.

"Laura, what's the name of that…" I'm thankful for the interruption from Nathan.

"Columbano." She replies without even looking over at him. Her eyes fixed on me. I've known her for years now, but this has never happened before. She's always been standoffish and fake. I thought she didn't even like me.

"… Artist. That's him, thank you, darling."

"Would anyone like coffee?" I stand up, leveraging the opportunity to move away.

Laura isn't unattractive by any measure. If I wasn't with Kirsty, I'd jump at this chance. But I am, and I don't play around. It's not in me to do it.

Kirsty looks up and nods with a smile. I'm being a delightful host. Might get a lay tonight if things go well. Another reason to keep away from Laura.

As the coffee percolates into everyone, Laura seems to stiffen up a little, losing interest in me, rejoining the conversation with Nathan and Kirsty as we adjourn to the living room. Another crisis averted. Probably best Dave didn't come tonight, as I know for a fact he'd have sniffed out horniness and found a way to drag Laura upstairs and sneak a shag in, leaving Michelle and me to discuss curtain fabric. She works in a home furnishing superstore place, so that isn't an exaggeration.

I perch on the arm of the sofa next to Kirsty, and try my best to contribute to the discussion, but the architecture and history of a distant country I know almost nothing about, is far from my field of expertise. If they wanted to talk about the history of the x86 Microprocessor, or server network architecture, well, that's more my cup of tea.

Chapter Two

"Morning, babe. Brought you some brekky." I clear a space on Kirsty's nightstand and put down a tray for her breakfast in bed. Surprisingly, I woke up early, no hangover, feeling fresh and chipper. A first for me in a long time. I took the opportunity to clean up the kitchen, drink my coffee on the couch, browsing on the iPad, and then make a nice brekky for Her Highness, all in the peace and quiet of a Sunday in the suburbs. I even plucked a daisy from outside and put it in a shot glass as decoration.

"Oh, wow. You shouldn't have, Andy. Thanks." Bed-head hair, eyes closed and no makeup, Kirsty is still beautiful. "But I'm not sure I can face food yet. What is it?"

"Glass of juice, freshly squeezed, pancakes freshly microwaved, and a bowl of mixed fruit freshly cut up."

"Aww, you are so good to me." Kirsty squints open an eye, then rapidly shuts it again. "Ugh, you couldn't add a couple of aspirin to that, could you?"

I chuckle. "Coming right up."

I return with a glass of water with two plink-plonks in it and drop it down on the tray. Kirsty is absent. I assume she's in the bathroom. As I turn to leave her to it, and get back to my news article on the fascinating subject of augmented reality and machine learning, Kirsty reappears from the bathroom. A vision in a purple nightie.

"Thanks, Andy. It was a lovely evening, wasn't it?"

"Yeah, not bad, after all." A white lie to keep the peace. I mean, it wasn't terrible, but it wasn't exactly much fun for me, either. Could have been worse, I suppose.

"I can't face breakfast yet, but you know what I do fancy?" A smirk bubbles onto her face, and she nods towards the bed. With a deft shrug and a nudge, her nightie falls to the floor. She stands in front of me, naked and inviting. Game on!

Startled from the dream-like haze of post-fun-time snuggles, the sound of heavy thuds from downstairs is enough to rattle us into reality. Another thud, followed by the shrill ring of the doorbell.

"Ugh." Kirsty groans and pulls a pillow over her head. "Andy, can you get that?"

"What time is it?" I turn over and pick up my phone. "Shit."

"What?"

"It's eleven. That's Rissa. I completely forgot."

"Ugh." Kirsty pulls the duvet up over the pillow.

"See you later, then."

I get up and go to the window. Sure enough, my sister is

standing on the path, jogging on the spot. I clamber to open the window and stick my head out.

"Be down in a second." She nods and jogs off down the path and up the road. That woman can't keep still for a moment.

I pull my sweatpants and t-shirt on, grab my phone, attempt to kiss Kirsty goodbye, but end up just reaching under the covers and grabbing something, probably an arm, and gently squeezing.

"Say hi to Clarissa from me." A muffled voice calls out.

"Yeah. Love you."

"I'm going back to sleep. Lock the door."

"Took your time." Clarissa has probably already jogged fifty miles this morning. She's here to take me for a run. A first step, literally, in my attempt at fitness, or something like it. Kirsty instigated this plan, with Riss ridiculously keen to pick me up as a student. I think my little sister just wants the opportunity to lecture me and laugh at my failings. I complained that my work is largely responsible for my situation. I do spend an inordinate amount of time sat on my arse at a desk. What can you do? Run, apparently.

"Forgot. Sorry."

"Never mind, here now. You ready?"

"Not really. But, whatever." I feel like I've already had my workout for the day, but I won't bring that up now. Should have had a shower. Never mind, I suppose. "Kirsty says hi, by the way."

"She should come with us, one day."

"Doubt if she'd be into that. She doesn't like to get too sweaty." Although… I clear my throat to hide a snigger.

"Right, well, off we go then. We'll start slow and build up."

"Okay." I take a deep breath and brace myself for disaster.

Rissa takes off and I follow, as best I can. She zooms away and by the end of our road, she's twenty paces ahead, not looking back. "Hey… I thought you said we would start slow!" I'm breathless already. Bloody hell. How did I get so pathetic?

"This is slow." She stops and turns to face me. Not a bead of sweat to be seen, but as I approach her and judder to a halt, I have to lean on someone's wall for support.

"Hang on a sec." I pant and wipe the sweat from my brow, pausing for a moment while Rissa rolls her eyes and tuts at me. When I can catch my breath again, I stand up, four inches taller than my very-little sister, but light years behind her in physical ability.

"I think this may have been a mistake."

"The only mistake was leaving it this long, Andy. You are making the right moves here. It's just going to take some time to build you up."

"Well, yeah. I've spent my entire career sat on my arse in front of computers."

"Yeah, and the rest of your days eating takeaway and watching TV."

I can't deny it, but that's what you do, isn't it? Is there something else I should be doing?

"Can we just walk the rest of the route? I was feeling great this morning until now."

She sighs. "Fine, but next time we're stepping it up."

"Don't tell Kirsty, yeah?"

"Andy…" She turns to face me. "Grow a pair of balls!"

"Eh?"

"Stick up for yourself."

"We're off soon on that holiday. She wants us to look beach-worthy. Nathan is a lanky twat, and Laura, I think she spends half her week in beauty parlours."

"Should have started months ago, then."

"Yeah, well… Which reminds me, can you water the plants while we're away?"

"Sure."

We get to the park and Clarissa can't help herself. She speeds up her walk by at least thirty percent.

"I thought you didn't like Nathan and Laura?"

"I don't. Especially Nathan."

"Why are you going to Portugal with them, then?"

"Kirsty's thirtieth."

"Yeah, I know, but… Still."

I shrug in a 'what can you do,' way. Riss flashes me a look. I change the subject. "Oh, can you give me a lift to the train station tonight?"

"Where you going?"

"Bloody work thing. Early meeting in the home counties. Staying in a hotel tonight and back tomorrow evening. Not looking forward to it, but Big Ron insisted it was necessary."

"Can't Kirsty take you? I'm a busy woman, you know."

"She's got a dance class. Some bloke she reckons looks like Antonio Bandyarse or whatever his name is, teaches a Spanish dancing class, so she signed up."

"Oh, yeah? Might try that myself." She flashes me a wink. "Is Dave going?"

"To the work thing, yeah. I don't think he'd be into Antonio strutting his stuff."

She chuckles. "No, probably not. Why don't you get a lift with him, then?"

I stop dead, dramatically. "Clarissa, I will NEVER get into a vehicle or any other means of conveyance with that man again in my life! Not a car, not a hot-air-balloon, not a fucking fairground bumper-car. That man should not be allowed a license nor a right foot."

"Safe driver, is he?"

"He thinks the speed limits are minimums. He thinks bridges are stunt ramps, he thinks the handbrake is for making right turns. The last time he 'gave me a lift' I had to spend the afternoon in therapy to recover. No, I would rather crawl all the way on broken glass than get into a car with Dave 'F1' Jackson!"

She can't help but laugh. "Fine, what time?"

"I need to be at the station at seven."

"Right. Better press on then."

Clarissa steps up her speed-walk into what I'm sure she thinks is a slow-jog, but after a few hundred yards, I'm back to panting and wheezing again. I slow down but carry on. Push through the pain. If I collapse and die here in the park, at least it's a nice day.

By the time I get home, I'm a wreck. I can't even muster the energy to say goodbye to Riss, so I vaguely wave as she casually speeds up to her usual pace, and jogs off home. She's like the Energizer Bunny, that one.

I flop down on the couch in a silent house. High town-house ceiling, the scent of green tea on the air, net curtains gently swaying in a light breeze, the room is carefully set up to be perfectly relaxing.

Kirsty is cither still asleep or gone out somewhere. I check my phone and there's no messages, but at one o'clock, I can't imagine she's still in bed. I'll have to let my body relax for a moment before I can climb the stairs to check. Instead, I fish for the remote on the couch and flick on the TV for some inane rubbish to numb my senses, before I have to pack my bag for the trip tonight.

"Wake up, lazybones!"

For the second time today, I'm shocked into the real world from the misty-haze of dreamland. Kirsty stands over me with several expensive-looking bags of shopping. Oh, no…

"Got some things for you to try on."

"What? I wasn't asleep. Just resting."

"Sure." She rolls her eyes. "Oh, how was your run?"

I shuffle off the couch and feel my leaden legs strain the muscles within. I'm sure I've torn or sprained something. "Yeah, not bad, actually." No, not bad. Bloody awful, in fact. Kirsty smiles.

"Come on, then. I'll show you what I got."

She skips off up the stairs and I slowly follow. Each step a mountain to climb. I'm sure that Rissa and Kirsty are right. I am unfit and in need of exercise. But does it have to be so painful?

Kirsty has laid out various items of clothing on the bed when I get to the bedroom. I know at a glance, these are not my thing.

"What do you think?" She seems excited.

"Err, about what?"

"I got you some holiday clothes."

I pick up a pair of khaki shorts that are basically old-man slacks cut down. Under a pile of shirts, I spot the same pink shade that Nathan was wearing yesterday. This is going to end badly.

"Try them on." She urges.

If there's one thing I hate more than jogging, it's trying on clothes. I don't want to be studied, and I'm no model.

"Thanks, Kirsty, for getting me some gear, but…" Her face switches to bitch-mode. "I already have some shorts and stuff."

"You needed an upgrade. I'm not walking around with you in your nasty old threadbare junk." There it is. The real reason. She is embarrassed to be seen with me.

"How much did you spend?"

"Just a few hundred." She waves it off.

"Bloody hell. Have you got the receipts?"

"Andy, you needed new clothes."

"Sorry, but these aren't really my style…" I pick up an orange short-sleeved shirt with a pineapple motif all over it.

"Exactly, your style is terrible. This is your new style." She waves a hand over the bed where it looks like a sixty-year-old American tourist has just unpacked his luggage.

"What's wrong with jeans and a plain t-shirt?"

"Don't you want to look good on holiday?" She huffs. "Anyway, I got you a pair of jeans" She points to a pair of faded blue jeans with carefully pre-made holes in them, just like Nathan wears.

"Not really, if I'm honest. I want to be comfortable." And I certainly don't want to be a clone of Nathan. "I didn't know you were going shopping today. I could have come with you, and we could have picked stuff out together."

"We'd have ended up with nothing, that's why I went alone."

Kirsty sits down on the bed, where only a few brief hours ago we made mad, passionate love. Now a tear runs down her cheek. "I was just trying to be nice and get you some new clothes."

I sigh and sit down next to her. "Sorry, babe. I know." She leans into me and buries her face in my chest. "I'll have a look through and try some stuff on, okay?"

A sniff indicates an acknowledgement. I stroke her hair and glance back at the pile of clothes I'm now obligated to wear.

I check my watch. "Shall we get takeaway now, before I go off?"

Kirsty sits back up, abruptly. "Oh, are you still going?"

"Work meeting in the morning. I have to pack and prep."

"I wish you didn't have to go."

"Believe me, I don't want to. A shitty hotel next to an industrial estate, then a long day of meetings is exactly what I don't want. But work, you know. What can you do?"

Kirsty stands up and walks towards the door. "Go order food, then. I'll have my usual."

Chapter Three

There's nothing so dull, boring and soul-sucking as a corporate hotel on the edge of an industrial estate, serving the visitors to the various factories and businesses within. Every corridor a reflection of the last. A burrowing maze of identical, reasonably priced rooms, each with an air conditioner that rattles, a kettle that leaks and an ironing board that wobbles.

Even the staff are dreary. And most of them look like they are still in school. Painted over with false smiles at seven in the morning, wishing me a wonderful day as I pour skimmed milk over a bowl of dried twigs, and decant a tiny glass full of orange juice that always somehow tastes off.

They know we aren't here for fun. Not one single guest in this hotel has ever come here for a holiday. This is work; boring, exhausting, inconvenient and annoying.

· · ·

I got here last night around ten, after a long train ride, and as I stepped out of the taxi at the hotel, a massive clap of thunder punctuated my arrival, quickly followed by a downpour of proportions that I haven't witnessed in a long time. I got absolutely drenched just running from the cab to reception.

Hopefully, not a portent of the day ahead, but it kept me awake half the night, rattling and shaking the windows with every flash, before the storm poured itself out around four. Must have been right over us. I think this place is at the bottom of a little valley.

My room is on the ground floor. Room thirteen… Not that I'm superstitious. However, I was a bit worried I'd wake up under six feet of water, but as it turns out, the only water in the room was the tepid dribble from the shower.

I thought I'd see Dave in the bar last evening, but he was nowhere to be found, and no reply from the numerous texts I sent. I presume he was either still on the way down, or already out and sampling the local hostelries. I downed a swift pint in the bar at the back of the hotel, then called it a night and went to my room to try and give Kirsty a ring, but she wasn't answering. Not unusual, she never has her ringer on. In the end, I just lay on the bed resting my aching muscles and watched some hotel TV, then looked out the window at the storm which was far more entertaining.

I didn't want to stay long at the bar in case I bumped into Ron. He can bore for England, that bloke. He'll talk for hours on end, with great authority, about obscure topics that no one else on the planet gives a single shit about. He once caught me off guard, and I was forced to listen to an hour-long monologue about the shingles on his roof, which then pivoted to such fascinating wonders as Bubonic Plague, the Pied Piper of Hamelin, and topped off with his take on why cassette tapes were the pinnacle of music distribution. That's an afternoon of my life I'll never get back.

Breakfast meetings… What absolute bastard came up with that idea? A pre-meeting before we go and have a day full of other meetings. For us to 'align' and 'get on the same page', apparently.

I'm not even reading the same book as most of these folks, let alone the same page.

Where the hell is Jackson, anyway? Texted the twat six times already this morning. I don't want to sit down without his buffer. No doubt he's still in bed, or, more likely, he's only just got to bed after draining some bar of every drop of piss-lager they had.

Bloody hell, there's big Ron Corbishley at the conveyor-belt toaster. Avoid eye contact, pretend to be getting fruit. I turn away and focus intently on a bowl of grapefruit pieces, obviously from a tin-can, floating around in syrup.

"Mr Clarke!" Shit. Spotted.

I turn around, a fake plastic smile borrowed from the waitress plastered on my face. "Morning, Ron."

"What's that, fucking badger food?" He nods down at my tray. "They do a nice full English here. Set you up for the day." He pats his ample gut with a hideous shit-eating grin on his mug.

"Yeah." I sigh. "Kirsty's got me on this diet, for the beach holiday, you know?"

Corbishley makes a whiplash sound-effect and mimes the

motion to go with it. "Bloody hell, mate. Didn't have you down as pussy-whipped?"

I laugh because arguing will only make it worse. "Too early for me to eat much, anyway, Ron." I change the subject. "Where's the coffee?"

"The lass will bring it to the table. Speaking of which, go grab a big one, so there's room for the laptop."

"Right."

"A table, that is. Don't go grabbing a big lass." He sniggers with a dirty wink.

I roll my eyes. Where the fuck is Dave?

I procure a suitable table, up against the wall, with a comfy cushioned bench seat along it, where I dump my jacket and phone to discourage anyone from sitting next to me. I need my space and I don't like people creeping up behind me. I like to be able to see the room.

But the view here isn't wonderful; Ron Corbishley, balding, overweight, red-faced and always far too cheery, lingering at the breakfast counter, apparently chatting up the girl who fries the eggs.

He turns to scan the room and I half-heartedly stick up my hand, so he can see where I sat.

"Some storm last night. Did you hear it?" Ron drops down his tray in front of me and digs in his bag, pulling out a laptop and notebook. Oh, boy. Am I now to be treated to an in-depth explanation of how thunderstorms work?

"I did indeed. Couldn't really miss it. Kept me up half the night."

"Girl at reception said they had an awful one here last week, too. Flooding in some places." He looks up at me. "Big day ahead. Hope you're up for it?" Ron is the account manager on this deal, he thinks this gives him authority. Nobody else thinks that.

I'm here only as a technical hardware advisor. Mostly to reassure all parties involved that we know what we're doing. Spoiler: We don't, really. We're just good at bullshitting. Ron and Dave especially. I try to stay quiet at these things as much as possible.

"Yeah, no worries." I flash a smile to keep the peace.

"I take it Dave is here?" Ron glances at his watch.

"As far as I know."

"Hope he gets his finger out, I want us to get fully aligned before the meeting."

I lean back. I don't like the look of the precarious wobble on Ron's fried egg as he stabs the air with his fork for dramatic effect.

I sigh inwardly and take a deep breath, then take a sip of my insipid orange juice, offering nothing but a shrug as response.

"Hey, hey, boys!" Dave Jackson finally appears from thin air, freshly showered and hair-gelled by the looks of it. Dapper in a dark blue suit he must have just bought. He slaps the back of Ron's chair and drops his laptop bag on the table. We have long since finished our breakfast and had the plates cleaned away. Left only with tiny coffee cups, dribble stained and thick ceramic in a sickly pale cream colour.

"Nice of you to join us, Dave." Ron sticks out a hand for a shake.

"Seven-thirty, you said?" Dave looks faux-worried, checking his watch.

"Pretty sure I said seven?" Ron looks back at me for confirmation.

"Eh, I can't remember." I flash Dave a look. He knows perfectly well it was seven. He's obviously been out all night.

"Ah, well. Here, now. Let's get cracking." Dave claps his hands together, far too loud and energetic for my liking.

"You eating?" I nod over at the food counter.

"Nah, mate. I'll grab some coffee, though."

Ron waves to get the waitress' attention. "She'll fetch you some. Now then, down to business, gentlemen."

He flips open his laptop and opens up a presentation. Death, by PowerPoint.

The urge to pull my phone out and scroll endlessly through some memes or news articles, or anything that isn't this bloody meeting, is strong. Dave seems focused, asking all the right questions that he already knows the answers to, and Ron is blabbering on as he always does. Dave knows his triggers and plays him like a broken fruit machine. I'm bored to tears, and I daydream off into my own world. I've got a bloody ear-worm tune stuck in my head since I woke up, going round and round driving me mad; some song I can't remember the name of. And fragments of a weird dream I had last night, in the short bursts of sleep I managed to get between the massive static-discharges from the cumulonimbus. Hard to remember now, but something about a church, then a forest and a train ride. I'm guessing my brain's unconscious interpretation of the storm sounds and the long day I had.

I should text Kirsty, but she probably won't be up yet.

Ron finally closes his PowerPoint and then the laptop. "We all set to do battle, then?"

"We'll slay them, Ron!" Dave plays into the act. You'd almost believe he was for real if you didn't know him.

"Right. To the chariot!"

"I've got to check out and pay, yet." I stand up to go.

"Andy, come on, that's a rookie mistake. Always check out before breakfast." Dave makes a tutting sound and I throw him a look of daggers. I've covered for his arse twice since Saturday and he's trying to throw me under a bus? Twat.

"I'll go get the Merc. See you out front in five." Ron stands up, which is a significant effort on its own and shuffles off towards the reception area.

I turn to Dave. "Where the fuck have you been, you knob?"

Dave checks to make sure Ron is out of earshot. "Went out last night to sample the local fare, you know? Then got stuck because of the storm."

"You were in a pub all night?"

"Well, no. We managed to make a run back to the barmaid's house between the worst downpours." He chuckles. "She was soaked through, couldn't just leave the poor lass to shiver alone and wet, now could I?"

"You dirty fucker. Did you even use your hotel room?"

"Yeah, course. Came back and had a shower, got changed, checked out. Well worth the eighty-quid."

"Bloody hell." Dave is the sneaky, bawdy twat we all want to be, but aren't because society says we shouldn't do these things. He shoves his hand in my face.

"Smell my fingers."

"What! Get to fuck, will you?" He takes a big whiff as I push him away.

"That's pure pheromones, that. Raw."

"Thought you said you had a shower?"

"I did. She survived it."

"Christ on a bike, Dave. I'm going to get my bag and pay. You owe me, by the way, for trying to cover for you, twice."

"Twice?"

"Yeah, Saturday, too. You left me high and dry at dinner with Nathan and Laura. God, it was boring. Oh, that reminds me, thanks for the photo of Michelle's tits that I had to delete immediately in case Kirsty saw." I roll my eyes.

"Eh? Michelle's tits? I never sent you a photo of Michelle's tits."

"You were drunk, and you stuck your finger up at me over them. Remember?"

"Oh! That weren't Michelle, that was Kayla."

"Who?"

"Michelle's mate, what works in Aldi."

"Fuck's sake, Dave. Keep it in your pants, mate. You are going to get yourself into massive trouble."

"Spice of life, Andy, my boy. You know what they say?"

"What's that?"

"If you ain't got them, then you hit rock bottom." He thrusts his hips, rather unnecessarily in my direction as he sings that Fun Loving Criminals song. I shake my head and go back to my room.

. . .

Thankfully, the drive to the customers' office is only five minutes through the industrial estate. Of course, Dave called shotgun, and I was forced into the back seats. Not before copious ridicule about my suitcase being huge. My small case fell apart last trip, and I never bothered to replace it, so I've had to endure the standard-issue ribbing. "Aww, could you not choose an outfit, sweetheart?", "Did you think it was a month-long trip?" I chose to ignore them, but I'll need to buy a new overnight case before the next work thing.

Ron parks in the visitor car park, and they exit, leaving me stuck, banging on the windows for someone to open the door.

"Sorry, Andy. Forgot about the child locks."

"Ah, so that's how you keep hold of women, eh, Ron?" Dave flashes him a wink and receives back a guttural laugh. I get out of the car and almost fall back down immediately. A belter of a headache hits me like a freight train out of nowhere.

"Sorry, not feeling great, all of a sudden."

"You all right, mate? You look pale." Dave looks at me with genuine concern.

"Yeah, just need a second." I clutch my head. "Fuck."

"What's up?" Ron checks his watch.

"Headache. Like a migraine. Must be the storm pressure or something."

"You gonna be okay for the meeting?"

"Yeah, I'll survive." I take another deep breath and follow the lads to the building reception. So far, not a great day. I guess this is what happens when you let your sister take you for a run the day before an early work meeting.

. . .

Crammed into the customers' small meeting room with one wall entirely glass, two stories up. Hot, stuffy, bright and awkward, really isn't doing my head any good. But what can I do but smile and nod in all the right places? My vision a little blurry, I try to focus on what people are saying, but the words just float through one ear and out the other. They are introducing themselves, and I've instantly forgotten everyone's name.

"Andy?" Ron raises his eyebrows at me, and I feel a roomful of faces looking and waiting for me to speak. "Oh, right. Yeah." I clear my throat. "I'm Andy Clarke, I've been with the company for about eight years now. I'm the hardware technical consultant, here to answer all your queries and concerns about our products. I work with Ron on these very complex deals like yours to make sure everything runs smoothly and on time."

My spiel flows out easily. Rehearsed dozens of times now. A few nods and smiles, and then they move on to the next punter. I look around the room at them. You can quickly weed out the ones that are only there for the free coffee and biscuits, and the ones that have waited a month to ask their very poignant question with a smug grin. I've heard them all before, but we always answer as if it's the first time anyone has asked. 'That's a great question'... Ron taught me that. It disarms them and makes them connect with us on a subconscious level or some bullshit.

Ron opens up his PowerPoint presentation again, and I switch off my brain. Can't wait to get back home this evening and feel the warmth of Kirsty as I snuggle up to her in bed.

Chapter Four

Honeysuckle on the summer evening air, cool but welcome. The aroma almost makes me feel drunk, so heady is the scent. I lie back and watch vast shapes in the clouds pass by in the tranquil sky. Clichéd, but worth it.

The peace is grounded by the sound of a lively stream close by. Its gurgles and bubbles form the foundation on which the tranquillity is built. Birdsong, rushing water, and a gentle breeze shimmering the trees. I'm happy here. Happier than I can remember.

In my periphery, she stands up, sprightly, and walks over to the water, kneeling down to take a sip from the cool stream. When she comes back, she flicks spots of water at me from her wet hands.

"Oi, you!"

She giggles and runs away, inviting me to chase.

"Where are you going?"

"Come and find out." She calls over her shoulder, gaining speed down the grassy hill. What can I do but follow?

At the crook of the valley, the stream widens. Still narrow, she hauls up her dress to step across. Bare feet glistening with spray, and a thin silver anklet on her right foot with tiny bells hanging down, jangling when she steps.

She turns to me, bidding me over to her. I look down at the river in front of me, now thirty feet wide, at least, and deep enough to be pitch black, cold and silent. I shake my head.

She laughs, steps back over, easy, dainty and elegant, then takes my hand, and we skip to the other side. I look back, confused. A haze where the river was, a thick mist where we lay at the top of the hill only moments ago.

She leads me through the landscape, running ahead at a lively pace, but I am able to keep up with ease.

Suddenly, she stops ahead of me. I almost slam into her, bent over, arms spread wide, holding me back.

"Wait!"

"What is it?"

She carefully sits down on the long grass, and delves ahead of her with long fingers. After a fumble and a mumbled curse, she pulls out a tiny white kitten, blue eyes, fur matted with Goosegrass buds and filth. He sits easily in her palm and emits a barely audible squeak, looking up at her.

She squeaks back and grabs the critter by its scruff, then shuffles the baby into her cleavage, where it seems happy. She gets up.

"We'll have to clean you up, won't we?"

One hand covering the kitten, she steps forward again and beckons me to follow.

· · ·

32

Some time passes, but I couldn't tell you how much. We cover a huge distance across tundra of unknown type and geography. Igneous bulges and sedimentary layers give way to a beach, a smooth hill meadow, then once again a river, this time snaking into the distance. She stopped once only to adjust the position of the kitten, who is now snow-white, clean and purring.

"Where are we?" When we finally sit down to rest on a bench-like stone, she looks around the vista in awe.

"I don't know, but it was fun, wasn't it?"

"Err, yeah." I try to focus on her eyes, but they twist away and blur.

"I think I have to go now. But see you another time?"

I look up again. "Sure. I hope so. But how?"

She smiles and tosses her hair back. "You can look, and you will find me." She touches me on my arm, her hand soft but freezing cold.

She laughs, then stands up from the rock and turns away. She takes a few steps, then turns back.

"Kitten says bye-bye." She waves its tiny paw, then giggles and fades into nothing. All around me, the scene dissipates into blackness.

Chapter Five

W hen I finally got home last night, I emailed work that I'd be out sick today. I decided to take a day off to rest after the horrific events of yesterday.

It was late when we finished up at the customer site. They really made a meal of it, and I thought the meetings would never end. They asked me all the usual questions, plus a load more that I have to do some work for and report back. Bugger that for today, though.

My head was pounding the whole time, even after Dave gave me a pain-killer he dug out of his bag at lunch. Think I must be coming down with something. I still feel like I have a killer hangover now, but I didn't touch a drop of booze yesterday.

I check my phone. Quarter past eleven. No text from Kirsty. I vaguely remember her getting up to go to work this morning. The sound of the shower and the smell of her shampoo permeated my sleep. She must have gone to work without waking me. I guess I slept like the dead.

I think it was almost ten o'clock when I got back last night. Oh, man. The trip home… No doubt that's why I'm still feeling so awful. Dave convinced me somehow to get a lift back with him.

My train was cancelled, and I'd have to wait two hours for the next one if it bothered to show up at all. In the end, I gave in and reluctantly got into his death-mobile. I figured if that was my time to die, then so be it. With the pain in my head, at least it would be a relief.

Three hours in the car with that nutter. Luckily, the traffic most of the way was so bad he couldn't speed. But the weaving in and out of lanes has done my nerves and guts no good at all.

He was on the phone with various people for most of the journey, work and women. A mix-tape of voices and tones. I faded out the world, closing my eyes to the impending doom that was almost inevitable.

When he eventually stopped outside my house, I was shocked that we made it home in one piece.

I roll out of bed and stumble to the bathroom. That bloody song in my head still circles around. Just a few words and a repeating tune. I know I know it, but I can't place what it is, and it's driving me bonkers.

The only way to get a song out of your head is to listen to it, I reckon. Sometimes you have to do it a few times, but eventually, it clears out and somehow resets your brain. Trouble is, I don't know what it is or where I heard it. Early Madonna, maybe? Some kind of pop, for sure.

I shake my head to try to make it stop, and turn on the shower.

. . .

They gave us a free lunch at the customer site yesterday, and I think there was something dodgy with the ham panini, as I'm feeling a bit weak today and liable to run to the bathroom at any minute. 'Hot butties what's been run over by a tractor.' Dave calls them, and I reckon he's right. I wasn't hungry after his drive home, more nauseous than anything, but now I could devour a mammoth and spuds, covered in gravy.

First, I need coffee, so I slip on a dressing gown and plod down the stairs.

My phone buzzes on the counter as I pour my black nectar. A text from Kirsty. 'Hey, fancy coming by for lunch?'

Oh, don't mind if I do. Kirsty is the manager of a Starbucks in town. I have to be honest, I'm not a huge fan of their coffee, but that isn't Kirsty's fault, I guess. The food is okay, and it isn't often I'm allowed to come and grab a free meal. I'll take what I can get. 'Thanks, babe. Yeah, see you in a bit, then xx.'

In the spirit of exercising, if not actually doing it, I take a walk into town rather than drive. There's never anywhere to park, and it isn't raining. May as well make use of the day. I'm in no rush. Ambling rather than striding. Still, burns calories, doesn't it?

We've lived on this side of town for almost a year now. I used to live a mile or so outside the town in a bland estate, then with Riss for a while when I was paying off debts. She has a nice place across town.

Kirsty chose this area. She thought it was up and coming.

Fashionable or something. Expensive, more like. BMWs in driveways, security cameras on every door. I don't have a clue who my neighbours are, and they probably think we're scum for driving a nine-year-old Ford.

I pass by streets I've never bothered to explore down, alleyways that aren't covered in graffiti, shops that sell things I have no use for. How they stay in business, I will never understand. Like those weird places at the airport selling five-hundred-quid handbags in an almost empty, brightly lit space. A taste of obscure luxury midst the filth and bustle.

I carry on walking, and that bloody tune pops into my head again. Can you go genuinely mad from an ear-worm? I reckon you can.

"Hey, Andy." Kirsty flashes her public-facing smile as I walk over to the counter. "You feeling better, now?"

"Hiya, Kirsty. Yeah, a little. Had a good long sleep, which helped." Kirsty has never been one for much sympathy, so there's no point in complaining, and she insists on no nicknames or terms of endearment when out in public. Especially at her work.

"That's good." She walks over to the staff room entrance and beckons me in. "Sit down, and I'll fetch you a sandwich."

"Nice one. Thanks."

"Coffee?"

"I've already had some, cheers. Just some water, maybe?"

"Coming right up." She flashes her manager smile. Very professional is Kirsty.

I look around the tiny room; it's the typical staffroom mess with dozens of notes, rotas and rules stuck to every surface.

Uncomfortable chairs so people don't linger too long, and a radio playing some local station. It wasn't busy out in the restaurant. I don't know why I'm stuffed in the back.

"Here you go." Kirsty bursts in and plops down a cheese and ham toastie with a bottle of water in front of me.

"Smashing, cheers."

"Enjoy, I'll be back in a minute."

I give her a thumbs-up sign and tuck in.

When she invited me over for a meal, I thought we might be spending it together, but I've scarfed down my toastie and drank my water and there's no sign of Kirsty, or anyone else. Oh, well. Free food, I guess. Can't complain.

I get up to take the plate back to the counter and see where my girlfriend has got to, but as I open the door, she bursts in.

"Sorry, Andy. I got caught up in some stuff. You finished?" She gives me her apology frown and a hand on my arm.

"No worries. Yeah, that filled the spot, cheers." I could eat three more of the same, but I'm still meant to be on a diet.

"Well, since you are in town and off work, could you do me a tiny favour?"

Here we go… "Err, I guess?"

She pulls a sheet of paper from her apron pocket. "I've got a few bits to get for the holiday, could you be a love and run out and get them for me?"

Shopping. Awesome. I try not to jump up and down with excitement. "Oh, right. Sure."

She hands me the list. Printed out and categorised into shop, then aisle, then product. At a glance, she wants me to stock up for the impending apocalypse.

"Just this?" I raise my eyebrows.

"Turn it over." She nods down at the sheet.

"Seriously?" There are another five shops with dozens of items listed on the back of the paper.

"Won't take you a minute."

No, more like four hours… "I walked in. I don't fancy carrying all this back." I complain.

"That's okay. Bring it all back here, then run home and get the car." She flashes her matter-of-fact face, and I know there's no point in arguing. My entire afternoon now booked up, doing battle in Boots, Marks and Sparks, and countless other shops I despise. I sigh inwardly.

"Right."

"Off you go then. Thanks, Andy. You're a star."

"Yeah." I step out of the door, back into the real world. Then a thought strikes me and I turn back. "Hey, you might know this song?" I sing her the lyrics that are still spinning around in my head, on infinite repeat. "Dumm da dee, you can look, do da dee dum dah, find me…"

"Time after time." She sings back, immediately.

"Yes! That's it. Thanks, babe. That's been driving me mad."

"Why you singing Cyndi Lauper songs?"

"I couldn't think who it was. I've no idea, to be honest, that lyric has been going round and round in my head and I couldn't remember what song it was."

Kirsty gives me a look I can't comprehend and ushers me out into the restaurant.

"Well, now you are showing your true colours." She sniggers. "See you later. Don't take long, I want to be out of here at four today." She pouts, "Girls just want to have fun, you know."

After my fifth trip back to the coffee shop to dump bags, I decide I need a break. I go to a rival café in the little shopping mall. Not a chain brand and they have decent coffee. I wouldn't mind a beer, to be honest, but my head is still ringing with a dull ache. Probably not a good plan.

I sit down with my drink and bacon buttie, that Kirsty doesn't need to know about, and pull out my phone. A text from Rissa is at the top of the list. 'I'll be out for a run this evening. Fancy coming along?'

I reply. 'No, thanks. I feel like I've done my five kilometres today. I'm doing a bit of shopping for Kirsty.'

She sends back a reply. 'lol, suit yourself. We need to get you built up though, Andy…'

I know she's right, but running is the last thing I want to be doing tonight. I feel the calling of the telly and slippers to try and forget this unplanned shopping spree. Speaking of forgetting, I plug my headphones in and find that song. Time after time by Cyndi Lauper. I play it once to try and erase the ear-worm, and then again just for luck. It's a nice enough song, but having it on repeat forever does get a bit much.

I haven't heard it for years. No idea why it's stuck in my head now? Must have been playing in the taxi or something when I went to that hotel. Or maybe Ron Corbishley was singing it? I bet he does a fabulous Cyndi impression…

I flick back to the Messages app, there's still an unread badge. I'm hoping it isn't from Kirsty with more shopping that she forgot to ask me to get.

It's from Dave. 'All right, mate? Big Ron was asking if you were okay and would be back to work tomorrow?'

Shit. I can't say I'm out sick if I'm pissing around in town doing shopping. No rest for the wicked, eh?

'Yeah, I'll be back tomorrow. Fuck's sake. Tell him to keep his knickers on.'

A message buzzes back immediately. 'Last thing I want to think about is Corbishley in a pair of knickers. That's put me right off me yoghurt, that has!'

I snigger. Mission accomplished.

The line from that song sneaks back into my brain, Cyndi Lauper singing 'Time after time.' over and over…

Ugh! I press play again on the song. I need to flush this out of my head, once and for all.

Chapter Six

"Have you ever had a moment of clarity?" She looks up from the tiny sink, trying to cram the kettle in under the tap, sideways. I can see her reflected in the enormous mirror. Half heated, so shower steam only clings to the cold side. She shines pale in the clear glass, blossoms in the haze.

"What?"

"Like a freeing of the mind. A revelation of sorts. Hard to describe, honestly."

"I'm not sure."

She clicks the kettle onto its stand and flicks the switch on. Harsh white-noise instantly filling the small room. Tiny cups already prepared with tea-bags and those little stringed-tags ornately dangling.

"Have you?" I prop myself up on the bed with one elbow, then shuffle up onto the pillows. So many pillows. Plump and bleached-white.

"I think so." She smiles and sits down next to me on the edge of the bed.

"Do tell."

"I was in a café, working on something in a notebook. A proper café, not a franchised branded coffee shop. Must be ten or more years ago, now." She looks at me, wistful.

I reach over and run my finger down the length of her spine, feeling each bump and notch. She shivers, then brushes back a strand of hair from her face.

"I was alone, and the waitress had just cleared the table. Then, out of nowhere, just à propos of nothing, this feeling explodes inside me." She spreads her hands out, eyes wide. "And at that moment, I knew that nothing at all mattered because I understood everything."

I sip from a bottle of water on the nightstand. "Everything?"

"Yeah. I knew everything. For a moment." She laughs. "This sounds weird, but honestly, everything made perfect sense. My life, the world, the universe."

"Well, what did you learn?"

"Absolutely no idea." She bursts out laughing.

"Well, that's a lot of use, isn't it?"

"Indeed, I want my money back." She chuckles. "No, I mean, it faded quickly. I can't remember much about it. Only the memory of the memory. But that feeling. At the time it was pure and raw."

"Nice." I lay back on the bed, curious to know more.

The kettle clicks off, and she stands up to pour the water.

She looks over at me from by the shelf. "I bring it up because I had a similar feeling again, recently. Well, not that similar, really. But in the category, you know?"

She twists open a packet of sugar for the teas, then brings them over to me, spoon on top. She puts both cups down on the nightstand, then pulls over a big wing-backed chair and sits down.

"What feeling did you have?"

"Are you sure you want to know?"

"Of course!" I laugh.

She pouts. "Warmth and safety. A flood of those. A memory, or a familiarity. I felt at home, where I belonged, in the bosom of a place I knew." Eyes wide and delicately glistening, a mischievous grin caves into a heartwarming smile. She glows. An aura of beauty radiating all around her.

"That's lovely. When did it happen?"

She pauses, biting her lip. "When I met you." She flashes a grin and picks up her tea.

Her cheeks flush red, and I feel a prickle of warmth spread through my veins to match. She moves to say something, but bites back her lip again instead, then takes a sip of tea, hugging the cup with her hands.

We linger for a moment.

Through the silence, the constant hiss of the air conditioner bulges out, from hidden to obvious. The drip of the shower joins in, then the distant drone of a jet engine. We are never far from distraction, here.

"There was an emptiness, at first, but then something changed. I wasn't alone anymore. It's really hard to explain." She squirms a little and turns to face me.

"You're a daft ape." I laugh and gaze into her eyes for an eternity until she blinks me away.

She pouts again, then puts down her cup and stands up.

Gathering clothes from the floor, she throws a pair of jeans at me. "You didn't answer the question."

"What question?"

"Have you ever had a moment of clarity?"

Chapter Seven

This week has been a ball of stress. Corbishley is on my back constantly to get the customer their answers for his big deal before my holiday. I've got most of it done now, but I'm going to have to bluff a couple of minor points and hope for the best. Oh, well. I think this is normal company policy, anyway. We should change our name to 'Blag and Scam Ltd.'

Kirsty has also been on my back to sort out all the last things for the holiday. I don't understand how there can be so much to do, but she keeps finding more seemingly unimportant things that are vitally essential and super-urgent.

I'm doing my best, but my best is hampered by interruptions, anxiety, apathy, and a thumping headache that still won't go away no matter what chemicals I ingest. Thankfully, the weekend is looming only a few hours and a couple of meetings away, and I'm out of here on the dot of five. Work will just have to wait, and the holiday will happen whether or not we have everything sorted. The only thing I'm looking forward to about this bloody break is that I won't have to work for two weeks. Saying that, all the work will be waiting for me when I get back. There's no escaping it.

Haven't heard a peep from Kirsty today, and I've been too busy wrapping things up to text her. She's on early shifts this week. Up and gone before I wake. I expect she's busy at work, too. She's training up someone to be the assistant manager, and she's been stressed about leaving the shop for two weeks. I'm sure it will all be fine.

Seriously, I'm almost wishing this whole thing was called off. Is it all worth it? I'm not certain if I can keep my happy-face up for two weeks of Nathan and Laura, either. If my headache doesn't go away, I might just spend the entire fortnight in the hotel bed. Now, that would definitely be worth the effort.

I know Kirsty won't let that happen though, unless I'm actually dead.

"Lunch?" Dave sticks his head over my cubicle wall with a grin that would sour milk at fifty paces. "It's where we get some kind of food, then eat together at a table, ideally with inane chat and observations."

"I know what lunch is, you knob-end. But I've got this crap for Ron to finish off."

"Have you not done that yet? Finger out, son!" He chuckles.

"Shut it."

"What is it? Can I offer some assistance?" He peers down at my screen.

"Network-card firmware versions and their comparative security differences and benefits."

Dave rolls his eyes. "Right. Burgers or Pizza?"

"Pizza."

"Excellent choice. Now, let's make like a tree and get outta here."

Thankfully, the pizza place is within walking distance of the office, so I'm not subjected to Dave's driving 'skills' again. Although he offered the spin.

There's barely anyone in here at lunchtime, which is kind of strange for a pizza restaurant. Suits me. It's always nice and quiet and there's a big table with comfy bench seats, that look out at the rest of the dining room. Dave favours this place due to the waitress, who is rather cute, it has to be said.

"Looking forward to the break, then?" Dave doesn't bother with the menu. Instead, he looks around, presumably trying to catch sight of his favourite server. Hannah, I think her name is.

"Not really, if I'm honest."

He turns to face me. "Heh?"

"Two weeks away with Laura and Nathan. Not my idea of fun… And Kirsty is making it into some kind of military operation. She's got me buying everything under the sun brand new, and organising insurance, cash, backup cash, special debit cards, translation books, you name it. I'm exhausted just preparing."

Dave shakes his head. "Dunno why you give in to it, mate."

"How do you mean?"

"You've let this get out of hand. Should be just you and her off for a romantic birthday thing. You never know, you might even get laid." He sniggers.

"I'll have you know I'm well catered for in that department." I grin. "Anyway, it's her birthday. She wanted this. I'm not gonna tell her no, am I?" I shrug.

"That Laura is tasty, anyway. You should be thankful."

I shake my head. "Some of us don't go around shagging their girlfriend's best mates."

"Spice of life, mate. Speaking of which…" He nods in the direction of Hannah, the waitress, who approaches the table with a grin.

"Hello, gents. What can I get you?"

Dave unsubtly licks his lips. "I don't think it's on the menu, my darling, but I'll tell you later if you like."

Suddenly, we're in the middle of a 'Carry On' film from the 70s, and I cringe inside, but Hannah is all smiles. She brushes it off, but her grin is genuine and reaches her eyes. She sweeps back a strand of hair from her face and laughs. "Usual, then, is it?"

"Yes please, Hannah. And a bottle of your finest sparkling water, if I may."

"You may." She nods, still grinning, and turns to me.

"Err, pepperoni and mushrooms, please."

"Coming right up." She taps on her little screen and heads off to the kitchen, a glint in her eye.

"How do you do it, Dave?"

"What?"

"Women eat out of the palm of your hand, yet you are an oafish pig."

"I'll try to take that as a compliment." He smiles. "You need to loosen up, mate. I'll tell you what your problem is, but you won't like it."

"Oh, yeah? Go on then."

Dave takes a deep breath, then slumps back in his seat. "How can I put this, Andy?" He pauses. "You always put the pussy on a pedestal. That's the phrase."

"Hey?"

"Believe it or not, but women are people, too. They aren't goddesses or delicate art, not to be touched or flash-photographed. They are humans with blood and desires, the same as us. And guess what, they fart and belch same as us."

"I know that…"

"Well, that means they want to have a laugh and some fun. When you treat them like their shit don't stink, they'll end up believing it. Like your Kirsty."

"What do you mean?" I'm feeling a bit attacked here.

"No offence, mate, but Kirsty is a bit… Snobby."

"Hey, come on!" I throw up my hands.

"Calm down, I'm just saying… You've not helped matters, lying down and rolling over whenever she says."

"I don't. I'm just in it for a peaceful life."

"Whatever you say, Andy. But just remember, she's just a person, same as me and you and our lovely Hannah here."

Dave throws a smile as the waitress brings our pizzas, just in time to defuse the situation. But now I've got that bloody song stuck in my head… 'Girls just want to have fun.'

Before we can ponder on the dessert menu, we are summoned back to the office by a notification on my phone. Another impromptu meeting that Ron has called, so we can 'catch-up and align' before I go off.

I grit my teeth, grab my laptop, and tread the path to the meeting room. Dave skulks off back towards his office to pretend to work, and no doubt flirt with the receptionists for half an hour. Nice life if you can get it…

"Mr Clarke." Ron is already waiting in the little meeting room. He's set himself up at the table with a tiny cup of coffee, a Snickers bar, and a bag of cheese and onion crisps. I come empty-handed.

"Ron. I didn't know it was a snack meeting."

"Grab yourself a chocolate bar and a drink if you want, I'll wait."

"Nah, you're all right. I'm meant to be watching my weight."

Ron makes the whiplash sound effect again and grins like a baboon. I take a seat opposite.

"Right, then. Let's catch up."

He opens up a spreadsheet of tasks and actions, filtered by my name. I take a deep breath and sigh.

Death, by Excel…

Nearly six o'clock when I finally leave the office. My plans for an early getaway blasted to smithereens by Ron Corbishley finding another dozen tasks that I was meant to get done, that I curiously had no record of. By the end of the meeting my head was fried, my chest tight and a ball of stress growing bigger in my throat with every breath. I can't wait to step off the plane in

Lisbon now if only to be far, far away from Big Ron and his bloody checklist.

Kirsty should have got home hours ago. With any luck, she's already made some dinner. I'm starving, and the pizza lunch I had seems like an eternity ago. I turn the key in the door and enter into a peaceful house.

At last.

I drop my laptop bag and go through into the living room. No Kirsty.

"I'm home, babe," I call up the stairs. Perhaps she's in the shower, or even better, waiting for me naked on the bed?

No reply.

I go into the kitchen, but there's no sign of any grub. Not even the scent of cooking. I head up the stairs.

"Babe?"

I go into the bedroom, and she's folding clothes into a suitcase.

She jumps as she notices me. "Bloody hell, Andy, you nearly gave me a heart attack."

"Sorry, I called out."

She points to her ears. "Headphones."

"Right. I just got home. Ron had me doing stupid reports till all hours. I'm starving."

"I've already eaten."

"Oh… I'll get myself something then, shall I?"

"Whatever." She shrugs and goes back to her suitcase.

"You nearly packed up?"

"Yup." She barely looks up.

"You okay, babe?"

She flashes me a cold stare. "Fine."

Oh, fuck. What have I done?

"I'll get myself a toastie or something, then."

"Whatever."

I escape back downstairs to the kitchen, trying to think what it is I'm guilty of. Kirsty doesn't do the 'Whatever' act very often, and it's usually only when I've fucked up something big time. I think the last time was when I got her the wrong size knickers by accident, and she assumed it was my way of saying she was fat. Took a month of flowers and apologies before that was forgotten, if such a thing is possible

As far as I know, I've done all the things she asked me to do, we're all set for the holiday, tickets, passports, cash and bookings all printed out. Everything is ticked off. The bins are taken out, the laundry done. I'm at a loss. Maybe she just had a bad day at work and this is nothing to do with me? Best to keep out of the way until it subsides.

I grab some slices of bread, ham and cheese and go about knocking up a fine toastie. That and a beer should keep me going and hopefully give Her Highness time to cool off.

As I take my first bite, Kirsty appears in the kitchen.

"You were late home today." She checks her phone.

"Yeah," I chew and swallow. "Bloody Ron had a load more stupid tasks for me to do before I was off."

"You've been late a lot lately."

"He's been on my back all week about this bloody deal. This customer is meant to be the biggest deal of the century or some crap." I shake my head.

Kirsty puts her hands on her hips and looks me straight in the eye. "Andy, who is Chloe?"

"Chloe? No idea. Who is she?"

"I asked you." She doesn't flinch, still staring at me.

"Hey? Not with you."

She bends down and leans over at me. "I said. WHO. THE. FUCK. IS. CHLOE?" She pauses between each word, yelling with bulging eyes.

"Err. Kirsty, I have no idea what you are talking about. I don't know anyone called Chloe."

"Yeah, right." She walks out of the kitchen and slams the door, then stomps up the stairs.

What the hell is going on?

I was going to eat my toastie and ponder on what just happened, but the sound of something crashing down the stairs stirs me from my meagre dinner. I sigh and stand up. I can't think of anyone I know called Chloe. I even scrolled through my phone in case there was some contact I'd forgotten about. Has someone pranked me? Is this something to do with Dave? I guess I better find out…

At the bottom of the stairs is my suitcase, all my new clothes spilt out down the stairs. I tiptoe a route through the carnage up to the bedroom where I find Kirsty, sitting on the bed, tears in her eyes and dismay all around.

"Babe, what are you doing?"

"Don't you fucking 'babe' me!" She throws a bottle of suntan lotion at me, which I dodge. It splatters on the landing. Cost twenty bloody quid, that.

"I honestly don't know what's going on."

"Sure, course you don't. Men never do, do they?"

"Hey?"

"You sneaky bastard, Andrew Clarke. There's no point

54

pretending any more. I know what you've been up to." She sneers at me through tears.

"Well, that's good because I haven't a clue."

I sit down on the bed next to her and try to put my arm around her. "Kirsty, I don't know what you think has happened, but whatever it is, I'm innocent."

"Don't you fucking touch me with your whore hands!" She stands up and backs away.

"Kirsty, will you please calm down and tell me what the bloody hell is going on?"

A sadistic grin spreads across her face. She points down at me. "Fine, we'll do it your way then."

"Hey?"

"You've been acting weird all week. Day off sick, late nights at the office." She does quote marks in the air with her fingers. "Singing Cyndi Lauper songs, and last night you gave yourself away, didn't you?"

"What?" I'm at a loss. What she describes is all accurate, but it was exactly what it said on the tin, not a nefarious coverup.

"You called out her name in your sleep."

"Whose name?"

"Chloe. Your little slut, of course. Pay attention, Andy."

"Kirsty, I don't know anyone called Chloe. For fuck's sake!"

"Right, I suppose you just call out names of random strangers then, do you, while you press your bloody rock-hard dick up against me in the middle of the night?"

"I… What?"

"I bloody knew it. I should have realised when I saw you flirting with Laura last weekend."

"Ah, you have got to be kidding me now. I was never flirting with Laura. It was all her!"

"Sure, course it was." She scoffs. "Beautiful Laura who has a rich, handsome and successful boyfriend would be trying it on with fat loser Andy Clarke. Right. You are pathetic, Andy. Pathetic."

"Babe… I mean, Kirsty. Seriously, you've got it all wrong." I plead.

"Yeah, well, tell it to your slut, Chloe, because I'm done with you."

"For the last time, I don't know anyone called Chloe!"

Chapter Eight

Much as I love a good nap on the couch, spending the entire night here was less than ideal. I woke up frequently; cold, disturbed and seriously uncomfortable, not to mention confused and miserable.

I cautiously open my eyes and the harsh reality slaps me in the face. Kirsty had some kind of freak-out yesterday, and I'm totally at a loss to explain it. She said I called out a name in my sleep; Chloe, apparently, whilst I pushed myself against her, ready for action, as it were.

From this minor infraction, she's concocted a whole scenario of mythical events to back it up. My late evenings at work, my tiredness and attitude all week, my humming a random song, even.

Those things may be true, but they are all utterly innocent. I have no way to confirm what happened in my sleep, of course. I don't remember it at all.

Was I dreaming about someone called Chloe? If so, that's bad enough, according to Kirsty.

She seems to think that instead of going on a work trip last Sunday and Monday; I spent the night with some woman.

Of course, I didn't. I've never done anything like that in my entire life. I wouldn't even dream of it. Well, so I thought…

I protested. I showed her my phone and scrolled through innocent messages with no mention of a 'Chloe' or any other woman, for that matter. She shook her head and said it was simple to hide or delete things. I told her to ask Dave for verification, but that was a bad move.

She cited Dave as the least authentic source of truth in the world, if not the universe, and a destructive influence on me. She even speculated that it was him who organised the entire thing since I'm 'pathetic' and 'no other woman would want to fuck me, anyway, chore that it is…' After that revelation, she concluded that Chloe must have been a prostitute and that I was a filthy, disgusting pig for touching a whore.

Clearly, this is all some big misunderstanding. But last night was not a good time to attempt to convince Kirsty of that fact. She went bat-shit crazy and threatened all kinds of things, including severing organs and gouging out eyes.

A woman scorned, as they say. Well, a woman who thinks she's been scorned, anyway…

I'm hoping that the night has given her time to see sense and reason, and we can get back to some kind of normality. We are leaving early tomorrow morning for our holiday, and I don't fancy two weeks of the silent treatment, and having to pretend that everything is okay in front of Laura and Nathan.

. . .

What a disaster. I thought Dave and his rampant cock would end up getting him into trouble like this, but it turns out that doing nothing wrong and worshipping your beautiful girlfriend can still end in tears. Who knew?

I move to stand up, but my knees are stiff, my back is killing me, and my neck is cricked and twisted. Ugh.

I try again and manage to get off the couch by sort of rolling off onto the floor. Now I'm tangled in a couch-throw that I used as a makeshift blanket, which provided little warmth. I ditch the throw and crawl back to the couch, using it to pull myself up. Standing feels like a monumental achievement.

I drag myself to the downstairs toilet for some much-needed relief.

Ignoring the carnage of the evening strewn down the stairs, for now, I check the time on my phone, which has only five percent battery left.

Still early, Kirsty is probably asleep. Could I try to make amends by bringing breakfast up to her? I think back to the events of last Sunday and how wildly different they are to this weekend. Dinner, wine, passionate sex. Compared to this weekend; half a toastie, a massive row, and the loneliness of the couch. How could things go so wrong in a week?

Probably not a good idea to go upstairs yet. I'll let her come down in her own time. Then we can talk like rational adults and straighten this whole thing out. Maybe even have wild make-up sex later if it all goes well. Then I can re-pack my bag and get ready for the holiday.

First things first, though. I need a bucket of coffee.

I find an old charger in the kitchen and plug my phone in, then ponder on the options for breakfast. We don't have much in, as the plan was that no one would be here after today. What's left is two eggs, a few slices of bread and half a cup of milk. Enough to scare up some scrambled eggs on toast.

As I take a bite, I'm treated to a flashback of what Kirsty said last evening; that I'm a 'fat, pathetic loser.' Is that what she really thinks, or was it angry talk from being upset? Either way, I'm a bit shocked, to be honest. I thought we had a good relationship. Another point noted and recorded for lifelong recall; she thinks Laura has a handsome, rich and successful boyfriend... I'm starting to see a pattern here. Not one I like, one bit.

Jealousy, it seems, is paying us a visit this weekend.

"You still here?" Kirsty appears in the kitchen. Pissed off, by the sound of it. She's dressed and made-up, which is unusual for her on a day off at ten in the morning.

"Where else would I go?"

"Oh, I don't know, maybe to your whore house?"

I sigh. It seems the night has brought no rationality to Kirsty, and she's still stuck in the same groove.

"Never been to one. I wouldn't even know how."

Kirsty ignores me and pours herself a coffee from the pot.

"I don't want to argue today. I'm going out." She announces. "And I've been thinking."

I look up. "Oh?"

"You never wanted to go on this holiday, anyway. I think it

would be best if you don't come." She looks down at me, matter-of-factly.

A shudder of adrenaline courses through me, and I feel my guts turn. "I… What?"

"I think we need some time apart." She casually gulps down her coffee. "This is an opportunity. Two weeks away. Would probably do us good. We need a little time, to think things over."

My mouth drops open, but no words come. "… But." My mind races, trying to find something tangible to grasp onto. Am I still asleep, midst a horrible nightmare? "Your birthday…"

"Yeah, a lovely gift you gave me, wasn't it?" She huffs.

"… I" I do have a gift for her, wrapped up and hidden away. I want to tell her how much I love her, that all this is a horrible misunderstanding, that never in a million years would I cheat on her and that I'm lucky to call her my girlfriend, but the words stick in my throat. She rinses her cup in the kitchen sink, before grabbing her bag from the back of a chair and keys from the hook.

"Where are you going?"

"Not that it's any of your business, but I'm going to Laura's."

"Oh."

"See you in two weeks, Andy. Please, try to get your shit together."

"Two weeks? You aren't coming back tonight?" Panic hits me as I realise what she's said.

"We're going to the airport from hers. No need."

My brain seems to be disconnected from the rest of my body, I can't move, can't protest. "Oh. Right."

"See you." She shrugs a vague wave and walks out. I hear a suitcase handle being extended and then the door open and close. The two brass knockers thud as she slams it shut.

"I love you…"

I find my muscles suddenly and jump up, going to the front living-room window. Kirsty gets into a red Tesla without looking back at the house. They silently speed off down the road, out of sight and out of my life.

Who the hell is Chloe, and why has she ruined my life?

Chapter Nine

Various beeps and notifications on my phone tell me that I've somehow managed to make a huge mess of everything in my life, without even trying. The first was early this morning when I should have been leaving for the airport with my gorgeous girlfriend for her birthday holiday celebrations. The second was that our plane was ready, and we should be waiting at the gate, the third, and most damning, that the plane had departed on time and was heading for Portugal. Taking my girlfriend far away from me.

I'm still in shock. I can't believe this is really happening.

I know I wasn't a huge fan of this holiday in concept, but to be left behind because of a raunchy dream I allegedly had? How can this be true?

The house feels weird now. Haunted with memories and the

ghostly spirit of my confusion. I'm not supposed to be here, alone, and feeling somewhat empty and desolate.

I've gone over the events that led me to this a million times in my head, and it still makes no sense.

Then there's the embarrassment of having to explain this to Rissa and even Dave. Do I lie and tell them I had a change of heart and made Kirsty go without me, for who knows what reason? Or, do I come clean and try to brush it off as no big deal?

It is a big deal, and I can't help but wonder if Kirsty will come back in two weeks.

I've barely left the couch since yesterday. Mostly staring at a dead black TV screen in a silent house. Our bed, better than the couch, but cold and empty without Kirsty, was of little comfort. Every time I tossed and turned, I was reminded of the reason I'm alone. My brain going round and round with the same thoughts. What happened? Why did it happen to me, and who the bloody hell is Chloe?

Most painful, though, is the thought I can't seem to avoid, no matter how ridiculous it may be, and how many times I tell myself to shut up and ignore it; that this is all some kind of charade, to hide the actual truth, which is that Kirsty is having an affair with Nathan.

A fresh problem presents itself. My stomach rumbling. I don't think I've eaten since yesterday breakfast. Food was the last thing on my mind. But now, an ache in my guts means I have to get up and deal with the situation.

As I open the fridge to an Arctic wasteland, I remember that there's nothing in because I'm not meant to be here. Another kick to the guts. Now what?

My phone presented an answer with a food ordering app.

I couldn't use any of our normal restaurants because every menu just reminded me of what Kirsty would get. In the end, I ordered from a place I used to go to years ago when Dave and I would go drinking until three in the morning, then top it off with a dodgy kebab. I can be sure that Kirsty would never lower herself enough to eat from there.

A jolly young lad brought it to the door, slamming it into my hand. I seem to remember it tasted better, back then, after twelve pints. Now it tastes dull and of bitter rejection. Still, it's sustenance, and vaguely healthy if you only count the salad.

I flick the TV on and some inane droning rubbish fills the screen. Better than the mess in my head, I tune out and hope I can forget, for a few minutes at least, that everything is very strange right now.

I'm startled from my sorrowful binge by a key in the front door. I scramble to my feet and run to the hallway. Could it be that Kirsty realised this is all a huge mistake and has come back? I feel pounding anticipation in my chest as the door opens.

"Oh, it's you…" My sister comes into the hallway, then jumps a foot into the air as she sees me.

"Andy, you scared the shit out of me!" She holds her hand to her heart and takes a deep breath.

"Sorry, I thought you were Kirsty." Another wave of sadness

flows over me as I realise the truth. There's no way in hell Kirsty would have come back, and now I have to explain it all to Rissa.

"What? Why are you here? I came to water the plants."

Instinct takes over my brain, and before I know it, my arms are wrapped around my little sister, and I'm literally crying on her shoulder. "She's left me, Riss!"

"Here you go." Rissa hands me a big mug of tea as I sit and recover in my favourite couch spot. "Now, tell me what happened?"

"Thanks, Riss." I take a sip and then a deep breath. "I don't really know, to be honest."

I explain, rather embarrassed, about the name I apparently called out in my sleep, how Kirsty wove this into a story of treachery and deceit that I couldn't convince her was all false. Then that she told me not to come to Portugal, so that we could have some time apart, for reasons that are way over my head.

Clarissa listened quietly, as she does. Shaking her head occasionally.

"That's absolutely mad, Andy. Wait till I see her."

"No, Riss. Don't say anything. I mean, it will just make it worse."

"Dreams are just dreams, though. How can she come to such a ridiculous conclusion based on a name?"

I may have skipped the other detail. "Err, she reckons I had a boner at the time." I look away. Talking to my sister about my dick feels odd, to be honest.

Clarissa splutters out a laugh. "Sorry! Oh, my god, sorry. I didn't mean to laugh."

"Sure." I roll my eyes.

"Men and their appendages, eh?"

"Indeed. Even so, I never shagged anyone called Chloe, in my dreams or otherwise. I don't think I've ever even met anyone called Chloe in my life."

Rissa shakes her head. "It was probably something on telly that you didn't even pay attention to. Subliminal thoughts, you know. Dreams are complicated. I don't think anyone really understands them."

"Kirsty always had this thing about dreams and how they show your genuine desires from deep in your soul, or some crap like that. She read it in a magazine. I dunno." I shrug.

"Still, I think she reacted a bit strong."

"No shit!" I bite my lip and pause. Rissa raises her eyebrows, expectantly. "It makes me wonder if there's something else going on, you know?"

"How do you mean?"

"Ah, probably nowt, but, she mentioned how Nathan was rich, handsome and successful. Then I saw him pick her up in his fucking Tesla outside the house."

"He's Laura's boyfriend?"

"Yeah."

"Well, if she stayed with Laura, she's hardly going to shag Nathan right under her nose, is she?"

"Yeah, no. You're right. It's crazy, but things just go round and round in my head…" I flash a weak smile.

"You daft ape." Rissa pauses, then smiles. "Remember when we were kids, and we had that cat, Marmalade?"

"Oh, yeah. Big ginger moggy." I smile.

"Remember, he went missing for a few days once, and I was really upset?"

"No, I don't think so?"

"Well, I do. I was crying day and night for ages, and you kept telling me it would all be okay, he'd come back soon enough."

"Really?"

"Yep. I was probably six or seven. You must have been nine, then."

"I don't remember that at all."

"You went and got all the money out of your piggy bank, and took me down to the shop to buy some sweets to cheer me up, and on the way back, we saw Marmalade sitting on a wall down a few streets from our house."

"Yeah, I remember, now. See, I told you he'd come back, soon enough."

Clarissa nods. "Yeah. He probably just got lost for a while. But he followed us back home and ate half a can of cat-food, then slept on my bed for the rest of the day."

"Big piggy, he was." I chuckle.

"Yeah. Well, I never forgot that, Andy." Rissa puts her hand on my arm. "Kirsty will be back soon enough. Maybe she just got lost for a while. Perhaps she's right, and you do need a little break."

"Hmm. Well, I don't know about that part."

"You didn't really want to go, anyway, did you?"

"I guess not."

"There you go then. Did you get your money back? For the tickets?"

"Bloody hell, I didn't even think about that. Probably can't now?"

"Worth a go."

"Yeah, might give the airline a ring tomorrow. I got all the insurance."

She nods. "Do you want to come stay at ours, tonight?"

"Ah, no. Thanks, Riss. I'll be fine, here."

"Well, if you are certain? It's no bother. Are you working tomorrow?"

"No. I mean, I'm officially on holiday."

"What you gonna do then?"

"I have absolutely no idea."

"Don't mope about all day. Get out and do something. Give Dave a ring, maybe?"

"Yeah, maybe. But he'll be working."

"That's never stopped him before." She chuckles.

"True."

My chat with Riss cheered me up a little, until I climb the stairs to bed again, facing another night of loneliness. Now I think about it, I'm actually annoyed that Kirsty would think I'd even be capable of betraying her like that, especially if she thinks I would actually have sex with a prostitute. I don't even think Dave has ever done anything like that.

Maybe Riss and Dave are right? I should be more assertive with Kirsty and tell her straight. It isn't right to treat me like this. I've done nothing to deserve it.

Exhausted, I run a hot bath instead of going straight to bed, to soak away my troubles, hopefully. I'll deal with it all tomorrow and give Dave a shout. Maybe go for a beer at lunch.

Chapter Ten

"Oh, hello." *I find myself in a cold, dark, empty place. But I know she's there, a beacon of light and warmth, already waiting. I walk over to her side. She nods and touches my arm, gently. Saying nothing.*

"Where are we?" I look around, straining to see anything.

"Where do you want to be?" She smiles and a brief flicker of fire burns in my chest.

"You choose."

She turns, leaving a light trail as she moves. Melting into the black.

There's no transition, not that I can notice, but suddenly, there's a landscape. A dark rocky plateau. Night, but a green glow slowly pulses in the sky. The air smells like a thunderstorm, charged with energy and ozone.

"What is this place?"

"I don't know the name. But it's a planet, far away. Uninhabited."

I raise an eyebrow. "Can we breathe, here?"

She looks over at me, rolls her eyes. "We aren't really here, are we, dummy?"

"Right, yeah."

A large bird swoops out of nowhere, landing in front of us. A huge owl. It looks us up and down, then coughs and flies away.

I turn to her. "What was that?"

She giggles. "He smokes too much, I guess."

"You nut-job." I laugh. "Well, what do you want to do here?"

She reaches over and takes my hand. "Just walk for a bit."

I nod, and we walk slowly in silence along a beach that wasn't here a moment ago. The sea is dark; the tide is flowing out.

For the first time, I notice her dress. Pale green, floaty. Bare feet, and her hair blows in the breeze. There's a sadness about her, it troubles me, but I say nothing.

Ahead, I notice a cave entrance in a tall rock face. We walk towards it.

Inside, there's a large driftwood fire burning in a cutout of the wall, and a complicated system of copper pipes, valves and gutters that lead to a pool carved into the stone floor. The water is hot, gushing in one side and draining out the other. In the firelight, it glows and sparkles.

"Shall we?"

"Rude not to."

In the water, she folds into my embrace. We lie facing the ocean outside, the firelight twinkling on the surface of the pool.

She puts a finger over my lips. "Just hold me, close?"

I do as she suggests.

We stay like this for some time. I don't know how long, but longer than I can count. Occasionally she'll twist, like she's being pulled away, but a flick of her foot brings her back to me. I stay silent.

At some point, I notice a white cat who looks over at us, blinks and tilts its head, then lies down and curls up in front of the fire, content and warm.

The tide has taken the ocean away, so far that we can't see the edge anymore, just a desert of sand and the night above it. The green glow morphing and flexing, casting shadows on our skin.

"I better go." Suddenly, she rises, and we are back on the plateau, dry.

"Oh. Right."

"Sorry, and thank you."

"My pleasure. As always."

She sings a line from a song, by Texas, I think. "... when you dream of me..." Sweet and passionate, but the sadness still lingers.

I nod, and she fades away into the black.

Chapter Eleven

"Chloe?" Dave looks at me over his pint, wide-eyed.

"Yeah, that's what she said." I hold my hands up and shrug.

"You bloody twat." Dave laughs. "First rule of women, Andy, is they don't like it when you call out the wrong name." He grimaces. "Made that mistake once, myself, and it weren't pretty." He shudders.

I shake my head. "No, you don't get it. I don't know anyone called Chloe, and I've not so much as looked at another woman since we've been together." I pick up my pint and drain the rest.

"Come on, mate. It's me. You can tell me the truth."

"Fuck's sake, Dave. That is the truth! Don't you start." I sigh. "I wouldn't even know where to begin, to be honest. I'm not much good at flirting and the like."

Dave nods. "Yeah, I'll give you that, you are a bit useless in the pussy department." He chuckles and I shake my head. "It is a weird one."

"Weird is one way to put it."

"She's gone on holiday without you?"

I sigh again. "Yeah."

"Right, well, you know what that means?"

"Means I'm alone, miserable, pathetic and arguing with the insurance company about getting my money back." I look down woefully at my empty pint glass.

"Well, that, yeah, but also…" Dave pauses for dramatic effect. "Piss up for the lads. Get your glad rags on, Andy, me old mate, we're going dancing tonight, boy!"

I must admit, going out on the piss tonight with Dave wasn't top of my list of things to do, but there's a part of me that does fancy going mad for a change. I haven't been out for a binge in years. Kirsty prefers wine over beer, and fancy restaurants over pubs and clubs. Sophisticated, she calls it. Dave calls it snobby. I suppose he's right, to a certain extent?

Dave wouldn't tell me what the plan is tonight, just that he'd pick me up at seven, and we'd take it from there. Normally, I'd be worried, but you know what? Sod it. I think I deserve a bit of fun after the weekend I've had.

Bang on time, I hear a beep outside and go to the window. A big black cab is waiting, and I can see Dave in the back. Looks like he's with someone.

"Here he is, the man himself." Dave waves me into the cab. "Andy, you know Michelle?" He flashes a wink and nods to his girlfriend next to him, done up in her tiniest skirt and top. Blonde hair, puffed up and dyed with pink and blue streaks, with bright, colourful makeup caked on around her eyes, and shocking pink lipstick to match. I smile and nod. "And this is Kayla." Dave motions across the cab to Kayla. I think she's the girl he mentioned before — 'Michelle's mate, what works in Aldi.' She's equally done up and scantily clad in a lot of black fishnet. Thick, dark eyeliner and black hair stuck up with hairspray. She smiles and pats the seat next to her, coy and pretty.

"Err, hi." I clamber into the cab and sit down next to Kayla. She smells strongly of a sweet and fruity perfume I don't know, mixed in with booze and smoke. Dave reaches over and taps the glass partition. The cab pulls away. "Where we going?"

Dave is dressed in a baggy suit. Black-and-white striped shirt with the top four buttons open. His jacket sleeves rolled up and his hair gelled even more than the usual gallon. Bloody hell. I've got into a cab with Madonna, Rick Astley, and Siouxsie Sioux.

"You're in luck, mate. The girls knew of an 80s night that was on tonight." He laughs. "We're going back in time, Andy." Michelle and Kayla squeal and laugh. I grimace. An 80s night?

"Oh. You might have said. I'm not really dressed for it." I look down at my blue jeans, black t-shirt and a leather jacket.

"You'll be fine, mate." Dave grins like a baboon. I suspect the alcohol has already been flowing.

Kayla puts her hand on my leg. "You look fine. Jeans are timeless, aren't they." She squeezes gently and giggles.

I'm not sure what Dave has told them, but I wasn't expecting a double date here. I mean, I am still with Kirsty, aren't I? I shouldn't be out with a girl… Then again, I'm not going to do anything. It's just a few drinks and a dance. Still, if Kirsty found out, she'd go absolutely insane.

A vivid image of Kirsty and Laura lying on a Portuguese

beach, in tiny bikinis, with Nathan rubbing sun-tan-lotion over both of them, slow and deliberate, flashes into my brain and I shake it away. Sod them all. I'm going to enjoy myself.

"Right, then!"

Kayla pulls a little silver flask out of her bag and opens the lid, offering it to me. "Now we're talking. Have a drink?"

I sniff the flask and recoil. "Damn, that's strong. What is it?"

"Jägermeister, Red-Bull and a drop of Absinthe." She laughs. "My special recipe."

Ah, I see we're going for maximum shit-faced here. "Bring it on…" I take a gulp from the flask and nearly bring it straight back up. It tastes as revolting as it sounds. Burning and tingling on the way down. Still, it probably does the job, even if it kills a few million brain cells.

The cab drops us off at a dingy-looking club on the edge of the less salubrious area of town. I can guarantee Kirsty would never set foot in this place, for fear of catching something. Dave pays for the cab, and we descend a narrow flight of stairs to a basement that's much bigger than it looks like it could be from the outside. There's a cloakroom, but I'm worried my jacket would be nicked if I leave it there.

We move through to a bar and a big open dance-floor. Not many people around yet. We sit down at the bar. The girls order drinks — some kind of fruity colourful cocktail, and then they depart for the restroom together.

"I wasn't expecting you to bring company, Dave."

"Be boring otherwise. Besides, the girls wanted to come for the disco."

"Kirsty would literally kill me if she knew I was out with you lot."

"Simple solution to that in't there?" Dave grins. "Don't tell her."

"I'm paranoid. What if I bump into her mates or something, and they tell her?"

"Andy…" Dave sighs. "Kirsty basically left and went on holiday without you." He pauses. "Sorry, mate, but that's a dick-move, in my book. You did nowt wrong to deserve that. Also, I very much doubt Kirsty would have any mates that would come to this place."

"Yeah." I feel a sinking in my guts. He's right. Even so, I can't get rid of the guilty feeling.

"Move on, have a laugh, get over it."

The barman plops down two lagers in front of us and the ornate cocktails for the girls. I move their drinks to where we can see them, in case someone tries to date-rape drug them.

"But I don't want to move on. I love her." I check my phone for the hundredth time today, to see if Kirsty might have sent me a message, but still nothing. She didn't even tell me she'd arrived okay. I had to check the flight status on the airline website. Maybe Dave is right, and it is all over. I should move on. But accepting that fact is harder than it seems. I'm still clinging on to the fact that Kirsty will come back, realising this was all a big mistake, and we'll get back to normal.

"I know, mate. But shit happens. Now, get that pint down you and enjoy the evening." He slaps me on the back. "One thing I'll tell you, mate, if I may?" I raise my eyebrows. "You have to keep farting to keep the flame alive."

I laugh. "What? You nutter."

Madonna and Siouxsie reappear next to us, both looking

rather tasty if I'm honest. Michelle sits down next to Dave. Kayla stands close to me and picks up her drink. She holds it up and giggles, a twinkle in her eyes.

"Well, cheers, Andy."

"Cheers, Kayla…"

Chapter Twelve

I've never been much good at dancing. Kirsty once called me a cross between an elephant and a squid, swinging around like a trunk and flailing my tentacles in all directions.

To be fair, I never pretended to be any good at it, but it turns out that dance moves and choreography aren't in the least bit important when the booze is flowing like a river, and the music is a mix of songs I vaguely remember from my childhood. I'll probably ache for a month, but I have to admit, it was just a tiny bit fun.

I spent at least half the night at the bar, yelling drink orders over loud music, and a good chunk of the rest of the time watching the girls dance. A pastime I am highly qualified to perform. They knew what they were doing and seemed to enjoy themselves.

Once the slow songs came on at the end of the night, Dave grabbed Michelle and draped himself around her, smooching around the dance-floor. I looked over at Kayla, who caught my eye from the floor. A pang of guilt throbbed through me, even after who knows how many pints of cheap lager, and I looked away, but she came and got me, pulling me onto the dance-floor and putting her arms around me. What could I do? Kayla smiled and pulled me close, and we drifted around for two or three songs like that. She smelled good, and I liked her warmth next to me. I forgot who I was for a moment.

Then they played that bloody song, Time after time, by Cyndi Lauper, and it dragged me back to harsh reality, remembering why I was there in a dingy basement nightclub, and not with my girlfriend in some fancy bar in Portugal.

I woke up this morning with the hangover from hell. I'm used to the constant daily headaches these days, but this was the real deal. It felt like the back of my head had been smashed in with a sledgehammer.

I stumbled bleary to the bathroom where I almost had a long conversation with God on the big white telephone, but somehow, I managed to hold it together. It was only then that I realised where I was. Dave's apartment, or his shag bunker, as he calls it. I would often end up here after a piss-up night out, but since I moved in with Kirsty, that sort of thing has been frowned upon.

I went back to the spare room and was surprised to find Kayla in the bed, still fast asleep.

I crept back in, trying not to wake her. I needed some time to get my thoughts in order, and perhaps for the pounding headache to subside a little.

. . .

I know we came back to Dave's around three in the morning, once the club had kicked us out, and we'd satiated ourselves in the nasty kebab place. A frequent venue for me, of late.

When we got back to the apartment, Dave and Michelle grabbed a bottle of something and retired to his room, leaving Kayla and me alone. I still felt awkward, but she led me through to the spare room.

Kayla sat down on the bed and urged me to join her. I hesitated, and she sensed my anxiety despite both our drunken states.

"You're a nice guy, Andy." She said, seemingly out of nowhere. I looked up at her, surprised. "I'm too tired, anyway. We can just cuddle if you like?"

"Err, yeah, sure. Of course."

She flopped back on the bed, then groaned and got back up. She motioned to her face and hair. "Be right back, I'll have to take my face off, or you'll wake up to a zombie!" She laughed and went off to the bathroom.

I wondered if I should wait. I stood around for a moment, feeling extremely awkward, then used the 'fuck it' principal. I was already in way deeper than I ever imagined I would be. Getting in the bed just seemed inevitable. I lay down and tried to keep the room from spinning around me.

Kayla came back, changed into a long white t-shirt and all her makeup and wild hair gone. She's really quite pretty. She climbed into the bed next to me, nary a care.

"You gonna cuddle me, then?" She giggled.

Well, it would be rude not to, so of course, I did. A stirring in my groin as I snuggled up to her, then another memory crashing my party — Kirsty telling me I pressed my boner up against her while calling out the name 'Chloe'.

"You okay?" Kayla swivelled around to face me. Just inches away, I could feel her breath on my face, hot and fiery from the alcohol. She smiled, sympathetic.

"Well, now you come to mention it… Not really, Kayla." I flashed a weak smile.

"Wanna talk?" She put her arm around me, gently stroking my back.

A good question. Blokes don't really talk, do they? I mean, I can't break down in tears and give Dave a big hug as I can with Riss. Maybe I needed an unbiased opinion.

"Err, well…"

"Dave told me your girlfriend left you." Kayla pulled me a little closer and squeezed my shoulder.

"Yeah, well… Not quite. At least, I hope not."

"I got dumped by my first love when I was nineteen. It hurt bad for a long time."

"I'm sorry."

"Not your fault, but thanks." She smiled. "I got over it, now I'm much better off."

"Do you have a boyfriend?" I realised the irony of the question as the words came out of my mouth. She was lying in bed with me, cuddled up, and only at that point do I ask if she's seeing anyone. A bit late, Andy.

"No, not really." She smiled. "After Shane broke up with me, I had a rethink about my life." She closed her eyes and paused for a moment.

"I don't blame you."

"Have you ever just been doing something mundane, like sweeping the floor or cleaning a window or something, and suddenly out of nowhere you have an epiphany, and everything just seems clear?"

"Err, I'm not sure, how do you mean?"

"A moment of clarity, I think it's called. You just click and the world makes perfect sense. All the troubles of your life, all the problems and things you think are important are just gone."

"A moment of clarity?" I felt a bolt of adrenaline pulse through me as she said the words. I'd heard the phrase somewhere else recently, but I couldn't think who said it.

"Yeah, it happened to me one day. I was at work, stacking a shelf full of beans at the time. I just stopped, with a can in my hand, looking down at myself from somewhere above. I was still for ages until the feeling subsided. Time stopped for a little while." Her eyes were wide as she recalled the event. "After that, I just felt a lot better. I knew Shane was a twat, and I was better off without him."

"You are probably right."

She giggled. "Yeah. I just do what I want now, I don't need a fella to be happy."

"Right." I looked into her eyes. She seemed happy, but maybe that was just the booze haze.

"Have you ever had one? A moment of clarity."

I shrugged. "No, I don't think."

"Your time will come, soon, Andy. I can sense it."

I raised an eyebrow. "You reckon?"

"Yeah, trust me. A woman always knows." She giggled again, sweet and warm. "I'm knackered, and I have to work tomorrow. Better sleep now."

"Right, of course."

Kayla kissed me gently on the lips, then twisted around, facing away from me, but she pulled my arm around her and snuggled close into my spoon cuddle. I felt stirrings again, but pangs of guilt knocked them aside. What was I doing? In bed with a beautiful woman who wasn't my girlfriend, my emotions and hormones confused and conflicting.

I guess I must have drifted to sleep soon after that. Until I woke with the pain crashing in my head.

"Morning." I'm startled from my thoughts by Kayla, waking next to me. I turn to face her as she blinks awake and rubs her eyes. Dave's spare room curtains aren't much good, and the harsh daylight of the morning streams in through the thin material, leaving shadow patterns on Kayla's face. She shields her eyes and turns away from the window towards me.

"Good morning. How you feeling?"

She yawns and turns away, embarrassed. I snigger.

"Yeah, not bad, considering." She jumps up suddenly. "Oh, my god! What time is it?" She reaches for her bag and fumbles a phone out, looking at the screen. She sighs in relief. "Ten. Thank fuck, I thought I was late for work."

I laugh. "What time are you starting?"

"Noon today, till eight." She makes a face. "Better get up, I suppose." She pulls the covers off and turns to get out of bed, but then changes her mind, turns back and leans down over me, kissing me on the lips, firmly.

"Thanks for being a gentleman, Andy." She smiles and jumps out of bed.

"Err, yeah, my pleasure. I mean, of course."

She laughs and flits out of the bedroom, presumably to the bathroom.

. . .

Of course, Dave has no food in the house, so after everyone has woken and dressed, we lumber and wobble down the street to a little café for breakfast. The girls discuss the disco and their mutual disdain at having to go back to work today, while Dave is all smiles, having rung in sick already. His boss is based in Boston and is none the wiser of Dave's schedule and general dossing. To be fair, Dave puts in the work when he needs to.

Kayla and Michelle are cheery, and the consensus is that it was a splendid night, and we should do it again soon. The pain in my head disagrees, but I can't deny I had a good time. I would like to do it all again. Then I realise, I probably won't be doing anything like it again, when Kirsty comes back. The fact that I did it at all means that I can never speak of it again, for fear she will find out and carry out her threat of cutting my balls off and mounting them on the wall. If I'm ever to get back to normal life with Kirsty, then this has to be a one-off.

I smile because there's no need to put a downer on the breakfast table. Kayla smiles back at me. Under the table, she squeezes my leg.

A thought occurs to me. "Kayla, you probably weren't even born in the 80s, were you?"

She giggles. "No, 1993."

I roll my eyes. "Youngster." I smile. "You both did a brilliant job of the costumes."

Michelle pipes up. "The 80s are in, now, aren't they?"

"How can a decade that was, err, forty-odd years ago be in?" Dave looks confused, then slurps back a mug of coffee.

"It's fashion, in't it?" Michelle slaps him on the arm, playfully. "Everything what's old is new again."

. . .

The girls leave us in a flurry of hugs and kisses to get to work. I'm in no rush, being on holiday, such as it is. May as well enjoy the moment.

"Good night, eh?" Dave claps his hands together, then waves the waitress over and orders more coffee.

"Aye, not bad."

"That Kayla is tasty, in't she?" He gives me a wink and a nod.

"She's lovely, yeah."

"You two get much sleep then?" He sniggers. He's obviously prying for gossip, and I'm enjoying making him wait.

"A gentleman never tells, Dave." I tap my nose.

"Aye, that's as maybe, but what about you?"

I shake my head. "We had a pleasant chat and a cuddle if you must know. That's the extent of it."

"A chat and a cuddle?" Dave scoffs, then shakes his head in disbelief. "I set you up a clear shot, Andy. I left the black ball an inch from the pocket. All you had to do is whack it!"

"Elegantly put, Dave, mate. But I'm still technically with Kirsty, aren't I? I can't just go shagging around, willy-nilly."

"She don't deserve you, mate." Dave pours himself another cup of coffee from the pot, shaking his head the whole time. I shrug. Maybe he's right, but I can't help who I am, can I?

Chapter Thirteen

A few days of bumming around with nothing to do can drive a man to ridiculous things. I mean, what else was I meant to do? Not like I'm going to walk around the zoo, or find a circus or something. Anything I could think of that I could do on my days off required me to be with my girlfriend. Not loping around on me tod like a weirdo stalker or something. No.

So as I didn't go off my nut, with thoughts and songs spinning around my head out of control, moping about the house on my own, watching rubbish on telly and trying to distract myself, in the end, I just went back to work.

'Sad fucker', Dave called me, and he's probably right, but, in fairness, what choice did I have? Rissa is busy with her life. Even Dave went back to work. I don't have any other friends.

I pondered going to visit my folks, but the questions would be too much to deal with. 'Where's Kirsty?', 'How did you bugger it up this time, son?' I need that like a hole in the head. Work was the easiest choice.

But now, sat at my desk, scrolling through all the drudgery of emails that had banked up, I somewhat regret my actions.

Well, I regret many things lately. Surprisingly, that night cuddled up next to Kayla isn't one of those things. That was special. Now I come to reflect on it. She's a great girl, and if the world was a different place, I'd be very tempted to ask her out again. Just us this time, and less booze, more bedtime.

But that's not the world, is it? I don't live in a dream, I'm stuck firmly in reality, and today is a particularly dismal one to be stuck in.

Today is Kirsty's thirtieth birthday, and instead of celebrating it with gifts, food and wine, sex and happiness; here I am at work, hundreds of miles away from her, while she no doubt has the time of her life with Laura and Nathan. Am I forgotten? Am I not part of her life, anymore? I don't know.

This morning I pulled out the present I got for her, still wrapped and ready to be packed in my suitcase, to be delivered in a five-star hotel room in Lisbon along with a tray of breakfast and a naughty smile.

I put it on the windowsill next to a daisy in a little glass, and took a photo, sending it to Kirsty. 'Happy birthday, babe.'

No answer, but I know the message was delivered.

I have to admit; I have been exchanging text messages with Kayla. She's quite insightful, and she's been doing her best to cheer me up, but I'm probably a tough assignment at the moment. I'm trying to be extra careful not to flirt with her. Professional and businesslike. Well, as much as I can be. She's sweet, and I appreciate the effort she's making. I don't want to let her down like she told me her ex, Shane, did when Kirsty comes back from holiday, and everything is forgiven and forgotten and I can get back on with my normal life.

I told Kayla the details of what happened. How it was a silly dream that triggered all this craziness. She 'lol'd' and said Kirsty needs to calm down and get with the picture. I agree.

It's nice to have someone to talk to about 'things.'

I don't want to keep droning on with Rissa and especially not Dave, who has little sympathy in this matter. 'Get over it' he'd urge, 'She ain't worth it.' Easy for him to say. The longest he's been with the same woman is probably about three months, not that I'm counting.

"Come on." Dave appears at my cubicle. "Pizza."

I look up. "Eh?"

"You've had a face like a slapped arse all day. We're going for lunch, and I'm not listening to any arguments."

I lock my computer and stand up. "No argument here, mate."

"Sound."

We sit down at our usual table, and Hannah, bubbly and cute as ever, takes our orders. Dave looks over at me and sighs.

"What am I gonna do with you, eh?"

"Kirsty's birthday today, in't it."

"I know, mate. Facebook told me."

I look up. "Did she post something?" I deleted my Facebook account years ago. Can't stand it, to be honest. The tabloid of the internet.

"Didn't see, but I got the notification this morning, 'Wish Kirsty Hughes a Happy Birthday'. I'd sooner wish her a kick up the arse."

"Hey, come on."

Dave raises his hands. "I know, I know. But sod her. Forget it. Don't say the K-word anymore, okay?"

"Fair enough."

Hannah brings us food and drinks with a smile, and Dave flashes a wink and a grin. I have to wonder if there is more between them than I know about. I wouldn't be surprised. Is there a woman in this town that Dave hasn't had some relations with?

Dave picks up a slice of pizza and stuffs most of it in his mouth. "What did you tell Ron?" He spits out the words between chews.

I chuckle. "Just that my flight was cancelled or something. He didn't seem to care much, as long as I was back and doing his bloody tasks."

"Sounds right. No compassion, that fella. Make sure you get your holiday days back."

I nod. "He reckons this deal is the biggest thing since sliced bread. Keeps going on about how it will set him up for retirement and then some, if we win it. He's talking about going back down to visit them again soon." I shake my head. "Fat lot of good that is for me, though. I don't get a penny of commission."

"Aye, and it's us who do all the work. Same old story, mate." Dave prods at his chest, violently.

"Dunno about 'us', Dave. I think it's me what's doing all the work, here!"

"Yeah, that's what I mean. You know, the camaraderie of us

workers at the front line, grinding the path so as the generals can walk it easy."

"The only grinding you do…" I tail off. "No, never mind." Dave's face spreads into a grin. "Dirty bastard."

"Spice of life, Andy, me old mate." He winks and nods toward Hannah who bends down at a table in front of us. "Speaking of which, get a load of that pert arse. Gives me the shivers, that does." He shudders and quietly wolf-whistles through his teeth. "I think I'll have pudding, today."

I shake my head and chuckle. "Cheers, Dave."

He breaks his stare at Hannah's behind and looks back at me. "For what?"

"You know. This… Caring and trying to take my mind off stuff."

"Don't get all soppy on me, mate. Just get yourself out there and enjoy life."

"Yeah, right. Maybe after I get all the reports done for Ron."

By five, I'm achingly aware of the boredom and stress of work. A feeling I know only too well, greatly amplified today as I shouldn't be here.

I begin the shutdown procedure on my computer, which itself can take an age, and start packing my stuff into my bag. I'm procrastinating and slow, I know, but there's a repelling force at home, keeping me away. The thought of going back to the empty, silent house now, on Kirsty's birthday, while she's far away and totally ignoring me, is unpleasant, to say the least. I should be with her, celebrating with fine food and wine, then a romp on a huge and soft bed, not here alone, miserable and cold.

Still, what else can I do? I meander around the supermarket on the way home, picking up a perfunctory list of easy to cook meals and, despite my better judgement, a six-pack of beer to ease me through to bedtime. I don't normally drink alone, but I feel like I can justify it this time.

I pierce the lid of a nasty ready-meal curry with a fork, stabbing over-enthusiastically until there're more holes than lid left, then I throw it into the microwave and slump back down on the couch, melting my brain, half watching a documentary on tree-frogs, waiting for the ding that signifies my dingy dinner alone.

A thud from the front door jolts me up off the couch. I'm not expecting anyone, and it's a bit late for a Jehovah. Kirsty? No, I'm not even going to let that thought enter my head. There's a snowflakes' chance she would fly back from holiday, on her birthday without saying anything just to surprise me. I go over to the window and peer out.

Rissa stands on the doorstep, holding a white plastic bag.

"Hiya. Err, I wasn't expecting you today, I'm not really in the mood for a run this evening, Riss."

"No running today, brother dear." She lifts the bag up. "Brought you dinner."

I feel a smile creep onto my face. "Oh, well. Come in, then."

Clarissa unpacks half a dozen takeaway boxes onto the table and opens the lids. Chinese from the good place. It smells delicious. Far better than the nasty supermarket curry that now sits untouched in the microwave.

"This is great, Riss. Thanks." I nod in appreciation. "What's the occasion?" As I say the words, I realise what the reason is. She knows what day it is, and she's doing the same as Dave did, earlier. Trying to make sure I'm not sat around in misery. I'm not going to complain, though. My stomach might tomorrow, but screw it. If I was in Portugal, we'd be having some kind of blow-out meal, no doubt.

"Nothing special. Nick is out with his football mates tonight, and I thought you might like some company."

I nod. I'm sure there's more to it than that, but I say nothing.

"Well, cheers, sister dear. Fancy a beer?"

"May as well." She smiles.

She's been with Nick for years now. They aren't married, no kids, and I'm never quite sure if that's what Rissa wants or what Nick wants, or even if they've ever thought about it. Nick isn't a bad chap, I suppose, but I've got nowt in common with him, aside from he's more or less related, at this point. He's something to do with procurement for a big factory. I've never been interested enough to ask the details. He's as fit as Clarissa is. Always running and playing something or other, as well as coaching kids and doing endless charity runs. There's nothing technically wrong with him, but I've never really liked or disliked him. I just acknowledge he exists and is a distant part of my family. When I'm forced to interact with him, the conversation is strained. I don't know anything about sport; he doesn't know anything about computers. We're left with the weather and the price of petrol. I vigorously avoid all talk of politics and religion.

I'm just glad my sister is happy. At least, I assume she is. Which is more than I can say for me, of late.

.   .   .

"Have you told Mum and Dad, about, you know?" Clarissa hides behind her glass of beer, the pint-glass huge in her hand after she drops that bombshell.

"No." I shake my head. "And I'm not going to. Don't say owt, okay?"

"Okay, but, they'd want to know if you and Kirsty are broken up."

"We're not!" That came out louder than I wanted. "Sorry. I mean, we aren't broken up, Riss. She's just… I don't know, having a moment or something. A couple of weeks apart to do us good." I take a sip of my beer. "She'll come back, and it'll all be forgotten, back to normal, or even better. Absence makes the heart grow fonder, and all that."

Riss flashes a sympathy smile. "Okay, Andy."

I can tell she doesn't believe me, and if I'm honest, I don't even believe myself. But hope and positivity is what people always say, isn't it? Misery just attracts more misery.

Our parents mean well, of course. They want the same as anyone; for their children to have happy and worthwhile lives, to be strong and healthy. I suppose that's why I don't want to tell them what's happened because they'd feel sorry for me, and I'd be letting them down. Plus, it's one thing telling Rissa about my boner dream, but I can't exactly relay that story to Mum with a straight face.

The first time they met Kirsty, they absolutely fell in love with her. Kirsty is perfect 'bring home' material. Pretty, polite and friendly. I think Dad likes her more than he likes me.

Mum was hinting at wedding bells in the first five minutes, much to my embarrassment. Perhaps, secretly, I wanted the same thing, but it just never felt like the right time. Given what's happened recently, maybe that's a good thing. The mess of divorce is a lot worse than a simple break-up.

Dad is very straight-forward about these things: You meet a girl, you get married, you have kids, you work hard, and you make sure the kids have everything they need. Then your life is complete. There's no need for dilly-dallying around with divorce or other women. There's nothing complicated about it; He managed it. Why can't everyone?

He was lucky, I suppose. Mum was cast from the same mould. Back in their day, things were so much clearer.

They read the Sunday papers, go to Blackpool for their summer holiday, take the Christmas tree down on New Year's Day, and enjoy their simple life. Sometimes, I wish I could be the same, but even though I value the stability and safety that comes from those choices, I've always felt something was missing; adventure.

Saying that, it's not like I've been very adventurous, but the possibility was always there. That's what I like to tell myself, anyway.

Adventure is only a dream away. I've often let my mind wander where it may, through road-trips around America on the back of a Harley, hiking through the Alps, or making a friend in rural China and exploring the local culture, learning the language, working in the rice fields.

Even though Portugal wasn't appealing to me, I think in the depths of my heart; I did want to go, just to experience something wildly different. It was mainly the company I objected to.

None of those things have happened, of course, even the one I had booked and paid for… But the others could one day, if I won the lottery or something. There's always the pull of responsibility, dragging me back to work and keeping me tethered to reality.

Bloody hell, what a mess I'm in. My life is far too complicated for the amount of joy I get out of it.

Suffice it to say, I don't need the stress of explaining to Mum and Dad what happened between Kirsty and me just yet, at least not until I know what is going on.

I drain my glass and get up to go to the fridge. "Another can, Riss?"

"Don't mind if I do."

Chapter Fourteen

A tunnel leading forwards, as far as I can see. Tiny glowing lights measure the distance low to the ground, a shining pearl necklace that spans infinity. I trudge forward. The ground is soft, covered in patterned carpet. Maybe not a tunnel? A corridor?

I glance up. Doors lead off on both sides. I stop and try one; number thirteen. Locked. I carry on.

In the background, there's a quiet hum of fans and an occasional distant rumble. Thunder, I think.

I look down at my feet, which are bare, then I notice I'm wearing a soft white robe and nothing else. It doesn't feel like mine; I don't recognise the texture. I'm clean, fresh from a shower, smelling vaguely floral. My skin pruned from being too long in water, my hair damp and slick.

Something knocks against my leg as I walk. I slip my hand into a pocket on the robe and pull out a cold, hard object. A key, but huge, ornate and old. Dark metal worn smooth, smelling of *iron and rust. I offer it up to the lock on a door, but it's far too big. Not even close. I put it back in my pocket and walk on.*

I have a sense of calm here. The narrow space envelops me and forms a barrier between me and... Well, whatever harm may be in the world. I'm sure there's plenty to choose from.

I pad steadily along the carpet, with no noticeable progress to the end of the corridor, if indeed there is one. I turn and look back, and the lights fade after a few feet. They slowly flicker off as I watch, stopping just short of where I'm standing. Now, the path I took here is empty black velvet, I dare not go back.

Some doors have no handles or frames. Instead, only a small keyhole and a subtle outline of where the door should be. You could easily miss them if you weren't looking. Some have big brass knockers that thud gently on the wood as I step my way through the endless passage. Some have peep-holes, and I stop and look through one. All I can make out is light and colour, but no shapes. I notice every door is numbered the same with a '13' in brushed, varnished brass. So many thirteens. If I was superstitious, this could be a problem. All I try are locked.

"Where did you go?"

Startled, I jump as I hear the voice behind me. I stop and turn. She's there, in a similar white robe to mine. Her black hair wet and starkly contrasting on the cloth. She smiles, sweet and gentle. She came from nowhere, silently.

"I... I'm not sure."

I hadn't noticed them before, but tiny spotlights shine down from the ceiling. She stands directly under one and a glowing halo of stray hair vignettes around her head.

She reaches out to hold my hand. I notice her skin is also pruned and clean.

"Well, never mind. You're here now."

"I suppose I am. Wherever here is?"

We walk together for a while, hand in hand, bare feet striding in harmony. Then I remember the key in my pocket.

"Do you know what this is for?" I pull out the heavy object. She lets go of my hand and takes the key from me.

"Wow, cool. Where did you find it?" Her eyes wide in awe.

"In my pocket, but I've never seen it before." I shrug.

"No idea what it fits, but it looks fancy." She hands it back, and I stash it away in my inventory again.

We carry on walking for some time. I couldn't say how long. There's an understanding between us that we need not speak to convey thoughts. I feel her desires and fears somehow deep inside, and I nurture them in my mind. Then I feed back my cravings to her, silently, and a tiny curl of a smile blooms on her face, but also inside her. I feel her warmth. I know her, and yet I know nothing about her.

"This is my room." She stops outside one door, a number thirteen, of course. I wonder how she can tell this particular one is hers, as they all look identical to me. "Come in?"

She opens the door with a card she pulls from her pocket. Inside is a room I'm familiar with. Nothing special. A bog-standard hotel-room. A small bathroom on one side, with a spacious bedroom beyond. She sits down on the oversized bed and beckons me over.

"There was a storm when I was here last, too." She looks over at the window. A vista of frequent flashes over a distant forest looms, awesome and disturbing in equal measure. We must be quite high up.

She gets up and pulls the thick curtains closed, then turns to face me with a smile. I stare into her eyes for a long moment. So dark brown, they are nearly black. Shy, she looks away, blushing.

"What?" She giggles.

"Nothing, just…" I pause. "You are beautiful." As I say the words, a tingle of heat pulses through my veins.

She turns away, embarrassed.

"Shush, will you."

"No, serious." I smile and take her hand again. She sits back on the bed and pulls me down with her…

"You, there." A voice, harsh and old, calls out from behind us. I turn in shock and a throb pulses in my chest. A man is sitting at a writing desk in the corner of the room. I could have sworn there was no one else here a moment ago. He's gaunt, grey skin pulled tight around his skull, bulging eyes and sunken cheeks. Dressed in dark robes and his head bald, aside from a perfunctory rim of hair around the back of his head, like a monk or something. "Trespassers, get out!" He shakes his fist at us. "Thou do not hail from my thoughts, nor my deepest dreads?"

"What? Who are you?" I turn to look at her, but she is as wide-eyed and stunned as I.

"Where did ye hail from? I've passed through the stones these long years, ne're did I meet the likes of you afore. What demon or devil sent ye?" His voice is raspy and dusty, dry like bone.

"Pardon?" I raise an eyebrow and stand up, moving towards the man. He flinches and waves his hands at us in a panic, shaking his head. I back up.

"Get out. Get out from the stones, quick. Afore the dynge traps ye forever!" He stands up and grabs a book from the desk, then waves it towards us. "You must leave, now." There is an urgency and threat from him, a stench like tar and an overwhelming sense of dread as he steps towards us, growing bigger with every step. A thick black mist blurs his edges, slowly enveloping the room into inky darkness. The thunder outside rumbles and I feel the shock waves deep in my belly.

The bed and furniture are gone now, and we're at the edge of an empty room, crouching in fear. The monk lurches forward and I'm paralysed. My throat constricts, my legs don't respond to my commands, my heart beats like a drum in my chest. I shrink into the corner and the room fades into black.

I'm shocked into consciousness as she grabs my hand and pulls me up, out of the room and back into the corridor.

We run, not looking back, past the endless doors, faster and faster until they blur into a streak of brown and grey. The colours change to deep green, then pale, and the musty atmosphere is replaced with a lush, moist scent. We slow down and the walls melt into a forest, dark and tall all around us, no longer clad in bathrobes. Instead, I'm in my usual jeans and t-shirt. She's wearing a long dress, blue and white.

"Who was that? What just happened?" I turn to her, panting out of breath. My heart thumping in my chest, my mind racing.

"I don't know." She looks back to where we came from, but there's no sign of the corridor, only the wooded path. Above us, a canopy of leaves shields us from the rain that drips occasionally, and slinks silvery down the tree trunks, enveloping us in a comforting sound. "I think we're alone, now."

I nod. "Where are we?"

"I brought us to my woods. The safest place I know."

"Your woods?"

"Yes, mine." She stretches her arms out wide and slowly spins around. Laughing. "These are my woods. No one else ever comes here."

"Except me?"

"Indeed. Except you, now." She raises an eyebrow, then grabs my hand again and leads me along the path. "I know a place." She squeezes my hand gently. "We'll be safe, there."

Chapter Fifteen

Bloody 'Tiffany' in my head today, that awful song 'I Think We're Alone Now' from the 80s going around and around. The usual method of playing it a few times to clear the blockage isn't working either, and now my music streaming service thinks I like 80s teen pop. Awesome. I had to hide my phone in my pocket in case Dave walked by my desk and saw me playing it. I'd never live that down in a million years. Where do these stupid ear-worms come from? How does your brain decide, oh — today, I think we'll put Tiffany on repeat for hours. What's next, 'Agadoo' and 'The Birdie Song'? Ugh.

I woke in a sweat and panic this morning, my heart racing, my thoughts confused and messy. A nightmare, I think. Someone yelling at me, a strange smell, and… A woman.

I don't remember much about her, but there was an intimate familiarity like I've met her somewhere before.

.   .   .

Clarissa, in her infinite wisdom, convinced me to meet her regularly and get back into our running regime. She thinks it will do me good on many levels; fitness, weight and mentally. She's not wrong, of course, but it still grates on my philosophy. I think I just expect that I should have all those things without the need to do the exercise. 'Unless you have a magic wand, you better get real and put in the effort.' Riss correctly pointed out to me. Lunch with Dave at the pizza place is cancelled for the time being, and my sister dragging me from my desk replaces the pleasantry. Dave will have to gaze at Hannah's pert arse on his own. No hardship there.

"Can we take it easy, today, Riss?" I grumble as she speeds off. "That Chinese was great, but it's still lingering if you know what I mean."

She chuckles and rolls her eyes, but slows down. "Just this once, Andy."

We amble through the park near to my work, which isn't so much a park as a playing field, plentifully dotted with dog shit and litter, with a few swings and a broken slide at one end. The broken glass bottles and cigarette butts all around the playground probably means that teenagers frequent the area, rather than the toddlers the council expected.

Wearily, I motion to a bench and Rissa nods, shaking her head a little. I drop, thankful for the cold metal supporting my arse. Rissa daintily sits down next to me.

"How are you doing, brother dear?"

"Been better, to be honest." I puff and wipe sweat from my brow.

She laughs. "We'll have you in shape, soon enough. I mean the other stuff…"

"Oh, yeah…" I sigh. "Keeping on, keeping on. You know?"

"Fair enough." She smiles and takes a sip from her water bottle, offering it to me.

A thought occurs to me as I take a gulp. "I had a weird dream last night. A nightmare, sort of."

Rissa raises an eyebrow. "Oh, yeah?"

"Hard to remember the details now, but I think I was in a hotel, then there was this woman…"

"Oooh. Do tell." Rissa smirks. "Who was she?"

"I can't really remember." I shrug.

"Not a 'moist' dream, then?" She giggles.

"No, nothing like that, you dirty sod." I pause for a moment. I do remember a bit of heavy snogging, now I come to think about it, but there's no need to mention that. "It was really… I dunno, vivid. Like it wasn't a dream, but it was." I look over at my sister, to see if she understands. "Anyway, then there was this weird old dude, yelling at us. It was paralysing and scary, but I don't know why."

"Dreams are weird, generally."

"True, still this was different, somehow." I shake my head. "It's hard to explain."

"Who was the old man?"

"No idea. He was dressed in a sort of robe, and he had a bald spot, like a monk, maybe?"

"A monk? What was he yelling?"

I have to stop and picture the feeling. I read something once about how dreams happen in a different part of your brain to normal events, and so they don't form memories in the same way that real life does. And as soon as you wake up, those chemicals are flushed from your head. You quickly forget it all. What you have to do is remember the dream as soon as you wake up, to capture it into your normal memory, where it will hopefully stay. "I'm not sure. Something about trespassing." I shrug. "I just remember the feeling of being freaked out and panicked. It wasn't nice, at all." I shudder.

"Not good." She pauses and scratches her head. "I saw this article recently about lucid dreaming. It was quite interesting if you're into that sort of thing?"

"What's that?"

"Well, you sort of take control of your dream, in your conscious mind. Instead of the crazy path your brain is taking you on, you make it go where you want."

"Oh, aye? How do you do that, then?"

"I think there are a few steps you have to take and prepare for. I'll dig it up and send you a link if you want?"

"Yeah, do."

"And maybe keep a dream journal. Write it down as soon as you wake up if you remember."

"Yeah, I thought that." I take another drink of water. "Dreams don't mean anything, though, do they?"

"Who knows, Andy... Brains are funny things, aren't they?"

"I suppose. Did you try the lucid dreaming thing?"

"No, I told Nick about it, and he said it was stupid. Then again, he only dreams about winning the match. Why would he try to change it?" She laughs.

"I might give it a go..." I think back to the reason my girlfriend is far away from me, because of a woman in a dream. I can't help but wonder, is it the same woman I remember snogging in my dream last night? Chloe? I still don't know who she could be, though. Perhaps some lucid dream investigation would be worthwhile? "While I was in the dream, in the good part," Rissa sniggers, "I remember feeling more awake and alive than I have in real life for a long time."

"How do you mean?"

"It's weird, but for ages now, I've had this never-ending headache, and a sort of soft, distant feeling about the world. Everything is dulled, somehow. I don't know how to put it. It's like everything is through a gauze, and I'm just drifting along, helpless." I think back to the night out at the disco, and wonder if I should mention it to Riss… On reflection, it seems like a bad idea. She'd probably tell me to go immediately and chase after Kayla, and I probably would because I don't think it would take much convincing me. But if I do that, I admit that me and Kirsty are over, and I'm not ready to do that.

"Maybe you should go to a doctor? Get everything checked up?"

"Nah, nothing like that." Last thing I want to do is see a doctor, who'd likely give me a sleeping pill, then tell me to drink plenty of fluids and get some rest.

"I don't want to have to worry about you, Andy. I've got enough of my own stuff to worry about."

I turn to look at her, detecting a sense of frustration in her voice. "Like what?"

"Oh, never mind." She shrugs it off.

"No, something's up, isn't it? You have to tell me now."

"It's nothing, Andy." She bites her lip.

"Bullshit." I grab her hand. "Remember, I've known you for your entire life, young lady. I know when something is up. Is it Nick?"

She lets out a sigh and shakes her head. "No, well, I don't think so…"

"There is something?"

"Yeah." She pauses. "I… Well, we… One or both of us, I don't know, can't seem to make babies."

"Ah." I find myself lacking words. I turn to Riss, and she's looking down at her fingers in her lap. "Sorry, sis." I reach over and put my arms around her and pull her close. She leans her head against my chest, and we stay like that for a moment, saying nothing, until the moment passes and Rissa sniffs away a tear and then shifts back to her side of the bench.

"Nick won't go to a doctor, same as all you stubborn men, but he reckons it's maybe the time he forgot his cup and got kneed in the bollocks playing rugby…" I look up at her to see if she's joking and a grin spreads across her face. "Rugby players have funny shaped balls, don't you know." We both burst out laughing.

"Have you had any tests done, or whatever they do?"

"Not yet… But I think we'll have to, at some point."

"They can work miracles, these days, can't they? I'm sure it will get sorted, whatever it is."

"Maybe." Rissa drifts off into a daydream for a moment. "That stuff costs a fortune, though. Money that we don't have."

"Oh, right."

"Maybe it's for the best, anyway…" She sighs again. "Not like we're ever going to get married, either."

"Oh…" Lost for words again, I'm suddenly feeling guilty of all my pathetic problems, now that I hear my sister's situation. I thought everything in her life was rosy and going how she wanted. She's fit, healthy, young and has a good job at the Uni doing admin stuff. She seemed to have her excrement well and truly centralised. "Sorry, Riss. You must think I'm an idiot for all my silly woes. I had no idea."

"No, Andy. Everyone has their troubles, and it isn't for us to decide if they are big or small to them. You are entitled to have problems, same as anyone." She reaches over and grabs my hand, squeezing.

"Thanks, sis." I offer a smile. "Shall we get back on the road, so to speak? I'm meant to be back at my desk."

"Shit, yeah."

On the walk back, which neither of us rushes, I ask Clarissa the obvious question I already know the answer to. "Have you told Mum and Dad anything?"

"Not bloody likely." She says, shaking her head. "Can you imagine the fuss they'd make?"

I can, which is why I haven't told them anything about Kirsty.

"Have you ever thought about it? You know, marriage and kids."

"Well, I have, on and off, of course, but… The time was never right. Not much chance of it now, is there?"

"Suppose not, but you'll get your chance again, soon. Mark my words, Andy."

"If you think, dearest sister."

I spent the afternoon researching lucid dreaming, instead of working. Riss sent me the article she mentioned, then I got deep in the weeds of Google, snuffling around for videos and articles, instructions and people's experiences. Quite fascinating. To think that a universe can exist inside your head, and you are free to roam around it, however you please. If it's as good as people say, I can imagine some never wanting to leave their beds. Sort of like a Star Trek Holodeck or Virtual Reality. The experiences are as real as anything.

If I can figure out how to do it, I might figure out what is going on in my dreams, and find out who the mysterious Chloe is, once and for all.

When I prove to Kirsty this was all a mistake and Chloe is a newsreader or something, and my imagination just ran wild for a moment, she has to see sense and forget the whole thing, and we can put this ridiculous event behind us and move on. Maybe I will 'pop the question' soon, show her I'm serious about this. No more messing around, we'll get married before the year is out, and I'll never have to think about this stupid misunderstanding again.

Chapter Sixteen

Harder than it seems, this lucid dreaming lark. So far, all I've got to show for it is a few garbled dream journal entries, a worse headache than normal, and feeling idiotic, repeating the mantra 'I will control my dreams, I will control my dreams' over and over, as I fall asleep. I tried playing some 'binaural' music that was suggested to ease my brainwaves into the mood, or something, but all I felt was queasy and tired.

As with everything, YouTube and blogs all over the internet make it seem simple. Just follow these five easy steps, and you can control your universe in five minutes. Bullshit. I've stopped short of some of the more ridiculous suggestions that I set an alarm for four in the morning and then sit up for an hour, before trying to go back to sleep. Bollocks to that, I have enough sleep issues as it is without creating more on purpose.

I'm going to continue the dream journal though because maybe that will dredge up some useful information. Or at the very least, be entertaining when I read it back one day.

I downloaded an app on my phone specifically for dream journaling, because my handwriting is utterly illegible at the best of times, never mind first thing when I wake up, and I can type much faster than I can use a pen. Speed is of the essence, so I immediately jot down the thoughts I have whenever I remember a dream.

I'm in a forest, old and rich smelling, and it's raining. I'm walking through mud, puddles, general twigs and brush, but none of these things seems to hinder my progress. I'm going towards a sound. Someone singing. A female voice, but I can't make out the words.

When I get near the sound, it stops, replaced by a soft silence. I look around, but there's no sign of anyone.

Suddenly, the forest fades away, and I'm now standing in a room. My parents' living room, I think. The TV is on and Bruce Forsyth gurns into the camera. "Nice to see you, to see you nice!" He bellows out to raucous applause. I turn away. Mum yells from the kitchen. "Dinner's ready." and I see Rissa jump up from the couch and run out of the room. I couldn't see her before, she was hiding under a blanket.

I follow her, but the passageway is ridiculously long. It should be about eight feet, but I walk for a long time and still don't make it to the kitchen. I don't remember our house being this big.

A door opens next to me. Inside is a musty old room, a stink of damp and smoke. I look up and a man is sitting at a writing desk. I stop dead in my tracks. He hasn't noticed me. I back out, slowly.

"YOU! Get out. I told ye 'afore."

I woke up then, sweaty and stressed like the other day. I've tried to focus on the man, but I can't picture his face or anything about him. I know I felt scared, but why, I have no idea.

Rissa couldn't make it today for a jog, but she insisted I take a walk myself to keep up the progress. I could almost match her speed for a while yesterday, but then I realised she'd slowed down for my benefit. I'm feeling a little more fit, I guess, after a few days of regular training.

I lock my computer and stand up. My cubicle walls hiding me from the grey dullness of the office. I'm progressing with all Ron's tasks, but his constant meetings and status updates interrupt my flow and slow me down. He doesn't see the irony of this and prattles on during our daily meetings, regardless. "See the big picture, Andy." He says as he types his notes into the Excel sheet.

My phone buzzes in my pocket. A text from Kayla. 'Fancy going for a drink tonight? No pressure.'

A pulse of heat floods my veins as I read the message. A pretty girl is asking me out? Am I still dreaming? I tap the screen to reply, but I hesitate. I can't do this, can I? Kirsty is due back home soon. She'll see sense and forget the whole sordid affair, and we can get back on with our lives. I can't risk the chance of reconciliation by going for a drink with Kayla, much as I'd like it. I type out a message. 'I can't make it tonight, sorry.'

"Andy." I turn around and Dave is behind me.

"Hey, mate." I double-take. "You okay?"

"Been better, to be honest." He sighs. "Got a minute?"

"Aye, sure. I'm just going out for a walk. Come along?"

"Yeah."

Dave slumps along with me through and out of the office, and we cross the road to the green.

"What's up?" I turn to face him. He sighs again, showing me a big gash on his hand. "Jesus! What the fuck happened?"

"I punched the wall."

I laugh, but he doesn't see the humour. "What?"

"Me and Michelle got into a big fight last night, she told me to fuck off and dumped me, I drank a bottle of vodka, then I went and punched a big hole in the wall." He shrugs.

"Shit, mate. Do you want to start at the beginning?"

"Not really, but…"

Dave tells me his tale of woe. Apparently, Michelle found out about his extracurricular activities with other women. Many, many other women, and decided that she didn't want to be part of a harem, and ended the relationship. I can't say I'm surprised to be fair. It was inevitable. I resist the urge to say 'I told you so' to Dave. What I don't understand is why he's upset. I thought this sort of thing was run-of-the-mill for him. He's had more girlfriends than I've had hot dinners.

"Were you serious, about Michelle?"

Dave pauses to think about the question. "I suppose."

"Well, maybe you shouldn't have been knobbing around then, like a whore?"

"Don't you start. I've heard it all already… I realise it now." He shrugs. "I've fucked up, Andy."

He seems genuinely remorseful. "Did you tell her that?"

"Nah, she wasn't gonna listen."

"She might if you approach it calmly." I nod towards his damaged hand. "What you going to do?"

"Dunno, I thought you might have some advice, seeing as you've been dumped?"

"I'm not dumped!" I retort. "Kirsty is just having a moment or some shite."

Dave nods. "Yeah, okay, mate."

I sense sarcasm, but I let it slide. "My advice is to think about your life, and what you want from a relationship. If you were serious about Michelle, tell her that and see if she'll understand you've had a change of heart about things. Maybe it took a shock like this for you to realise you've got old, and you can't be shagging anything that moves, anymore."

Dave stays silent. I can sense the cogs in his brain ticking around.

"Do you want to settle down?"

Dave shudders at the thought. "Even the words make me cringe, Andy, but something ain't right now. The shags haven't felt as good, lately, you know?"

"You're shagged out, Dave." I chuckle. "It happens to all of us, in the end."

"There are blue pills for that." He smirks.

"True, but I mean, the thrill is gone now. What your body wants is safety, warmth, cuddles and companionship. Not random sex with people you barely know and will never see again."

"You could be right, mate." Dave looks into the distance, thoughtful. I never expected this day to come, but here it is. Shagger Dave ends his career with a record-breaking goal history, inelegantly stepping down as King, for some new stallion to step up to the mark and ride his way around the United Kingdom and all Her Majesty's territories.

I'm a little sceptical, to be honest, if this revelation will last, and if he won't just go back to his normal ways by the weekend.

My phone buzzes in my pocket. Kayla again. 'I'll be in the pub around 8, if you want to come along :) xx'. I realise I didn't send my reply to her before. I look up at Dave and his face like a wet weekend in Blackpool, and ponder on the lecture I just gave him about not shagging around. I come to a rapid conclusion and send the message I wrote earlier. 'I can't make it tonight, sorry.'

She replies instantly. 'Shame, maybe another time, then? xx'

I put my phone away and turn to Dave. "Come over tonight if you like? We can get kebabs and watch some shit on Netflix and wallow in our respective miseries."

"Sounds champion." He puffs out a laugh. "No bloody rom-coms though, I've had enough women troubles."

"Fair enough. I'm with you there." I look down at his hand again. "You up to date with your tetanus shot?"

"Yeah, since I rolled over onto a broken fencepost last year." He grins. "That Lucy bird, do you remember her? She liked a roll in the hay, she did." He takes his phone out of his pocket and scrolls around, then shows me a photo on his screen with a gurning smile on his mug. "Tasty, weren't she?"

I raise an eyebrow. "That lasted all of five minutes, didn't it?"

"What?"

"Your shagging remorse." I sigh.

"Oh... Yeah, thanks for being a downer, Andy."

"All part of the service, mate."

A thought springs into my mind, and I sit down abruptly on the same bench that Rissa and I frequent during our lunchtime jogs.

"Sorry, Dave. I just have to write an email quickly. Something just came back to me. See you later, yeah?"

"No worries, yeah. I'll call over. Cheers, Andy." He smiles and heads back towards the office.

"A moment of clarity?" Someone asked me the same thing, recently. I can't say that I have. "No, I don't reckon." A woman leans down over me, deftly delivering a kiss to my lips, so soft I barely feel it. She smells like honeysuckle, and she lingers above me, staring into my eyes. I feel an aura of warmth coming from her, an electrical tingle, exciting my atoms with her presence. My hand runs down her back and I feel every notch in her spine. She quivers, giggling softly, and rolls over. I look up and clouds gently pass overhead in the cobalt blue sky.

We're outside, next to a gurgling stream, a landscape of rolling hills and unspoilt country laid out in front of us, an idyllic and warm setting. She gets up and walks over to the stream, kneeling down to take a sip of the cool, bubbling water.

"I have." She walks back over to me, sprinkling me with drips from her fingers.

"*Oi, you.*" *I sit up, brushing away the cold water from my skin.* "*Have you? Do tell.*"

"*It was a while ago. I think I was in a café somewhere, and all of a sudden, à propos of nothing, this feeling just exploded inside me.*"

She spreads out her hands, and her eyes are wide. So dark they are almost totally black. I stare into them, and it's as though I'm connected to her. "*And in that moment, I knew everything.*"

"*Everything?*" *I hear myself speak, but I'm distant from my body, I'm drifting in third-person view and my avatar acts out my side of the story.*

"*Yep, everything. Just for a moment.*" *She laughs.* "*And then it sort of faded away.*"

"*Well, that's a lot of use, isn't it?*"

"*I know, I want my money back.*" *She chuckles.* "*No, I mean, it was great, for a moment, but it went away so quickly. At the time, though, it was pure and raw. I didn't know what it was at first, it took a while before I realised.*"

The scene switches to a beach, but there's no sign of an ocean. The sky above us is dark, lit with aurora in vivid green, melting and flowing silently, dancing light on the moist sand where we walk.

"*What did you do, then?*" *I reach over and take her hand. Her fingers are freezing cold, but she gently squeezes in acknowledgement.*

"*I didn't know what to make of it, not for a long time. But I asked a friend who knows about these things, and she told me it was a sign, to follow my dreams.*"

"*Can't argue with that, can you?*" *I smile.*

"*Exactly. So I did, and here I am now.*"

We walk up to a cave in the side of a cliff facing the beach, inside I can see a fire gently burning and a little pool of water with complicated plumbing that connects it to the fireplace. Who could have built such a strange bath? Without question, I follow her into the cave where she slips gently into the hot water.

"Just hold me?"

I nod and slide in next to her. Because what else can I do?

She sings softly, and I have to strain to hear the words.

"... when you dream of me..."

Chapter Seventeen

I wasn't going to do this, but in the end, I couldn't stand it and I gave in to my insecurities. Here I am, waiting at the airport for my girlfriend to come back from her holiday without me.

I got here super early, and I've been pacing up and down, sick in my stomach, a knot in my throat, and a killer headache all combining to make me into a complete nervous wreck. The plane has landed, and I'm trying to stay away from the arrival gate because I know it will still be a few minutes before they come out, and a security guard has already been giving me the evil eye.

The bookshelf at WHSmith provides little in the way of distraction. Still, I pick up a book on the history of Apple Computers to take my mind off things. Jony Ive smiles at me from the cover, mocking me… 'If you didn't have filthy dreams, you little pervert, then you wouldn't be in this shitty situation, would you?' he seems to say, from the page. Feck off, Sir Jony. What do you know about ridiculous dreams? Probably quite a lot.

. . .

I was half expecting Dave to suggest we go out on the pull when he came over the other evening, but he was still filled with melancholy and woe. Instead, we had a comfortable night in, with food, a few cans, and a selection of films that Dave knew contained nudity and bad language. Always a win. He's perked up a bit since then, but I can tell at work he's still a bit dejected about the whole Michelle thing. I suggested he give it a few days, or even a week, before he tried to contact her again with any kind of reconciliation plan.

I can give advice, apparently, but following it myself is almost impossible — as evidenced by me lingering here at the airport, skulking around, pretending to read a book. Part of me wants to go home now and be nonchalant about the whole thing. When Kirsty shows up, I'll pretend I didn't even know she was gone. 'Oh, hi. Did you grab some milk?' But of course, that will never happen. I'm about as nonchalant as Mr Bean, on speed.

I peek out of the shop window at the arrivals gate. Still no one coming through. A couple more minutes to come up with a plan... Ridiculous, of course. If I haven't come up with something good in the last couple of weeks, what chance do I have of preparing a suitable speech now, in the last ninety seconds? I'll wing it, I suppose.

A small crowd gathers around the arrivals gate; the usual suspects. People with Bluetooth headsets and an iPad with someone's name in big text. Families waiting to greet loved ones, dealers waiting for their mules... And me, sad, lonely, pathetic boyfriend, hoping that his girlfriend is coming back with a change of heart.

Travellers start to come through the gates, blinking bleary-eyed, weary, colourful, noisy and excited.

I spot Laura first, she's gaudy and blonde, heavily tanned and gushing to Nathan about something. She sees me, makes eye contact and pauses, turning around and going back through the gate. Nathan quickly shuffles away and avoids looking in my direction. Prick.

Laura comes back through the gate and barely nods to me, then walks away in the direction Nathan took. Where's Kirsty?

My phone buzzes in my pocket. I pull it out, while also trying to keep my eye on the gate. A text from Kirsty, the first one in over two weeks. 'Why are you here?'

Cold, curt, succinct, but not out of character.

'Came to pick you up! :)' I reply.

'I didn't want to do this here, Andy, but whatever. I'll see you in the coffee shop in a minute. Please, don't make a fuss.'

'Oh, right. Okay, then…'

Do what here? She's never been one for public displays of intimacy. I look around and find the nearest coffee shop, which is where I presume she means.

"Hey!" Kirsty approaches, wheeling a suitcase behind her. She looks different somehow. Tanned as Laura, but there's… something. "You look good."

"Andy, why did you come to the airport?" She sighs.

"I said, already. To pick you up." I try to fake a smile, but it comes out like a scary clown. I look away. "Do you want a coffee?"

"I suppose." She sits down at the table I've procured. I go up to the counter.

It isn't a Starbucks, but I get Kirsty the nearest equivalent of what she usually has at her work. Some kind of complicated concoction that costs a bloody fortune. I get myself a simple black coffee, but they don't call it that. I have to order an 'Americano,' whatever that means in real life…

"Good flight?" I try to break the ice, but Kirsty is deep in her phone, rapidly typing on the screen, fingernails clacking. She looks up, nodding thanks for the coffee I plop down in front of her.

"A kid was behind me, kicking my chair every three seconds, a fat bloke was next to me, stinking of BO, and turbulence made the hostess spill red wine on my skirt, but other than that, yeah it was fine." She flashes a fake smile, then looks back at her phone.

"Oh, dear."

Finally, she puts her phone away in her bag and looks up at me. "Andy, as I said, I really didn't want to do this here, but since you've come, I guess I have no choice." She takes a deep breath and a sip of her coffee. "Laura and Nathan have kindly offered that I stay with them for a while, so we can sort everything out."

I feel a thud in my chest. "Why would you need to stay with them?"

"I think it's best until we all get things straight."

"Sorry, I'm not with you. What things?" It strikes me suddenly what's different about her. She's done her hair exactly as Laura does. Fringe and all. Even died the same shade of blonde. They must have been to a spa or salon together, I guess.

"Us, Andy. I'm still not sure where this," she raises her hands, "is going."

I pause, trying to stay calm. "Well, I had hoped we could just go back to where we were, Kirsty." I flash a smile.

"I don't think so, Andy." She takes another gulp of coffee. Mine sits untouched. "I don't think we can, now, can we?" Her tone is as if I'm interviewing for a job in her café. She's switched to the authoritative 'manager Kirsty' voice.

"Well, I don't see why not?"

She puts her hands up to her temples and closes her eyes for a moment, taking another deep breath. I hear her phone ding in her bag.

"Look, I have to go." She moves to stand up. "I'll come to the house tomorrow to collect some things. But, I think it would be best if you weren't there when I come. It would just be easier."

"What?"

"I don't want a fuss, Andy." She raises her voice a notch.

I feel anger building in my chest. I'm still not sure what is going on here, but it seems a lot like I'm being dumped, and my presence is just an inconvenience to her. I fucking live in the house, don't I? Why should I evacuate just so Kirsty doesn't have to endure the risk of any drama?

"I… Right."

"Good." She stands up and fishes in her bag for her phone. "Look, it's for the best… I mean, it's not as if we ever really loved each other, was it?" She pulls the handle up on her suitcase and starts to walk away. "I'll be in touch."

Stunned, I'm paralysed for a moment, clutching my paper cup of bitter coffee, watching my beautiful girlfriend walk away from me, out of my life… Forever?

"But… I do love you, Kirsty."

· · ·

A millisecond long movie plays out in my brain, me running after her, grabbing her into an embrace, passionate kisses, tears and apologies, and we go back home and shag like bunnies all night, only pausing for bathroom breaks and food. But instead, I sit at the table, staring down at my lukewarm coffee, the noise of the surrounding airport dragging me slowly back into reality. Kirsty has gone, she's different somehow, and I'm alone, miserable, and I have no fucking change left for the car-park machine.

Automatic pilot drives me away from the airport. I'm vaguely aware of the road and cars, but everything is hazy, a veil of numbness draped over the world. I aimed for home, but when I shake my head back into awareness, I find I'm in the driveway at Rissa's house. My subconscious brought me here for a reason, I guess.

I get out of the car and knock on the door, hoping that Nick doesn't answer.

"Hi, Andy." Riss answers, in her usual leggings and sweatshirt. "I wasn't expecting you?"

I feel my knees collapse, my stomach churn, and I fall onto my sister's shoulder. "She's gone, Riss. She's fucking left me!" A burst of tears floods my face and I clutch hard onto my sister, shaking. She squeezes back, and we stand on the doorstep for an awkward moment before she gently pushes me away and wipes a tear from her face.

"You'd better come in, Andy."

. . .

Clarissa brings me a cup of tea. I'm flopped onto the couch, staring into space. Tea fixes all ails.

Her house smells of roses and sandalwood. A familiar scent, warming and comforting, the same as when I stayed here for a while. My house smells different, like green tea from various scent dispensers around the place, to give a sense of calm and meditation, or something. A thought occurs to me. "Is Nick around?"

Riss shakes her head. "No, he's gone to Cardiff for a match. Back tomorrow."

"Right." A brief wave of relief. Last thing I need is for Nick to see me like this.

"So, do you want to tell me what happened?" Rissa sits down next to me, clutching a big mug in both hands.

I sigh. "I went to meet Kirsty at the airport. She was due back today from holiday…" Riss nods. "… and, basically, it went exactly the opposite of how I hoped."

I explain how Kirsty seemed different, and she announced she'd be staying at her friend's house for some indeterminate amount of time until 'things' are sorted out. As I say the words, I can't believe they are really what happened. This seems like a horrible nightmare, going round and round in my head. Her matter-of-fact attitude, and those damning words — 'I mean, it's not as if we ever really loved each other, was it?'

Clarissa reaches over and grabs my hand. "Sorry, brother. That's a big load of shit." She squeezes gently. "God, she's a real cunt, isn't she?"

Shocked, I look up. I don't think I've ever heard my sister use that word before. I have to laugh. "She really is!"

Chapter Eighteen

I'm on a train. Not a modern one, but old-fashioned. Compartmented seating areas. A lot of wood and thick pile carpet on the floor. A smell of old tobacco and sweat.

Dirty and worn, but neat and well-kept. The constant clatter of wheels on tracks is reassuring.

I'm alone in my section, staring out of the window. We pass an endless string of undulating fields, dotted with sheep or cows, broken with forest and occasional houses. I don't recognise any of the places, and the train doesn't stop. I've been here as long as I can remember, and I don't recall how I came to be here. I just am.

This is life. A journey where I don't know the destination. How long will it take, where will I end up?

. . .

The door of my compartment opens, and a woman enters. She's dressed in black, tight-fitting, with a discreet hat that carries a gauze that effectively hides her face.

She pulls a suitcase in and closes the door, slowly and quietly, with purpose. She glances around the cabin and moves to the seat directly opposite me. I am presented with her shapely behind as she adjusts her purse, then bends down to pick up the suitcase. I notice her legs are clad in nylon, and they are just the right delicate Bézier curve that excites me. She hasn't acknowledged my presence.

She lifts the case up and tries to put it on the luggage rack, but she's too short and can't quite reach it. But as she struggles, I get another glimpse that sets my heart to race. Those legs extend all the way up, but the nylon stops short on her thigh. No suspender, just the darker band of stocking that holds them up. After that, the split in her skirt doesn't reveal, but my thoughts probe that crevice and wonderful treasures linger just inside.

I shiver at the thought. She turns around, looking down at me hiding behind my book.

"Excuse me?" Her voice smooth like chocolate, sticky. I look up, pretending to only just notice her existence.

"Yes?"

"Would you mind?" She nods to the suitcase and then the rack.

"Of course."

I stand and take the case from her. It isn't heavy, and I slide it into the rack above her seat.

"Thank you."

I nod, smile and sit back down. She takes off her jacket, gloves and hat, releasing her dark hair in the process. Then she sits down in front of me, prim, and organises her things on the seat next to her. Pulling out a book from her purse.

There's a moment, as she glances back at me. I see her face clearly for the first time. She's immediately familiar, yet I can't place where I know her from. I don't notice any recognition in her eyes, and she opens her book and begins to read.

I look away, feeling rude to stare. Back to the endless landscape that persists, undeterred.

A scent drifts in, presumably from her. Fragrant, feminine, floral, but not overpowering. Honeysuckle, I think. I look down at my book, but the words won't stick in my mind. Where do I know her from?

A thought occurs to me. Where did she come from? The train didn't stop, and I understood that it was utterly empty, but for me.

Is she real? I look up again, she's busy reading, her legs crossed now, I am blessed with a tempting view of those stocking tops once more. Lace edged, black and sheer, hugging those legs that tell stories of delight.

She sighs, closes her book and puts it away in her purse once more. She looks over at me. I'm trying to focus on my book, but I see the scene play out in my periphery.

"I've been a naughty girl."

I look up, startled. She has a mischievous grin on that face that I know so well.

"Pardon?"

"I didn't pay for a ticket. I've been awful."

"Oh, well. I don't think there's an inspector." I smile.

Her grin remains, and she slides a hand along her skirt from knee to hip.

"Do you think I should be punished?"

I laugh. "Oh, I think you can be let off, just this once."

She flutters her eyelashes. "I get off at the next stop."

"No harm done, then." A thought occurs to me. "Where is the next stop, do you know?"

"Where do you want it to be?"

"Sorry?"

"It's your choice, tonight."

"I'm not with you?"

She begins to answer, but the train slows, gently, but noticeably, then firmer, and she is thrown forward, off her seat and across the cabin, I open my arms to catch her as the train comes to a full abrupt stop. But there's no station visible from the window. She looks up at me.

"Oh. Thank you."

"That was sudden, wasn't it?"

"Where did you choose?" She stands up, brushing down her skirt and moving to peer out of the window.

"I... I don't know?"

I stand up to look, but as I do, the environment around me changes, with no transition that I can notice. I'm no longer on the train but in an elegant hotel room. A four-poster bed, a large dressing table, sumptuous chairs and thick plush curtains that frame a window looking out onto a mountain vista.

I pause. This isn't right. "Hang on." I try to remember what the thing was. I look at my hands. "That's it." I push my finger from one hand into the palm of the other. It passes through with no resistance. "I'm dreaming."

She looks at me. "Well, yes, I know." She rolls her eyes. "Don't ruin it."

I raise an eyebrow. "No, you don't understand…" She flashes me a look, and I stop. I know what she wants.

"You're Chloe, aren't you?"

She nods.

"Where are we?"

"I'm not certain. Do you want to look around?"

"That might be useful."

She takes my hand and leads me to the door of the room. We exit into a hallway, long and narrow. Little lights near the ground flicker on, showing us a path. We both shrug and follow it. What else can we do?

We amble slowly, hand in hand, along the passageway. We don't speak, but I can sense her, somehow. She's happy, curious and, rather interestingly, she's a little horny. I squeeze her hand. Her fingers are cold, but she squeezes back. We'll go back to the room in a minute.

I feel something in my pocket. It's a large metal key, rusty and heavy. A huge thing. Must be ancient.

"Do you know what this is for?"

"Nope. Still don't know." She looks at me strangely, and I put the key back in my pocket.

We come to a corner in the passage, and then a stairwell through a set of double doors. We push through and the steps only lead down, so we descend. The plush carpet of the passage is replaced by white marble steps, but as we go down, they become dusty, filthy and dark stone, but worn smooth from decades of constant travel. We arrive at the bottom and a small door faces us. Ornate and thick wood, with a brass sign attached.

'Lodestone Bar.'

"Fancy a drink?" I turn to Chloe, who sniggers.

"Don't mind if I do."

The bar is empty but clean and tidy. As though set up and ready for customers to come in, but we're the first. No staff. I look behind the bar at the beer taps. There are various ales and stouts. I try one tap and beer flows.

"Pint?"

"Go on then." She smirks. "Do you think we'll get in trouble?"

"There doesn't seem to be anyone around..." I flash a grin. "Anyway, this is a dream, isn't it..." I tail off, she doesn't want to spoil the experience. "Never mind."

I pour us two drinks, and we take them to a small table. I sit down first, so I can get a glimpse of her legs as she sits opposite. Tempting, I'd be inclined to go straight back to the bedroom and while away the rest of the night, but I need some answers. What is this place? Why are we here? Who is Chloe, and why does she haunt my dreams and, consequently, make a mess of my life?

"Where do I know you from, Chloe?"

She shrugs and takes a sip of her beer. "I was wondering the same thing."

"Thee should've heert myn waer-words, for I fear ye be fast, now for gud." I'm startled by a voice behind me, Chloe looks up over my shoulder. I turn and a man in dark brown robes is standing at the bar, "Not that there's gud in it."

"Sorry?"

"Leave, now. Curse the stones, ye'd deny myn soul eternity."

I stand up. "I'm not sure if I understand? Who are you? What are you doing here?"

The man, who I assume is a monk of some kind, going by his robes and hairstyle, such as it is, approaches me, glaring through his ashen pallor. He grows as he gets closer, towering and suddenly smouldering a thick black smoke from his robe. A stench of tar clings at my throat and a deep throbbing bass pulse churns at my gut. I feel myself shaking, nauseous, and shrinking down into myself, unable to move or speak. The room around me fades into blackness and I fall to the floor, helpless.

I sense a hand grab mine, and I'm pulled up, the monk instantly zooms away, out of focus until he's nothing but a dot on the horizon, I look up and Chloe leans down over me, whispering in my ear.

"Fly, Andy."

Suddenly, the ground beneath us is miles away, and we're falling, fast. I look in horror as the landscape looms towards us. My stomach lurches inside me and I twist and flap like a leaf in a storm.

"Fuck! We're going to die!"

"No, we aren't." Chloe laughs, and, still holding my hand, squeezes tight and takes a deep breath. "Fly…"

We slow down our rapid dive, and fields, roads and lakes become visible as if we're browsing on Google Earth. She nods down towards a town. A grey grid of buildings and roads that grow organically from the surrounding green. "I live there." She points down to a house that's just outside the centre, next to an area of forest.

No longer falling, we seem to hover thousands of feet above the planet. Clouds drift by above and below, but I'm not cold.

"Holy shit, this is amazing!"

"Yeah." She laughs. "But it doesn't last. We should go somewhere else."

"Okay."

Chloe snaps her fingers and the world beneath us melts and twists into a brown mess. Replaced quickly by blue seats and a big window beside us.

"We're on a bus?" I look around at rows of empty seats in front of us, we're at the back and there's no one else visible except the driver at the front.

"Yeah, going to my Gran's in Felixstowe."

"Really? Why?" I laugh.

"No idea." She chuckles and grabs my hand, squeezing tight, "But Gran makes a wonderful walnut cake."

"Fair enough." I sit back and watch through the window. The endless fields and hills remind me of the train journey I was on, going nowhere. A thought occurs to me. "Chloe, who was that old bloke, the monk?"

"Yeah, I'm not sure, to be honest. But he's strange, don't you think?"

"I do. I think I'd prefer it if he buggered off and didn't come back. Something about him puts me on edge."

I turn to Chloe, but she's not there. Then the seats in front of me fade into nothing. The bus flicks out of existence, and I'm left sitting on the couch in my living room, the TV blaring snow and white noise. A cool breeze comes in from an open window.

If this is my dream, which I'm pretty sure it is, then these characters must be from my memory, but I can't think where this monk bloke could have come from, let alone Chloe. At least she's pleasant, unlike the monk.

I get up and switch off the TV, then the light, and head up the stairs to bed.

Chapter Nineteen

R iss makes a damn good lasagne. First decent home-cooked meal I've had in ages. I stayed at her house last night; there was a bottle of wine and a good amount of reminiscing with the lasagne, which meant getting up early, and going home for a change of clothes before I went to work.

I left Kirsty's present on the bed, so she'd see it when she goes over to get her stuff. I won't be home when she calls, as instructed, and now I've had a night to mull it over, I think I also prefer not to be there when she collects things. Every item she picks up triggering a memory of when we got it, or who bought it for whom. We've been together long enough that the list would be long and painful. I'll let her with the cold, dead heart pick apart our lives. Ignorance, as they say, is bliss.

Anger and betrayal are what comes to mind now when I think about what's happened. My gut tells me that this has very little to do with me calling out a name in my sleep and that Laura and, especially Nathan, have a lot more to do with this whole situation than my dream-woman, Chloe. Never liked that Nathan. Slimy little twat. I bet he's filled Kirsty's head with ideas that she could do much better than sad, nerdy hardware technical advisor, Andy Clarke, who doesn't even drive an electric vehicle.

Bunch of arseholes. Maybe I am better off out of it? Try telling my guts that, though. I don't think it has hit me properly yet. I'm shell shocked. This has to be a huge mistake, doesn't it? Kirsty did love me. I know she did. We had many good times together. Sure, we had some arguments, but that's normal life. You don't stay with someone for six years if you don't feel 'something'… Do you?

My phone buzzes. Riss waiting for me outside work for our jog. I asked for a day off, but she said — 'That second and third helping of lasagne isn't going to magic itself away, is it?'

I can't help it if I enjoy eating. I've got bugger all else to look forward to these days.

"Hey."

"How you doing, Andy?" She flashes a sympathy smile.

"Fine, sis." I sigh. "You don't have to keep asking, you know."

"Sorry, just concerned about my big brother."

"Ugh, I know. Sorry, that came out wrong… It's just, I don't want to think about it. I'm fine. Thanks."

I give her a brief hug.

"Come on then, I've got to get back today. We can't linger."

· · ·

She's right, I ate way too much for dinner last night. Our jog around the green is harder than I remember. I push on, though, so she doesn't give me any more lectures, but my stomach doesn't much care for this exertion, and a stabbing pain causes me to stop and double over.

"You okay?"

"Just need a second." I pant.

A flashback memory; My stomach churning, my knees buckling, a horrific sense of dread and a stench of tar.

"Hey, I think I had one of those lucid dreams, last night." I slowly stand upright again and motion towards the bench at the end of the park.

"Yeah?"

"Yeah, there was a bar and a train… That woman again, and we went flying!"

"Oh? Sounds interesting."

"She's Chloe." I turn to look at Riss.

"That's the one from the dream that…" Rissa pauses. "Started it all?"

"Yeah."

"Who is she?"

"No idea."

"You don't recognise her from anywhere?"

"Nope. Not that I can think of. She's not from the telly, or work, or supermarket. I'm stumped, but it's definitely the same woman, in all the dreams. There was that monk bloke again, as well."

"Maybe it's a sign, Andy. Your religious calling." She guffaws.

"Oh, definitely." I scoff. "I don't think the robe would suit me… Mind you, it does look like I'm headed for a life of celibacy…"

"Pfff, don't be silly, Andy. You'll find someone decent. There's nowt wrong with you."

"Thanks, dear sister."

"Are you going to try again, with the lucid thing?"

"May as well give it a go." I ponder. "I wasn't even trying last night, it just, sort of happened."

"Aye, and that's how you'll find someone. Better than that bitch, Kirsty." Riss flashes me a look.

"Riss…" My instinct is to defend Kirsty. I still have feelings for her. It isn't a tap I can just turn off. Kirsty has been a part of my life for a long time, and I wasn't expecting her to stop being a part of my life anytime soon. There's a spark, somewhere deep inside me, that still hopes this is all a simple misunderstanding, and Kirsty will wake up from her 'moment' and come back home and life will just go back to normal, like a sitcom episode. My logical brain knows that will not happen, but our bodies and brains are in a constant battle to figure out what reality actually is. Our eyes see something, our brains filter it and brush it up, 'no — this is what you need to see…' Then, when we're unconscious, our brains invent a whole alternative world, filled with strange characters and ridiculous situations. How can you trust anything you seem to see or feel? I'm confused and tired most of the time, lately. All I know is I've had the same headache for weeks now and the world is a cold, loveless place. "Never mind." I sigh. "Thanks. Thank fuck I've got you, eh?"

She smiles and reaches over for a cuddle. "You daft ape." She stands up from the bench. "I gotta go, Andy. Nick is getting back soon."

"Oh, okay."

"I'm ovulating." She screws up her face in hope.

"Ohhh… Right!" I pause. "I was going to say, give Nick my best, but…" She laughs. "Err. Just.. Yeah, you know."

"Thanks, brother."

"God. I nearly said — I'll be thinking of you, but I absolutely will not be doing that! Fingers crossed." I smile.

"See you soon." She walks away with a snigger.

The second I opened my front door, I knew Kirsty had been. I could smell her scent, and I could also smell a fruity vape lingering in the background. Peaches or something. My hallway tainted with the vaporised effluent of Nathan's lungs. It persisted throughout the house. I opened the windows and lit an incense stick. I don't need the constant reminder that my life is cracking like thin ice beneath me.

My rational brain told me not to even look for what things Kirsty had taken, but my emotional instinct was having none of it. She's taken most of her clothes and jewellery. Makeup, trinkets, towels… And the gift I left for her. The wrapping paper dropped into the wastepaper-bin in the bedroom. When I saw it, dread and nausea filled my guts. The gift I got her for her thirtieth birthday opened while Nathan stood by and mocked me.

I'm thankful I didn't go whole-hog for the engagement ring now. That was an option I mulled over for a long time when choosing a gift. That could have been an expensive and even more embarrassing mistake. The white-gold necklace, with ruby heart pendant, for her birthstone, was bad enough. The little card I put inside the box read: 'My darling Kirsty, I gave you my heart a long time ago, but here's another one. Happy 30th. I love you.

Xxx'. I didn't need to recall the words I wrote, weeks ago, I could read them back from the card that was on the floor, next to the bin.

I sat down on the bed, which is where I remain, fifteen minutes later. A silly thing; I notice she's taken the alarm clock from the nightstand. That was the first gift I got her years ago. It could play 'soothing' rain forest sounds to go to sleep to, but it was terrible. Rain forest, through a shitty little speaker that makes it sound more like toilet flush. We never used the 'soothe' function, but every morning it woke her up with tweeting birds and a gushing, gurgling stream.

My phone buzzes. A text from Dave. 'Pub?' and never has that word been more inviting. I reply. 'Fuck, yeah. See you there.'

"I needed that." I drop my glass onto the bar and wipe my mouth after necking a whole pint in one gulp. "Another?" I nod to the barman.

"You're keen, tonight, mate."

"One of those days." I look over at Dave and sigh. "You were right… We're both now official residents of 10 Dumping Street, Dumpstown, County Dumped."

"Ah. Sorry, Andy." He flashes a sympathy smile.

"Yeah. Kirsty took a load of her stuff today, she's staying with Laura, apparently."

"I knew she was trouble, the moment I met her." Dave shakes his head.

"Kirsty?"

"Yeah, a real bitch, I thought she was."

I double-take. I had no idea Dave didn't like my girlfriend. "Really?"

"Yeah, why do you think I didn't want to come to dinner that time? Fucking Kirsty."

"I... Wow, I mean... You never said owt?"

"You don't tell your best mate his girlfriend is a bitch, do you?"

"You just fucking did!"

Dave picks up his pint and gestures with it at me. "Ah, well, she in't your girlfriend now, is she? That restriction no longer applies. All bets are off, or is it on? Either way, now I can tell you the truth."

"Oh... Right." I feel like I've been kicked in the guts. Not that I needed approval from Dave, but Riss didn't much care for her either, now I come to think about it. Was I so blind I didn't see the real Kirsty all these years? I mean, she was a bit controlling and funny about things, but everyone has their foibles, don't they? I decide to change the subject, in case things get any more awkward. "You heard from Michelle, at all?"

"Nope. And I doubt I will now. I think I've moved on." He shrugs. "Not like we was gonna get married or owt."

"Fair enough."

"Might give that Kayla a bell, see if she's up for some fun." He sniggers.

"Oh, Kayla... Right." I pick up my new pint and take a gulp.

Dave jolts his head back. "Ey, up. What's going on here?"

"Nothing?"

"Don't try to pull one over my eyes, mate. I know summat's up." His eyes narrow.

I sigh. "Well, if you must know… I've been chatting, on and off with Kayla. She asked if I wanted to go for a drink the other night, but I stayed in with you. You fucking cock-blocker."

"Oh, aye. You like little gothy Kayla, eh?" His grin spreads as wide as the bar.

"It isn't like THAT… I mean, she's nice, pretty and all, we got to talking that time at your house… And. Well, I was assuming Kirsty would be back… Nowt happened." I shrug. "Anyway, I feel weird going skinny dipping in the same lake as you've been in."

Dave chokes on his beer. "You dirty bastard. There's nowt wrong with my oats."

"That's as maybe, but I don't fancy stirring your porridge."

"Shut it." He sniggers, then looks up, a lightbulb shining above his head. "You know what we need, Andy, my boy?"

"A break? A lottery win? A private jet to the Bahamas?"

"Aye, all that, but…" He pauses for effect. "A boys' weekend away!" He waits for a reaction.

"Eh, I don't know about that, mate."

"What? That's a brilliant idea. We'll go somewhere neither of us have been before, where all the women are fresh and fair game. We'll drown our sorrows in booze and fanny, and by the time we come back, we won't even remember who Kirsty or Michelle are. Boys' weekend, fucking top idea!" He slaps the bar with gusto.

Dave seems excited about the prospect, but I can't seem to muster the enthusiasm. Years gone by, I'd jump at the chance. But we never had the money then. "Where are you thinking?"

"I dunno, Prague? Amsterdam?"

"Oh, I thought you meant somewhere here in England?"

"No, bollocks to England. We need to go big."

"Right… How about Paris? I've never been there."

"I'm not going to romantic Paris with you, you twat."

"Right, no… Let me think about it, we'll see. I'm not exactly flush right now. I never got any money back from the holiday I was meant to go on. Insurance companies are tighter than a gnats chuff."

"No surprise there. It doesn't have to cost a fortune, you can get great deals, these days."

"I suppose. It would be a laugh to go somewhere, I was meant to have a bloody holiday, after all." I mull the idea over.

"Oh, I've got it."

"Well, don't give it to me." I snigger.

"Shut it. I mean, I know where we're going, Andy…" He looks into the distance, misty-eyed.

"Where?"

Dave pulls out his phone and taps away at the screen for a moment.

"What if I told you there was a place where beautiful women are abundant, booze and food are cheap, there's live music, loads of hotels, with vibrant culture and history, easy flights and loads of things to do and see?"

"Jesus. Have you started working for Lonely Planet guides or something?" I chuckle.

He shows me his phone screen. "Kraków, Poland."

I remain unimpressed. "Poland?"

"Yeah, man. Fucking brilliant place."

"Have you been before?"

"Well, no, but I was seeing this bird from Kraków for a bit.

Magda. Fuck me, she was tasty." He shudders at the thought. "Dirty as hell." He winks.

"That doesn't mean they are all like that."

"Have you ever seen an ugly Polish girl?"

"Well, no… I suppose not."

"There you go. Right, that's that sorted. I'll start looking at the details tomorrow."

"I still don't know if this is a good idea, Dave. I mean… We could end up robbed of our internal organs or something."

"That could happen in bloody Manchester… No, we could have a brilliant time and a break from reality. Don't be bloody negative. The deal is done, we're going. Now, get the drinks in to celebrate." He slaps his hands together. His mug sculpted with a massive grin. At least he's cheered up from the other day. I guess Michelle is long forgotten, which is more than I can say about Kirsty.

It still feels weird, to be thinking about going out on the pull, when I can still smell the scent of Kirsty's perfume in my nose. Then again, what am I waiting for? Will anything change in a week or month? Probably not. I'll either be more miserable, or more jaded… Likely both. I make an executive decision.

"Fuck it, we'll go to Kraków."

"That's the spirit!"

I might regret this choice, no, I WILL regret this choice, but sometimes you have to push the boundaries of your life and shift out of your comfort zone. Experience different cultures and language, break the monotony and drop a rock into the still waters of your life. Let the ripples flip you over and see where the tide takes you…

· · ·

"Remember, I told you about that dream I had, where I called out the name, Chloe?" Slightly worse for wear, after half a dozen pints, we move to a table at the back of the pub and sprawl across the cushioned seats.

"Oh, yeah. Did you figure out who she is?" Dave leers over his glass.

"No, but, I've been having a load more dreams, and she's almost always in them…" I feel my eyes blur out the vista of the pub, wistfully gazing into nothingness.

"Your dream woman, eh?" Dave laughs.

"Must be. She's bloody gorgeous…" I try to focus on the memory of Chloe's face. Hard to do through a haze of booze and dreams, but those dark eyes permeated my brain.

"You dirty bastard." Dave sniggers.

"No, it isn't like that… Well, it can be." I chuckle. "There's something more, though. Hard to explain it. I feel like I've got a genuine connection to her."

Dave looks at me sideways. "Andy… These are dreams, right?"

"Yeah. I know…"

"Those aren't real, you know that, don't you?" Dave looks at me, wide-eyed.

"Well, yeah, course. But her face, her voice, her mannerisms and stuff. It must have all come from somewhere. Perhaps I know her from god knows where, and I just can't remember it?"

"We need to go on that trip, fast. You're losing the plot, mate."

"How do you mean?"

"You're falling in love with a woman you've conjured up in your dreams. You need to get out more. Experience the real world, shag some Polish girls, drink a load of vodka and generally have a bloody good laugh."

"I'm not falling in love!" I scoff, incredulous.

Dave tilts his head. "You've got that stupid far-away look in your eyes, your pupils dilated when you mentioned her, you're talking about a deep fucking connection with a gorgeous woman… You're in love, Andy, my boy… Which is bad enough in itself, but worse, you're in love with a woman who doesn't exist."

I ponder for a moment. "You know, you might be right. That is a real problem."

Chapter Twenty

"He's absolutely loving this," Dave whispers to me from behind a hand. "I bet he has a massive wank when he gets home…" I stifle a chuckle and nod, giving a thumbs up from my lap. The thought of Ron jerking the gherkin is not something I ever want to conjure up in my worst nightmare.

Big Ron Corbishly does seem to be lapping up the attention. He's called an emergency meeting for the whole team on the 'Eternitive Medi' account. Dave and I shuffled in at the back of the conference room, next to the coffee flasks and the plates of biscuits that Ron must have organised. We're trying to be inconspicuous… At least, I am.

Ron claps his hands at the front of the room to get everyone's attention. There must be twenty people jammed in here. I don't even know half of the faces. Where did they come from? "Thanks, everyone, for coming at short notice." Ron fiddles with his laptop, trying to get the projector to pick up the screen. "Ah, there we go. Isn't technology great?" A forced laugh comes from the front row and Ron's desktop appears up on the wall, eight feet wide, hundreds of icons littering all over the wallpaper.

"Well, I expect you are wondering why I've called this meeting?" He scans the room to silence and blank expressions, then clicks on a PowerPoint presentation file. God help us... "Eternitive Medi, the biggest supplier of pharmaceutical software in Europe and Asia, has asked us," He motions around the room, "to assist them with a new appliance product range." I sigh, quietly. There's no need for this recap; everyone here already knows the spiel. We've been working on this stupid account for ages.

"Fake news!" Dave shouts out. I nudge him hard with my elbow. Last thing we need is attention.

Ron laughs, "No, it's all gospel, mate." Dave flashes a wink. Ron continues. "And as you know, the deadline for completion was next quarter." Oh, no. I can sense where this is going. "But," Ron beams out a horrific grin, "EM has just won a massive deal in Japan, and we need to be up and running by the end of next month." Silence and shock floods around the room as Ron drops his bombshell. He taps on his laptop and moves the screen to the next slide. A big red line of text in the middle of the page stands out — **All leave is cancelled for the duration** — Ah, for fuck's sake.

We are then tortured for fifty-five minutes with Ron's slides and explanations of how he thinks we're going to achieve the massive tasks ahead of us. Timelines, contingency plans, overtime and stress. I need this like a hole in the head. Finally, the presentation ends, and we stand up to go.

Someone switches the main room lights on, and everyone blinks as if they are moles coming up from out of the earth for the first time. Never before seen the surface daylight.

"Andy, Dave, John — if you wouldn't mind staying on for a few?"

Shit.

John is a chap I vaguely recognise from around the office. Marketing, I think. I've never had to work with him before. Dave nods in recognition as we shuffle up to the front of the room.

Ron smiles. "What do you reckon, then, lads?"

We look around at each other. No one wanting to make the first move.

After an awkward pause, Dave pipes up. "Got to be worth a try, eh, Ron?"

"Exactly. That's the right answer, Dave." Ron looks me in the eye as he says it. I nod in acceptance. I'm hoping for a promotion at some point, ideally before I die, so I have to play the corporate game.

"We'll be going back down to EM next week for a follow-up meeting. Book a room for two nights in the same hotel. Use my cost centre code."

Awesome… Two nights away in that dingy corporate hotel again. I think back to the last time when my life was totally different, and I had a girlfriend to miss sleeping with… That's not the case anymore. What have I got to miss now?

"Two nights?" I look at Dave, who shrugs, then up at Ron.

"Yeah, thought we could have a team meal the first night, get everyone nice and friendly." He beams a grin around. Wonderful, a meal out with work people, just what I always wanted. I have a feeling there will be a good amount of liquid at that meal. Free booze, I suppose.

"Right. Will do, Ron."

I click open the 'Priory of St Augustine Hotel' website and browse through the rooms they have on offer. If we're being forced to travel for this deal that's going to make Ron stinking rich, I want to make sure my room costs as much as possible. If there's a luxury upgrade option, I'm fucking taking it.

I find an executive suite on the third floor, with views over the canal, a hot-tub Jacuzzi en-suite and a king-size bed, with included options from the pillow menu. I click the button to book it. If Ron asks, that was all I could find available, when I checked… I have a sneaky feeling he's probably staying in a similar room, himself.

I scroll around the website some more, to see if there's a menu for the restaurant.

'The Priory Grill.' — *Enjoy the traditional atmosphere, soft lighting and intimate booths, perfect for a romantic dinner or a family celebration. Bookings essential on Friday and Saturday. Then relax and sip a cocktail while sinking into a comfy armchair, or treat yourself to a fine wine in our Neo-Gothic 'Lodestone Bar' Open 24 hours a day to guests.*

·   ·   ·

Sounds delightful.

Hang on… Lodestone Bar? That rings a bell, for some reason.

My dream. That was the name of the bar in my lucid dream. That must be where I got the name from, as I had a pint in there last time. Funny how your brain picks up on silly details like that. I hadn't even noticed the bar had a name when I was there. Come to think of it, the dreams I've been having started around that time.

I wonder if that's where I saw Chloe? Maybe she was in the bar and my subconscious noticed her? Maybe Chloe isn't even her actual name, and my brain just invented a persona to go around the memory of her face. Or, maybe she works in the hotel, and she had a name badge on? Suddenly, going back to that boring corporate hotel is a bit more interesting.

I met Dave for a quick pint after work. He was a bit annoyed that our trip to Kraków will have to be postponed, due to Ron's 'all leave cancelled' notice. But he says he won't forget, and we'll just have more time to plan for a crazy trip. I hadn't even thought about it, to be honest. It was one of those drunken bar ideas that never actually go anywhere. Dave still seems keen, but he's equally eager to go back and meet up with the barmaid he banged last time we were at the hotel. Bethany. 'Tasty, she was.' He said, licking his lips. Dirty bastard.

I open the fridge to a barren Arctic wasteland. A lone lettuce leaf that has seen better days, and the dregs of a carton of milk are all

I have left. I can't face shopping now. I call up pizza delivery via an app on my phone, and settle down on the couch, ready to while away the rest of the evening filling my head with empty rubbish. At least it blocks out the miserable reality.

The doorbell rings, followed by a thud of the knocker. I jump up, half asleep. Must be the pizza. That was bloody quick.

I open the door, hungry, but I'm immediately disappointed. "Oh… Hi."

Kirsty stands on the doorstep, prim and proper. Her perfume instantly filling my nostrils. She's in jeans and a pale top, a light jacket. Make-up and lipstick.

"Hi, Andy. Can I come in?" She hesitates.

"Yeah, course." Has she come back? I glance out at the road, but there's no sign of a Tesla anywhere. Our car still sat on the driveway. Kirsty goes through to the kitchen. "How did you get here?"

"Laura dropped me." She flashes a smile.

"Right, well, what can I do for you?" I lean on the counter. "Cuppa?"

"No, thanks, Andy." Kirsty uses her official tone. No emotion. Polite and efficient. "I just came to grab a couple of things I forgot, some paperwork and bits." She pauses. "And I thought you should know what's going on…"

"Hey? Going on with what?"

"Me, Laura and Nathan."

"You're staying with them at the moment, I thought?"

"Yeah, I am…" She takes a deep breath. "Andy, we've become a throuple."

"Pardon? A what?"

"You know, a three-person relationship. We're all in love, together. The three of us."

I look Kirsty in the eye, expecting her to burst out laughing or something at the joke. But she's dead serious. Stunned, I can't find any words.

"I…"

"I thought I should be the one to tell you."

"Err, thanks… I guess?" I find my legs weak, and I move to the kitchen table, sitting down.

"Can I get you a drink of water?" Kirsty looks down at me. "You look a bit pale."

"No, I'm fine. Thanks." In truth, I'm not fine. Not remotely, but I have no precedent here to fall back on. I have no idea what I should be feeling, but fine is not it. I try to sum up what has happened. Kirsty, Laura and Nathan went on holiday, and now suddenly they are all an item? Two beautiful women, one man. He must be the smuggest bastard in England right now.

My girlfriend left me for another couple. How do I even parse this information? I keep expecting the punchline of the joke, but it doesn't come.

"I mean, how does that even work? Are you all crammed into one bed? Is it turn-based? Do you draw straws who gets the dick?" I feel anger rising in my belly. I'm insulted and offended and generally confused. But numb, somehow. No tears strain at my eyes.

"It isn't all about sex, Andy." She tuts. "But if you must know, we share everything, between all of us. It's very loving and real."

"I'm sure it is." I think about the scenes I've seen when browsing through Pornhub. Bloody hell. I'm living on the sidelines of an adult fantasy film. "How long has this been going on?" I look up at Kirsty. She sits down at the table next to me.

"About four months."

"What?" I blurt out, incredulous.

"Remember that spa weekend I went on with Laura, in April?"

"Yeah?"

"Well, we all had a few drinks that evening, and… It sort of blossomed from there."

"Jesus, Kirsty!"

"I'm sorry, Andy. I know you must be upset." She uses her sympathy smile as if she's a vet telling a child the family dog has to be put to sleep.

"You've been fucking Nathan… And Laura? All this time. You strung me along for months? Made me pay for half a holiday that you had no intention I went on…" I stand up. "I'm more than upset, Kirsty. I'm fucking livid!"

"It's not like that, Andy. I didn't plan it to happen like this!" She sighs. "I did want you to come on holiday. We had discussed that maybe you could be part of it, with us… Then you went and spoiled it."

"I spoiled it?"

"Yes, with your 'Chloe' thing. If you'd been unfaithful, then it would never work out between us all. Just because there's more than two of us, doesn't mean we're in an open relationship. Quite the opposite."

My jaw goes slack with disbelief. I can't even fathom any logical reason in what she's saying.

I raise my voice. "You're the one who's been unfaithful, Kirsty!"

She shakes her head. "I should have known you wouldn't

154

understand." She gets up. "I need to grab those papers I came for, and Laura will be waiting." She walks out of the kitchen and up the stairs.

When she comes back, I'm still standing in the kitchen. My body dysfunctional, my legs not responding to instructions. I can't cope with this amount of bullshit all at once. I'm going into shutdown. "I'll pay you back for the holiday money. We can take it out of the car value."

I look up. "What?"

"Well, I presume you'll want to keep the car, so you can buy me out of my half. But as a show of goodwill, I'll take the hit on the money you spent on the holiday." She pauses. "Seems fair?"

"Err, right. Sure." The words leave my mouth without my brain intervening.

"Bye, Andy. I'll see you around. Okay?"

"Yeah, sure…"

Kirsty goes back out to the hallway and I hear the front door opening and an exchange. She comes back carrying a pizza box and drops it on the table. "Your dinner, Andy… Bye."

I look down at the box and my stomach turns. I seem to have lost my appetite.

Chapter Twenty-One

"Fuck me, you drive like an old woman." Dave hasn't stopped moaning the entire trip. I didn't fancy going in his rollercoaster, so he came along with me, in the car that I've somehow been coerced into buying my ex out of her share.

I spent some time at the weekend, cleaning out all of Kirsty's crap from the glove compartment and boot, and putting it into a box. She can collect it at some point, or I'll dump it in the bin. Sunglasses, headphones, makeup mirror... I don't care, anymore.

I told Dave about the 'throuple' situation on the way down. His jaw dropped and hung slack for at least forty miles worth of motorway. 'You're fucking kidding me?' Then the inevitable; 'If I'd had known she was into threesomes, I'd have been over more often.' I explained that Kirsty claimed it wasn't about the sex. But, honestly, how can it not be? Everything is about sex, even chocolate bars.

Rissa had a similar, if less lewd, response. Not surprising, but reassuring to know I'm not the only one who thinks this is bloody weird. I remain numb. I'm waiting for the shock wave to hit me.

"No, Dave. I drive like a sensible, normal human. You drive like a fucking nutter. Everything is slow in comparison."

"We would have got there hours ago if I'd driven." He scoffs.

"You got a date or something?" I chuckle.

"Meeting that Bethany later." He smirks and rubs his hands together. I shake my head. I guess Dave is well and truly over Michelle. I wish I was as easily repaired.

"Well, I'm sure she'll keep. We're here now. Stop whining."

I pull off the road into the hotel driveway and roll to a stop outside. No thunderstorm this time, and we're here exactly when my phone predicted. No point in rushing.

My room is as elegant and vast as the website promised. Dave checked into his boring standard ground-floor room, and I chuckled as I walked past him through the long corridor to the lift, and tapped my card on the panel, which took me up to floor three: Executive suites. I sent Dave a photo of my Jacuzzi, and he replied. 'You jammy fucker.' No, not jammy, Dave. Smart. 'Meet you in the bar in 20 mins.'

The room and Jacuzzi is nice and all, but it would be better if I had someone to share it with. Feels a bit silly now, me alone rattling around in this huge room. Massive four-poster bed, and the vista over the canal and distant woods. Very fancy. Oh, well, may as well enjoy it. A nice soak in the tub later sounds great to ease away the stress of the last month.

. . .

Dave is already in the bar when I come down. He's been cornered by Ron and John, yapping away about something or other. By the tone of Ron, he's on one of his epic, boring monologues about architecture and history. If we don't stop him now, he'll happily talk into the small hours. Loves the sound of his voice, does Big Ron.

"Gentlemen." I sit down on a stool next to Dave.

"Hey, Andy. Can I get you a drink?" Ron offers.

"I think you know the answer to that, Ron." I chuckle. "Pint, please."

Ron calls over the barman. "I was just telling John and Dave about the fascinating history of this place." He motions around the bar.

"Oh, really?" I glance at Dave, raising my eyebrows a mere nanometre. He understands.

"Did you get a nice room, Andy?" Dave can barely hide his smirk. Bastard… That wasn't the diversion I had in mind.

"Yeah. Lovely."

Ron looks up. "What floor are you on, Andy?"

I pick up my pint and take a gulp. "Yeah, up on third."

"Third? Isn't that the executive suites?"

"That's all that was left when I booked." I swallow another swig of beer and narrow my eyes at Dave, who looks away.

"I'm on fourth." John pipes up, thankfully taking the focus off me.

"Bloody hell, spread out aren't we? I'm on the second floor."

I roll my eyes at Dave, who is enjoying the trouble he caused. Hardly containing his giggles. My expenses better not get questioned now.

"What's for dinner? I'm starving." I clap my hands together, changing the subject.

"She let you off the diet, then?" Ron grins and makes the trademark whiplash sound effect.

"Err, yeah, something like that." Ron sniggers. I don't fancy having to explain my relationship situation to him.

"Looking good, anyway, Andy." Dave chimes in.

"Thanks, mate. My running is starting to pay off, I think."

"Running? Fuck me. The only running I do is from the taxman!" Ron guffaws, spraying the bar with beer and peanuts. "We'll have one more and then grab dinner in the restaurant. They've got a nice grill here. Do a smashing steak."

I nod. "Sounds good."

Ron goes back to his diatribe on ancient history that no one gives a shit about, and I tune out. Dave is scrolling around on his phone, pretending he's doing work emails, but I'd bet he's busy setting up his evening shag.

I noticed the brass nameplate on the door of the bar as I came in this time. **Lodestone Bar**, just like in my dream. There's no doubt now. My subconscious noted this place, and for some reason kept it recorded for future dream locations. I mean, it's a nice enough bar for a business hotel, but there's nothing special about it. I don't know why this place would stick in my head.

I was curious about the name, so I did some online searching for the word 'Lodestone'. It's a naturally magnetic rock, also known as Magnetite. An odd thing to call a bar. Maybe that's why it stuck in my head?

I found an article that said the ancients used lodestone as a sort of compass, and that the earliest reference is from 600BC when a Greek philosopher named Thales of Miletus noted that iron was attracted to this stone. He therefore assumed that the stone had a soul. Bit of a stretch, but fair enough, I suppose.

It's always a Greek philosopher, isn't it? Never a Greek barmaid or Greek kebab maker. What are these philosophers doing roaming around picking up rocks for, anyway? Maybe there wasn't much call for philosophy that week, and he was branching out... Regardless, dreams are weird. I don't care what anyone says; I don't think they will ever make any sense or can be explained. It's just a random dump of memories made into a crazy story. The Lodestone Bar could as well have been the Guildford Wetherspoons for all my brain knew.

Still, I'm on the lookout for any female staff, especially if their name badge says 'Chloe' on it. Even if she is just a distorted memory, Chloe is a rather sexy one, and I'd love to meet whoever sparked these dreams in real life. Dunno what I'd say, if I bumped into her... 'Oh, hi. Are you Chloe? I've been having erotic dreams about you, fancy a drink?' That's the sort of opener that would get me arrested rather than laid.

Receptionists and bar staff so far do not match my memories. I'll keep looking.

As it goes, the steak dinner is delicious, and there's plenty of it. Washed down with copious quantities of wine and beer.

Our waitress isn't a Chloe, either. I almost asked her if there was anyone working at the hotel by that name, but it seemed a bit 'stalker-ish'. I have no good explanation why I'd be asking. It's a long shot, at best. Perhaps I should just forget this whole thing. There's something niggling at my brain about it though, that keeps me curious.

· · ·

I'm feeling quite merry after the booze. I can tell Dave is itching for an opportunity to leave, as he's surreptitiously text messaging someone under the table on his phone, no doubt Bethany. He thinks no one notices, but when he looks down and a huge shit-eating grin appears on his mug, it's kind of a giveaway.

Fair enough, I suppose. If I knew I was on for a shag later, I'd be eager to leave. Given the choice, the company of a delightful young lady is far preferable to a bunch of boring old men any day. Sadly, I seem to be stuck here with the old blokes.

"Shall we adjourn to the bar, good sirs?" Ron waves over the waitress for the bill.

Dave yawns. "Actually, I think I'm going to call it a night, Ron. Big day tomorrow." I raise my eyebrows. Dave winks at me.

"Yeah, I think I'll do the same."

"Ah, yeah. That's probably a good idea, gents." Ron smiles.

We escape out to the reception area before Ron can question the logic, and coax us back for more drunken history lessons.

"Nice one, Dave. Very smooth."

He chuckles. "I weren't going to sit with them all night listening to him prattle on."

"Off to see that Bethany?"

"Aye." He grins.

"Right, well, have a good one. I'll see you bright and early, then for breakfast."

"What? Where you going?"

"I was going to have an early one. Soak in the Jacuzzi and chill out."

Dave shakes his head. "No, no, mate." He grins. "Bethany has a friend…"

"Ohhh, right!"

Walking back up to my room, through the long, narrow corridors, I notice that the little night-lights they have at floor level come on when I walk by, and go out again a short while after I pass. I turn and look back, and the path I took is now draped in black velvet after a few feet. Ahead of me they stretch out like a pearl necklace into the infinite distance.

I made sure Gemma got safely into a taxi, but I didn't fancy coming straight back to my room. I took a slow circuit of the hotel grounds, the cold night air sobering me up, somewhat. I needed some air and space.

The evening was going pretty well… Gemma was cute. A little shy at first, but after a few drinks she eased up. Dave did the bulk of the chat. I'm not much good at flirting. Dave had somewhat exaggerated the reason for our being here, tonight; We're key members of the project team for this huge, groundbreaking technologically advanced deal, according to him. The girls seemed impressed, but I have a feeling they knew a lot of it was bullshit. Didn't matter, the drinks and laughs were flowing.

Gemma works at the local swimming pool as a trainer and lifeguard. Fit as a fiddle. When Dave suggested we all have a dip in my fancy hot-tub, both the girls were up for it, despite Dave's jokes about needing the kiss of life.

I was a bit nervous, even with the booze bravado. Never done anything crazy like that before. It was one of those 'leave the comfort zone' things, and it was exciting. I didn't want to see Dave in the nip, but the bubbles hid most evils... Gemma slipped off her clothes and jumped in next to me. We'd brought a load more booze back from the pub, and things were progressing very nicely, until Gemma jokingly asked, "Are we having a foursome, then?"

It was then that my blood froze, my guts turned, my head pounded with pain. My brain firing images of Kirsty, Nathan and Laura, all in bed together, all fucking and fingering, kissing, caressing, laughing together at how they got one over sad, pathetic Andy. All the fun of the evening suddenly washed down the plug-hole and left me cold and naked, vulnerable. The shock wave hit, and it overwhelmed me.

I excused myself and grabbed a towel. Before I knew it, I was out on the balcony, shivering, tears running down my face. I couldn't go back like that. I sat there for a good ten minutes before Gemma came to find me.

I could tell she was being kind, but she didn't want to babysit a pathetic loser. She came for some fun, not a counselling session. I wasn't surprised when she asked for a taxi home.

To be honest, I wasn't in the mood anymore. Dave and Bethany went back to Dave's room.

I apologised, tried to explain, without going into the gory details. She assured me it was fine, and she understood. "Perhaps you aren't ready, yet?"

I think she's right.

Chapter Twenty-Two

I t isn't possible to measure time in this place. Things happen, seasons change, but time itself, here, is like putty. Sticky, then stretching, moulded, and finally solid. You move through each stage without knowing and start again when you think it is all over.

I'm in a forest. Deep and lush. Dark from the green canopy above, heavily scented in sap, pine, earth and the occasional invisible wisp of Honeysuckle flower on a light breeze. I follow into the wind, for lack of a better choice. There are no paths, only gaps between the trees strung with ivy vines, clinging to life. Struggling for light.

The wind changes direction. Blows from all around. I stand still and wait. There's a throb of distant thunder, so strong that I feel it in my chest rather than hear it. The air chills and a fresh scent arrives on the breeze. Electrical and fizzing.

. . .

"Hey." A voice from somewhere near me, I spin around, but I can't find the source.

"Up here." I look up, and she's above me, balancing on a thick branch, perhaps twenty feet up a tree.

"Oh, there you are."

"There I was." Suddenly beside me, she laughs, taking my hand and dancing off towards a darker patch of woods. Moss covers everything, thick and green as if a plush rug by a fireplace.

"Where are we?"

"My turn, isn't it?"

"I don't know."

She nods. "I know a place. Come on."

Skipping with the elegance of a ballet dancer, she moves effortlessly into the gloomy wood. I follow, somewhat more cumbersome, yet keeping up, unfathomably.

She giggles when I ask where we are headed. She doesn't look back, mumbles something ahead of her to invisible ghosts who care to listen. I can't hear. The wind on our backs now carries her voice away. Undeterred, she carries on her gleeful jaunt.

I look around at the passing canvas, painted in dark green, deep brown, the occasional split of gushing white from a nearby star. There's no chance of harm here, there's no fear, despite the darkness. I know I'm safe with her.

It could be hours, seconds or months, I don't know, but eventually, she stops, abruptly. I almost crash into her, but she steps aside.

I stumble but manage to stay upright.

Ahead of us is a clearing, a circular gap in the trees with gigantic oaks at the perimeter. I look around, there's thirteen of them making up the circle. Each one must be eight feet thick at the base and stretching up so high I can't see the tops. This place is ancient. In the middle of the glade, there's a cabin made of logs, but none of it looks cut. The wood has grown into the shape of a house. A doorway swung with ivy creepers, windows drawn and divided with branches, a plume of white smoke coming from the chimney.

"Here we are."

"It's wonderful."

She nods, smiles, and motions for me to go in.

Inside is warm from the fire. Thick moss covers the floor. The walls a soft, rough bark. Light comes from a hanging crystal that sparkles and sprinkles glitter into every corner.

She motions to a bench next to a table. A teapot sits on top, with two cups and saucers, two spoons and a plate of wooden biscuits.

"Shall I pour?" I nod down at the pot.

"Yes. Pour and sit."

I pour two cups, but instead of tea, a thick black tar liquid oozes out of the pot. Disturbed, I look up at her, but she beams me a smile. I look back down at the cups. They are full of freshly brewed tea. I shake my head. This place is slightly off-kilter, a little askew and a shade unnatural. I'm not sure what to make of it all.

The biscuits are solid, polished mahogany, with an engraving on one side. Looks like a map compass symbol.

She picks up a cup and takes a sip. "Ahh. That hits the spot." Then she takes one of the wooden biscuits, dunks it in the tea and takes a bite. Nary a care.

"Are they good?" I nod towards the plate.

"Delicious. They're Cardinal Bourbons."

I pick one up, carefully examining the symbol, and tentatively biting down on the wood. It's as hard as nails and tastes bitter. I shudder.

"Dunk first, silly." She giggles.

"Err, I'm not a dunker, traditionally."

"Be adventurous, try it." She insists.

I plunge the wooden disc into the cup, then take a bite. It has softened up and is now quite edible. A mixture of vanilla and hazelnut. "Oh, wow."

"See?"

I smile. There's a childish grin on her that is devastatingly attractive. I find myself staring into her eyes as the patterns of light play over her face. She giggles and stares back. I shake away the moment, feeling a little nervous.

"What do you want to do here?" I glance back at her eyes. Dark and inviting.

"Oh, I don't know... Whatever comes to mind." A mischievous smile erupts on her face. She twists a strand of hair around her fingers and raises an eyebrow ever so slightly.

"Would there be a bedroom, in this treehouse?" I glance around the room. There's a ladder at the back, each rung is a thick branch, worn smooth from use and time.

"Well, of course. Wouldn't be much of a house without a bedroom."

"Perhaps we should take a look?" I let a smile reach my lips. She stands up. "Follow me."

She climbs nimbly up the rungs ahead of me, then, when she's safely up high enough, I do as she suggests and follow up the ladder.

We climb for a long time, the route twists and turns, and at one point it becomes horizontal. We traverse through a narrow tunnel, lit with a light cast from who knows where, and sometimes out in the open, looking down upon the surrounding forest. In the distance, a canal snakes across the horizon, a long barge skating like an insect over the water.

At one point, I lose her completely as she twists around a corner. I speed up to catch her, but above me, I can only see an infinite span of ladder rungs. I panic, turn, and look behind me. Has she fallen off? I carry on, feeling the sweat of exertion on my brow. I must be far above the trees now. I pass into a dark area, and the ladder ends.

I step out into a corridor. A sign on the wall says 'Level 3'.

I hear singing coming from somewhere and follow the sound, growing louder as I approach a doorway into a room. Spacious, with a complicated four-poster bed at one end, and a huge picture window showing a sweeping vista of a twilight forest below us. I turn around and find her sitting on the edge of an ornate bath-tub, with a few dozen tiny candles all around casting their soft amber glow on her body.

"Fancy a dip?" She smirks.

"Don't mind if I do."

She slips into the water and beckons me with a finger. What else can I do?

"You didn't listen… Now you can never leave."

We lie moist on the bed, tangled in sheets and blankets. A proliferation of thick bleach-white pillows all around us forming a barrier. Startled by the voice, I sit up. A man sits at a writing desk. He's familiar, but I can't think from where. He's clad in a dark blue suit. Balding, gaunt and ancient.

"Pardon?" I reach for her hand, but she isn't there. I turn and find myself alone in bed. I look back and the man now stands at a bar, and I'm sitting on a barstool, clothed and dry.

"My name is Thomas." He reaches out a thin, bony hand for me to shake. "Since we're stuck here now, for eternity, we may as well become acquainted."

I shake his hand. Stick thin, rough and sharp at the edges. "Err, hello. I'm Andy." Where did she go? Where am I now?

"I know." He picks up a pint from the bar. "Cheers." He nods towards a drink that sits in front of me. I pick it up. A cold, amber ale.

"Oh, yes. Cheers." I clink my glass against his.

He drinks deep and long. Then sets his glass down on the bar.

"What do you mean, stuck here for eternity?"

He shrugs. "There's no leaving the stones. Lord knows I have tried."

"What stones?"

He looks up at me, eyes wide. "The lodestones, of course…" His voice dry and croaking, he mutters, "Potentiam lapis, corporis libero animum." and then he withers and fades. Where he stood moments ago, now a thick cloud of black mist stands in the vague shape of a man. It dissipates into nothing, and I'm left in the bar alone.

Chapter Twenty-Three

Blokes are amazingly skilled at completely avoiding a subject and pretending something never happened. If you don't think about it, then it ceases to exist and the problem just fades away into nothing.

I was dreading the journey back from the hotel to home because of what happened with Gemma. I thought Dave would mock and joke about how pathetic I am, and that even when naked in a Jacuzzi with a beautiful woman, I still can't get my oats. But he never said a word, and I'm grateful for it. I gathered that he and Bethany had their fun, continued in his room after I made a fool of myself.

Well, at least they enjoyed themselves.

Of course, we never said a word about the evening to Ron or John. As far as they knew, we slept soundly in our respective hotel rooms and were up bright and early for his bloody breakfast meeting before we met the customers again.

We were coerced into attending another meal the second

evening. This time Ron thought it was a good idea to bring a few of the customer team out. I think it was the most awkward dinner I've ever had — on our best behaviour all night. I stayed off the booze, despite Ron paying for it.

We had to laugh at all their boring business jokes, and pretend to be super interested as they explained in great detail a new machine their customers use, which we'll need to interface with. They seemed excited, and I kept exchanging glances with Dave, who no doubt was as enthralled as me.

I phased out in the end, remembering the awful night before, when I totally made an arse of myself in front of the two girls and Dave. I don't know which was the lesser evil.

The evening was worse than the first and last time we ever went to Kirsty's parents in Hinckley. Maura and Jack Hughes. Nice enough people and Jack seemed to take a liking to me after I fixed his laptop and upgraded his operating system. Maura kept hinting at babies and marriage, and Kirsty had a look of daggers on her face all night. She couldn't wait to leave. We never spoke again about that evening, either.

At least Ron is happy, the deal seems to be going well, and we're making progress. The daily status meetings are painful, but as long as Ron can tick something off his list, he stays off our backs. He's already talking about going back down to see them again to finalise the whole thing. I might try to get out of that. I don't fancy going back to that place.

A text message buzzes into my pocket. I pull my phone out and the name on the screen causes a judder in my chest. Kirsty. 'Can you call over to the restaurant at lunch?' A thousand thoughts flood my brain. What does she want me to come over for? What possible bullshit could she drop on me now? Is she going to marry Nathan and Laura in some weird ceremony? Is she pregnant with their throuple child? I consider ignoring her, but I know she won't go away. 'What for?'

I watch the dots that indicate she's typing a reply, … … … and for some reason, a song starts playing in my head. Pet Shop Boys, I think. 'What have I done to deserve this?'

The text finally arrives. 'It's just easier if you come over.'

I sigh. I'm meant to be meeting Rissa for our normal jog. Which one is easier to postpone? I decide Rissa will be more understanding and send Kirsty a reply. 'Fine.'

"Thanks for coming, Andy." Matter-of-fact, manager Kirsty greets me at the counter in her Starbucks. She's always preferred to call it a restaurant than a coffee shop. Makes her feel better about it, I reckon.

I shrug. What else was I meant to do?

She ushers me to a table. Out in the main area, this time. Not hidden away in the back. I expect she wants me to remain calm and not make a scene.

I sit. Kirsty sits opposite. A fake smile etched into her face.

"Can I get you a coffee?"

"No, ta. I'm fine." I try to keep any emotion out of my voice. Seeing her surfaces all kinds of thoughts I don't know how to handle. The image of them all tangled in an orgy of flesh and juices won't leave me, and it brings nausea and an ache in my gut.

"I'll just say it then…" She sighs. "The rent is due next week, and, well, since I don't live at the house anymore, I don't see why I should pay my half."

I look up at her, stoic and calm. "What?" I hadn't even considered this situation. I paid her for the car last week and that pretty much cleaned out my bank account. This is the last problem I need now. "I can't afford the rent myself, Kirsty!" I raise my voice and she shushes me. Looking around the room in case anyone noticed my outburst.

"Well, you'll have to move out, then."

I stare at her, incredulous. "You wanted to live in that stupid house, double the price of anywhere else."

"I did, but I'm not there now."

"I…" I stop because there's no point in arguing. She's justified this all in her mind already, no doubt with the advice of Nathan the hipster accountant. I'm going to be kicked out of house and home, and I haven't got a clue where I'm going to live.

"I'll be picking up the last of my stuff at the weekend. A few bits of furniture and whatnot."

"Right." I can't focus. I can't even look up at her. She's a cold, evil and dangerous woman. No emotion, no compassion. She pushes back her chair and gets up.

"See you then, then."

"Yeah…"

I stumbled back to my car in a daze and drove on autopilot, not knowing where I was headed. I had vaguely made a list in my head of things I need to do; get some moving boxes and tape.

Start packing up my stuff. Send in the notice to the landlord, change my Amazon shipping address. Then I woke from my confused thoughts and found myself, once again, outside my sister's house. I knocked on the door and hoped Riss was home.

"Er, can I stay with you for a bit, Riss?"

Over a cuppa, I explain what happened and that I'll have no choice but to move out. I don't have much stuff, once Kirsty has taken all her furniture. The couch, fridge, table and all that came with the house, so there it will stay. I can probably get my bits all in one carload.

"Yeah, course you can, brother dearest." Riss smiles and looks down at her fingers. "I'll have to clear the room out, but that's no hassle."

It occurs to me that 'my' room, the only spare room they have, would be where a baby slept if they had one... Then a throb of guilt hits me. I can't intrude on their lives like this, especially if they are 'trying.'

That's the last thing I want to wake up and hear. Talk about nightmares. But if the choices are this or going back to my parents' place, I know which I prefer.

"Shit, sorry, Riss. I wasn't thinking, you probably need that room."

"Not yet." She smiles again. "No, it's fine, Andy. It won't be forever, will it?"

"No. God, no. I'll get looking for somewhere proper straight away."

"Well, that's settled then. Give us a day or two to clean up, and you can come whenever you like."

"Thanks, sis. I owe you one. I owe you a load, come to think of it."

"That's what family's for, in't it?"

"Aye." I pause. "Will Nick be okay with it?"

She waves a hand. "Yeah, course."

I should probably get myself a pair of those earplugs, so I don't hear any nocturnal activities.

I went back to work for the afternoon shift, but rather than working, I browsed through the endless listings of terrible apartments I can afford with my meagre budget. There's a couple of places I might go look at, but I know the area and I don't want to live there. Having lived in the fancy part of town for a while, I suppose I'm spoiled. But going back to an estate where you fear they will nick your wheels every night when you park the car, isn't exactly where I saw myself at this stage of my life.

If I'm honest, none of what's happened in the last month is where I saw myself at this stage of my life. I can safely say I never saw this coming. Girlfriend lost to a modern, fashionable relationship, taking my comfortable home with it indirectly. I suppose I should be grateful I still have my job.

I guess I can keep looking for a while more. There's no major rush. Even if Riss gets pregnant, I'll still have a few months before I'm kicked out.

Riss invited me back for dinner this evening, so we can break the news to Nick together. I pick up a bottle of wine and a few cans on the way.

"Hey, mate." Nick opens the door and a blast of delicious smells waft over me.

"Nick, how you keeping?" He's in a sports jersey and shorts. Probably just got back from coaching or a game.

"Not bad, pal. Come in."

"I grabbed this for dinner." I hand him the bag of booze.

"Cheers." He ushers me through to the kitchen. Riss is busy cooking. "I'll just jump in the shower. Back in a second."

I nod and Nick bolts off upstairs.

"How you doing, Andy?" Riss peers into the bag of drinks with a grin.

"As good as can be expected, I guess." I flash a fake smile. "Have you told Nick, yet?"

"Yeah, he's fine. Told you he would be."

"Oh, brilliant. Thanks. I didn't want to intrude, you know…"

She waves a hand. "Don't even think about it. You've got enough going on."

"I didn't want to go back home, you know. To Mum and Dads'"

"Bloody hell, no." She giggles.

"I suppose I could ask Dave…" As I say the words, I know that's not a good idea. We'd end up hungover every morning, and I'd most certainly be hearing bedsprings creak at his house.

"Well, if you like, but you are more than welcome here."

"You make a better dinner." I grin. "I'll pay you rent. I'll do my share of cleaning and whatnot. Just like before."

"We can figure it all out later. Andy. Just get yourself sorted and don't worry."

"Thanks, sis."

. . .

Before Nick came back down, I told Riss about what happened in the hotel, how we came back to my room with two women, but I broke down and ruined it all. I didn't mean to say it, but since I'm going to be living with her again, there's no point in secrets. She was sympathetic and pointed at the bag of booze. "Beer or wine?"

"Yes, please." I smile, and she sniggers, opening the bottle of red.

"I see you have started without me." Nick comes back down, heavily scented with aftershave.

"I'm sure you'll catch up." Riss grins.

Over dinner, Nick asks me about the deal we're involved in. He seems interested, says he knows the company 'Eternitive Medi' as he deals with them sometimes at his work. Small world.

We get along okay, and it keeps my mind off the situation. We don't talk about their fertility issues, and I don't mention the love triangle threesome thing.

As blokes, we're good at ignoring the actual problems and just getting on with life. Yeah, I think it's all going to be okay, as long as we don't think about it too much.

Chapter Twenty-Four

There's no escaping the daily jogs now. Riss drags me out twice a day, sometimes, if I'm not careful. Sleeping in the morning is not something she approves of. Running down the road at six in the morning on a Sunday is not something I approve of. We compromised, and she let me sleep until eight.

"I notice Nick gets a lie-in."

She humphs. "Don't get me started... Besides, he runs around all the time."

"So do you. So do I, now."

"Sooner you stop whining, sooner we'll get back."

"Yes, sister dearest." I speed up and pass her, but not for long as she zooms way down the road. Leaving me in her dust wake. "Hey!"

She slows down, and I catch up. I'm getting better, but she's still got many years of edge on me.

She chuckles. "Is the bed okay, in that room?"

A single bed is not really what I'd call okay, but at least it doesn't have any lumps. Small, no room to spread out, but better than nowt. It feels like I'm a kid again. However, that novelty wore off quick.

"Fine." I shrug.

"You sleeping okay, then?"

"Yeah, I mean, same as usual."

"Only, I heard you talking in your sleep last night."

"Oh, no… Sorry. What did I say?"

"I couldn't make much of it out. Just garbled words and mutters." She chuckles. "Don't worry, it didn't wake me up. I was awake anyway. Nick can sleep through an earthquake."

"I don't remember a dream last night."

"I say talking, but it was more like yelling. I think you said the name, Thomas. Something about stones. Yeah, 'where are the stones, Thomas?' does that ring a bell?"

"Not really. I don't know any Thomas." I ponder. "Stones?"

"God knows, Andy. Dreams are weird."

"What time was it?"

"About four, I think."

I double-take. "Why were you awake at four?"

"Ugh. Don't ask…"

I turn to look at her. "You okay?"

"Yeah, just woman stuff. It's fine." She waves a hand.

"You'd say if it wasn't okay, wouldn't you?"

"Yes, Andy." She flashes me a look.

"Okay, sis-Riss." She chuckles. I used to call her that when we were kids.

A flashback memory snaps into my brain. "Thomas, you said?"

"Yeah."

"I do remember now, a bit. There was an old guy in my

dream. He said his name was Thomas. Shook my hand and bought me a pint. He said something like I couldn't leave."

"Yeah? Leave where?"

"The bar, I guess." I chuckle. "It was that bar in the hotel again."

Riss sings the famous line from that Eagles song.

"Right, 'Hotel California' in the home counties."

She laughs. "What do you make of it?"

"I've sort of given up trying to make any sense of my dreams. They are bloody weird."

"Did you have any more luck with the lucid dreams?"

"Haven't bothered much. Too much crap going on in my actual life, let alone having a second life to worry about."

Moving out of my house was about as much fun as you'd expect. Kirsty and Nathan showed up one day to collect her futon and a coffee table, some boxes of books and a drawer of cutlery. I stood by, watching my life taken apart like a jigsaw puzzle. Nathan avoiding eye contact. Kirsty, clinically distant and practical. They rented a small van for the task. In and out in thirty minutes.

As expected, my stuff all fit into the car. I had to make three trips, but most of that was going back to clean up the place, before handing back the keys.

I suppose that was a closure, of sorts. A chapter of my life well and truly over. Still feels surreal and distant. How did it change this quickly, without me knowing anything was going on? Am I that out of touch with my own life that I can miss something so obvious? Perhaps I should listen to my instincts more, delve into my subconscious and wake myself up.

"Might give it another go, I suppose. Would be nice to get to the bottom of what's going on with these characters. Chloe, Thomas… Maybe they represent something in my psyche, or whatever." I shrug. "I dunno."

"Don't stress it, just see what happens."

"Aye."

Against my better judgement, I fire up my work laptop, even though it's Sunday afternoon. I've got a few more things to do for Ron, and getting it done at the weekend is theoretically less pain than having to listen to him whine about it on his daily calls. We're dangerously close to getting this deal done now, and the pressure is building.

After about ten minutes of staring blankly at my list of tasks to do, all the, admittedly small, amount of enthusiasm I had for working has deflated out of me like a farting balloon in a sigh of dismay. If I start one thing, I'll have to do three other things, and before I know it, the afternoon becomes evening, and I've wasted my entire day.

Sod it. I pick up my phone and open the messages app. Before my brain can properly engage, my fingers have typed a text to Dave 'Pint?'

He replies quickly 'Meet you in the pub.'

"If you could custom design your perfect woman, where would you start?"

Dave looks up at me over his drink, "Kidding? Obviously, I'd start with Scarlett Johansson and mix in a bit of Shakira." Dave grins as wide as the bar and shivers at the thought.

"Sure, I mean, yeah… But, what about a real everyday woman? The type you might stand a chance with, mate."

He snorts. "Hey, I could bag Scarlett no problems. Eating out of the palm of my hand, she would be."

"Right. Gorgeous, wealthy, fit and an actual superhero, Scarlett would be begging you for a ride. Sure… I have a feeling it would be the other way around." I laugh. "And she'd be calling her bodyguard to rip your knackers off within three seconds."

"If she walked in here right now, I'd be happy to prove you wrong, pal."

I look around to the door and an old chap staggers in, shaking the rain off his flat cap. "Tell you what, if Scarlett, or indeed any Hollywood movie stars walk into this dingy pub in the next ten minutes, pints are on me tonight."

Dave slaps the bar. "Deal!"

"What I mean, is, I suppose we all have an idea of our dream woman, buried somewhere in our subconscious. Not just how she looks, but how she talks, how she smells. The way she wrinkles up her nose when she smiles. The little sighs she makes when she's… You know."

"I do know." He sniggers.

"But where does it come from? I mean, is it based on all the women we've ever seen before, a mix of all the good parts blended? Is it just an instinct that we have? Beauty is in the eye of the beholder and all that, but it's your genes, in't it? You choose a partner who will produce strong, healthy and intelligent children."

"If you're going to get all philo-bloody-sophical on me, Andy, mate, I think you better go get a round in now, before you're drunk off your wistful romance." He chuckles at his observation. "Anyhow, I choose a partner by how quickly I can get her OUT of her jeans. Never mind any kids."

"Well, that I agree with. You definitely do."

Dave suddenly lights up. "Hang on. Is this about that bloody Chloe dream you're having?"

"Might be."

"It is. You've become obsessed with a character you've, literally, dreamed up. She's not real, Andy."

"Seems bloody real, from the memories I have."

"In't healthy, mate. You need to get out, forget about bloody Kirsty and mythical Chloe. Move on, sew your wild oats, allow yourself to have a laugh and some fun."

He pauses. I sense he's about to talk about the incident at the hotel in the Jacuzzi, but he skips over it if he was.

"We have to go on that Kraków trip. Soon."

"I thought you'd forgotten about that."

"Nah, mate. I reckon it will do you good. Do us both good."

"Yeah, you could be right. But…" I sigh. "I'm just no good at this stuff."

"You're just a bit rusty, Andy. Bit of Polish vodka will loosen you up."

"That nasty stuff would take the paint off a ship's hull. No, ta."

"And the knickers off a lass." He grins. "Serious, Andy. This dream stuff is worrying me."

"Hey?"

"If you let yourself get all sulky, you'll convince yourself that you'll never find a real woman. You'll never leave the house, never talk to anyone, and your prophecy will come true. You'll end up deeper and deeper into this dream world, and that road only leads to misery and loneliness."

I sigh. "Aye, you could be right, mate. But the dreams are bloody vivid and real… Especially the good bits." I feel a burning in my cheeks. "Chloe is one hot chilli-pepper."

"Stands to reason, you aren't going to dream up a boring old spinster who wears a girdle and support stockings, are you?" He grimaces. "Unless that's what you're into? You sick bastard."

I choke on a gulp of beer. "No, she's bloody gorgeous. Black eyes, long hair, curves that make me go weak at the knees… She's got an amazing voice when she sings."

Dave snaps his fingers at me. "Andy. WAKE UP! Chloe is not real."

"I know… I just can't get rid of the feeling that maybe she is."

Chapter Twenty-Five

W ork has an eerie feel about it at the weekend. The office is empty, but for me. The silence is a vast chasm that I can't stop myself gaping into, teetering at the edge, almost falling into the depths, where unknown torments lie.

It feels voyeuristic to walk around and gawp at other people's desks. Yet, that's exactly what I've been delighting in doing.

I put toothpicks into the gap between every key on Dave's keyboard, sticking up like a bed of nails, and I turned everything on Ron's desk upside down, including his monitor.

It's the little things that amuse us.

I sit down at my desk and power on the computer. The screen flickers, a message pops up for a brief moment but then vanishes. I think it said 'Guru Meditation Error' in red text. The screen goes black and three loud beeps come from the tower case under the desk.

I slide my chair back with a sigh and slip down under the desk to pull the power cable out. 'Have you tried turning it off *and on again?'. Under the desk is dark, dusty and dank smelling. The carpet has worn smooth where my feet normally rub back and forth. A tiny flashing light draws my attention up to the underside of the desk. Red, then green, on and off. I reach to touch it, but my fingers slide on bare wood. The light comes from a gap behind the desk that I've never seen before. I shuffle up close and peer into the hole.*

There's a passageway behind my desk. I can see a long string of lights fading into the distance. I squeeze through the impossibly tiny gap and fall forward onto a plush carpet.

I get up and look back to where I came from. Darkness is abundant, but there's a slit of light and I can see the bottom of my office chair and the water cooler in the distance. I turn back to the passage.

Rows of doors line each side of the corridor. Each one locked. A number thirteen in brass. I pause. This seems familiar.

I turn back and there's nothing but blackness.

I think I'm dreaming? I look down at my hands, but I can't focus on them. They seem larger than they should be, and a shade too yellow. Yes. This is not real.

I walk around a corner and randomly try some more doors. All locked, but if this is my dream, I should be able to… The next door creaks open when I push. A small room beyond with thick, white canvas sheets draped over everything. A ladder daubed in paint splatters in the centre. I lift up a sheet. Underneath is a baby cot. I think I've got the wrong room.

Other doors lead to storerooms, a kitchen, empty spaces and a multitude of identical bedrooms, each with a bathroom that has a mild damp smell. There's nobody around. I'm bursting for a piss.

I try a toilet, but it won't open. The next bathroom doesn't have a toilet at all, and in a third, the toilet is a small toy on the floor. Not connected to any plumbing.

I give up and walk to a window. Outside, there's the faintest hint of sunrise over some woods in the distance. A streak of glowing pink watercolour in the night sky. Still-silence envelops the world.

"The beauty of creation never ceases to amaze, no matter if you witness it a hundred or a hundred thousand times. Don't you think?"

A voice from behind jolts me from my gaze. I quickly turn as a bolt of adrenaline pulses through my veins. A gaunt, old man stands in the doorway. He nods towards the window to back up his statement.

"Err, indeed."

"Apologies, if I startled you." He smiles, thinly, but calm.

"No, not at all. I just thought I was alone here."

He scoffs. "As did I, young man. As did I."

"You're Thomas?"

"Correct." He bows slightly. "Thomas Bonham, keeper of the stones. And the stones, the keeper of me." He chuckles a dry, scratchy laugh.

"Do I know you?"

"Oh, you will. There's time for that yet." He waves a dismissing hand. "We aren't going anywhere, after all." That laugh again, with extra splutters. He staggers and sits down abruptly on the edge of the bed.

"Are you okay?"

"Tired, Andrew. I am so very tired." He shakes his head

slowly. "Godforsaken and tired." He bursts into a fit of coughs, then, as I watch, he expands and fades, a thick black cloud where he sat, dissipating rapidly into nothing. I move towards the space, but the room dims and drops away from under me. I'm left in a warm space of velvet blackness.

If this is my dream, then I don't seem to be in control of anything. Who is that chap? What did he mean? What did any of that mean? I look around me, but the blackness engulfs.

I close my eyes, metaphorically, I suppose, as they are already closed in real life. I let my mind wander. There has to be something interesting to do in this place?

Tentatively, I open one eye, then the other. I'm in a building. A church, perhaps? No. But a vast wide open space with a high ceiling. I look around.

I'm standing in the middle of an empty room, but there are some wooden cabinets around the edge. I walk towards them, and it becomes evident that they are glass-topped. I peer into the first one which is full of small crystals and gemstones laid out on a green cloth. Each one is labelled; 'Iron Pyrite', 'Peridot', 'Lapis Lazuli', 'Hematite', 'Magnetite.' This must be a museum. I vaguely recall visiting somewhere like this as a child on a school trip. I move around the cabinets and each one has a display inside. Some contain taxidermy animals, some skulls and bones. One has a huge old book open to a page with words I can't read. The label underneath says: 'Corporis libero animum'.

. . .

"What you looking at?" Another jump in my chest, but this time the voice behind me is female. I recognise it instantly and turn to face her.

"Chloe!" I grab her in an embrace. She smells of honeysuckle. She's warm and soft and she squeezes me tight playfully, then kisses me.

"Did you miss me?" She chuckles and steps back. "Where are we?"

"I did, yes." I feel a blush in my cheeks. "And I think this is a museum I visited as a child. I can't remember where it was, though."

"Fancy." She looks around the room. "Bit boring." A smile creeps onto her face.

"I suppose it is a bit." I laugh. "But I think there are some dinosaur bones, further along." I motion towards a doorway.

"Fascinating, but maybe another day?"

"Fair enough." I smile. "What did you have in mind?"

It seems strange to ask a dream character what they'd like to do, but here I am, so I may as well run with it.

Chloe ponders for a moment, sweeping her hair back from her face.

"Shall we go to a concert?"

"To see a band? Oh, err, sure. Who's playing?"

"Me." A shy smile blossoms on her lips. She spins around and the scene behind her changes. A stage, with a grand piano to one side. A stool and microphone in the centre. I'm seated in a theatre. Halfway up and in the middle. I look around and there's no one else here. An audience of one. Chloe laughs a little nervously, but sits down on the stool and picks up an acoustic guitar.

"This one is for you, Andy." She points to me from the stage *and a flush of heat spreads across my body. She strums the guitar, a tune I don't recognise. Then she sings. Her voice clear and delicate, original in her own style. She's talented. The song is about a lonely girl who wakes up one morning in a sweat, she's had a strange dream and suddenly, her life has changed. She met someone in the dream and can't get them out of her head. It could be written about me, and I suppose it was. She's amazing, but the niggle I can't get out of my mind is that she's a dream I'm having. How is my brain coming up with this stuff? I'm about as musical as a wooden post. There's no way I could have composed this song. Maybe I heard the tune on the radio or something and the rest is interpolated and mixed up from the world. The brain remains a weird and undiscovered realm.*

She sings so sweetly, and I feel tears prick at my eyes. Just her and a guitar, but she's stirring emotion that I didn't know existed. She fades out the song, repeating the last words of the chorus over and over. "Only in my dreams, you are only in my dreams."

When she finishes, I stand and clap. As I do, an audience of hundreds appears around me and we give her the thundering ovation she deserves. She stands up and bows, smiling.

"Another, please?"

She nods and I sit down. As I do, the crowd around me fades into nothing, and I'm left sitting alone in the theatre again. A spotlight appears on the piano, and she sits down in front of it.

She plays, and quickly I recognise the tune, heavily embellished with her own version of the song 'Cornflake Girl' by Tori Amos. She sings the lyrics, changing her voice to sound almost exactly like the original song, playing with elegance and flourish. When she mouths the words, she looks up at me and there's a smile in her voice. She's in her element, thoroughly enjoying herself. I sit, slack-jawed, watching the show with wet cheeks now, I dare not look away as she beats the piano into submission, teasing out humour and sadness with every twist of her fingers. The song reaches a crescendo, and she becomes one with the instrument. The edges of both merge into one thing, flooding the room with sound, reverberating through me, and I find myself standing and running towards the stage. I jump up, and she beckons me over to sit next to her on the bench. I place my hands on the keys, but I could never play anything beyond three blind mice, badly. Yet, now, when I move my fingers, a bass melody trills out, and she moves higher up the keys, in harmony with the tune I'm playing. She laughs and repeats the chorus again, staring directly at me as she does. I'm mesmerised, but my fingers keep playing, somehow knowing what to do without my intervention.

We reach the end of the song, and she fades out the notes. Then she shuffles over to me on the bench seat and plants a kiss on my lips. I feel the heat from her face, the beads of moisture from her sweat, the scent of her flooding my senses.

She puts her arms around me, pulling me tight. I close my eyes and let the moment take me, feeling her hands on my back, caressing on my skin. I peek open an eye, and we're no longer in the theatre, but in a smaller room. A bed under us.

"That was wonderful, Chloe. Thank you."

"Thank you, Andy. It was fun, wasn't it?" She smiles and looms above me, naked and coy. "What shall we do now?" A huge grin spreads over her face, and I stare into her black eyes as she leans down and bites gently at my neck...

I gasp. "Well, I have an idea..."

Chapter Twenty-Six

M y sheets were soaked in sweat when I woke this morning, among other fluids that I won't mention to Clarissa. I put everything in the laundry first thing and then got to the shower before anyone else woke. Monday back at work looms ahead of me, and tasks line up in my head like fairground ducks I need to shoot off a shelf.

Ron will no doubt want an update at his nine o'clock meeting. How he thinks we'll have anything new when we're all still supping our first coffee of the day, I don't know, but you can't tell him. He likes an early start, does Ron.

Memories of my dream flood back with the shower rain. Chloe. Holy crap that was some hot stuff. Some of it a bit x-rated to be written into my dream journal, in case Riss picks it up one day and blushes her cheeks off.

I feel a smile crawl onto my face at the thought of Chloe. She played me some songs, then we switched to a bedroom and bounced away like bunnies on speed. Nothing like it ever was with Kirsty. Chloe is adventurous, kinky and just a bit dangerous.

I never know what to expect with her, and that brings nervous energy that she seems to lap up. She's taken me to heights I didn't know existed. Teasing me to the edge of a precipice and then pausing, dancing around me for an endless moment, then together we leap off, falling, screaming and swooping into the chasm. Exploding when we hit the waves at the bottom. Floating back to shore slowly on a warm tide, until it deposits us in a heap of arms and legs on the hot sand, totally spent.

I pause. This is real insanity, no doubt about it. I'm feeling emotions for a woman who doesn't exist. Dave would slap me right now if I told him what I'm thinking. I have to remind myself that Chloe is a dream. Dreams aren't real.

Shame, because this is by far the most erotic and intense relationship I've ever been in. I loved Kirsty, and we played around often, especially at first, but there was something pragmatic and perfunctory about our love-making. Kirsty told me what to do, and I did it. She had a ritual and a plan, and I guess I was just there to carry out her bidding. Like phoning up to a call centre for an insurance quote, we never strayed from the script for fear of litigation.

In the car, driving to work, I allow myself another peek at those sweet dream memories, and they bring a warmth to my belly that I desperately need right now. The dullness of work, the emotion of my recent betrayal. The apathy of boring life and the burden of having to go hunting for a proper place to live, all sum up to a stress level that threatens to break the mercury out of the thermometer. I sigh and think again about Chloe and the songs she sang for me. At a traffic light, I tap the music app on my phone and find Tori Amos and play the song 'Cornflake Girl'.

So what if she's a dream? It's a bloody wonderful dream, and it does me good. No matter what Dave says, living is living, isn't it? Emotion is always real, whether it is for an actual human person or a character in a film, or even in a dream. You still feel it… And boy, do I feel it.

Big Ron Corbishley opens up his laptop and, once again, as he does every morning, he taps the wrong buttons and his screen is not projected, eight feet wide, onto the wall in front of us. I sneak a sideways glance at Dave, and we quietly roll our eyes in unison. Ron coughs and splutters as he pulls out cables and plugs them back in again.

I take a deep slurp of coffee and allow my eyes to close a little.

Ron's wheezing reminds me of something else in my dream. Thomas, the strange gaunt man. He was there before Chloe. He said something again about 'not going anywhere' I wonder if he's a metaphor for my life. I'm stuck in this rut, in a job I can do easily, but that I can't summon any enthusiasm for anymore.

I've been doing this too long, I suppose. I should look around for something else, to challenge myself and keep my brain interested. Most of what I do is pointless when I think about it from a rational point of view. If my Dad, or even Rissa, asked me what I'd done all week, I'd find it hard to put anything tangible into words. Yet, I'm always busy, always stressed and struggling to get this nothing done. What am I doing here, wasting my life away?

I look around the room, half the folks are missing today and there's an empty row of chairs in front of me and Dave. He's turned the chair in front around and has his feet up on it. Ron hasn't noticed.

"Sorry folks, normal technical issues." He bats away at the laptop again and finally, his desktop wallpaper appears on the wall in front of us.

"Here we go. Right, shall we get started on the tracker?"

My heart sinks into my gut, and my brain puts me on hold. Tinny music drowns out the words Ron is saying. I settle into my chair and hope that everyone else has unfinished tasks, and he can argue with them until the meeting is over, with any luck skipping my outstanding points.

Dave's head appears over my cubicle wall. "Lunchtime, Andy. And don't give me any crap about jogging today, I've got important information for you."

I look up. "Hey, Dave. Riss is busy today, anyway. You're in luck." I stand up and lock my desktop. I kick my chair back and catch a glimpse of the floor under my desk.

A flashback memory; there was a passageway or something under my desk. Crazy. There can't be anything under it. I'm against a wall on that side.

"Actually, mate, it's you who's in luck." He smiles.

"Oh?"

"Come on. All will be revealed shortly."

. . .

We sit down in the pizza place, and Dave's face is plastered with a smug grin.

"You owe me a hundred-and-seventeen quid, Andy."

"Eh. What for?"

"I hadn't finished… But, I'll let you off it, and you can pay me back in booze."

I ponder. I don't remember borrowing any money from Dave, ever. What is he playing at? "You'll have to remind me what this is about?"

He reaches into a jacket pocket and pulls out a few sheets of paper. "A flight to Kraków." He dumps the paperwork in front of me with a chuckle and folds his arms in satisfaction. "We're going to Kraków, mate. This Friday. Pack your bag and get the sulk off your mug because women can sense a miserable git a mile off. We're going on a boys' weekend away and there's no ifs or buts. It's all booked, and we're going."

I feel my mouth open and I try to say something, but words don't come out.

Eventually, I find my voice. "Are you serious?" I look down at the paper. It's a flight booking in my name. Direct to Kraków this Friday at noon. Dave nods. "But, Ron will shit the bed if he knows we're taking leave now."

"That's the beauty of it, Andy, me old mate. We won't tell him."

"But…" I stutter and Dave waves me down.

"We'll go to the normal morning meeting, give him the updates he wants to hear, then go back to our desks like nothing is strange. We go off for an early lunch, but instead of coming here to this delightful pizza emporium," he winks toward Hannah the waitress. "We adjourn to the airport and off to sample the delicacies that old Kraków has to offer. Fine food, beautiful women, strong booze and good music. Then, we'll enjoy the shite out of it until we fly back on Sunday evening. Back to work on Monday and Ron will never know we've gone." He slaps his hands on the table at the conclusion of his master plan.

"I guess that could work…" I ponder on the details. Spontaneous, fun, and a bit dangerous. I like it.

"Course it will."

"Why didn't you say you were booking it? I could have paid for my flight."

"Because I know you would have whined and complained, and we'd never have got it booked. Now it's done, you can't argue."

"No, I'm not trying to argue. It's great, mate. Fucking brilliant. Can't wait."

"That's the spirit!" He pulls out his phone. "I've booked us two rooms in this hotel, but you can pay for your room, after." He shows me the screen and the details of the hotel. Looks nice enough, right in the middle of the city. Cheap, an' all.

Over lunch, we discuss the plan. He's found a gig that's playing in a bar called 'Lizard King' on the Saturday night. A Polish band I've never heard of, but Dave sends me a link to their tunes and assures me its good old-fashioned rock, and we'll have a blast. During the day he's got a huge list of bars that we can visit. Underground dives, dimly lit, with lots of cobblestone, brick and alcohol. I can almost smell the atmosphere from the photos on his phone. Heady with sweat and beer suds. Loud music, youthful excitement and testosterone swagger. The sort of place that Kirsty would never in a million years visit, but I can imagine taking Chloe there if she was real. She seems like she'd enjoy the culture and atmosphere. She'd probably lead me to a strip bar and dance on the tables…

.　.　.

Dave is right. Good music, strong beer, beautiful women… It all adds up to a break that I need to take my mind off things. There's that sense of danger. Like we could get caught by Big Ron and sent to detention or something. We'll be sneaking off surreptitiously, and that always brings a high of adrenaline. It'll be like the good old days. Dave and Andy, the two boys going on an adventure. I feel a warmth building in my chest and I slap Dave on the back as we head towards the office. "Cheers, mate, for doing this."

Chapter Twenty-Seven

I hate flying. Not so much the flying part, which isn't bad, most of the time, but the ordeal of getting to the airport, getting through the miles of corridors, stripping for security checks, waiting and queuing, then cramming into a metal tube with hundreds of hapless passengers. The overall experience stresses me out.

Dave, cool as a frozen cucumber, is oblivious to the whole thing. Bastard.

This week has been hellish, to be honest. In order to be sure that Ron wouldn't throw a curveball and ruin our plans, we've had to stick to him like chewing-gum on his shoe every day and jump on each task he throws at us. Four steps ahead, we've been aiming for. If Ron thinks of something else that needs to be done, we've already done it and the next three things. He's gushing with praise for us now, which is great in one way, but it also means we'll have no way to escape going back to that bloody hotel to visit the customer again soon. Ron thinks we're doing this because we deeply care about the deal that will make him, and not us, a tidy sum of money. Not at all, we're doing it so we can sneak off early.

If he wanted us to work this hard all the time, he should dish out free holidays as incentive rewards.

Dave sits by the aisle with his sunglasses on like a prize knob, gawping at the attendants and other passengers. He's already pointed out to me several times that the flight to Kraków is loaded up with hot women. 'Just wait till we get there, mate. It's going to be like heaven.'

That's as maybe, but I'm still shite at flirting and pulling. I'm going to enjoy myself, no doubt. I just doubt I'll end up in bed with anyone other than myself.

Never mind. It'll be a blast either way. Maybe I'm getting old, but random sex doesn't seem like it's very fulfilling any more. I don't need to jump on every woman I see to prove anything. I'm not a teenager anymore. I know I can't expect Dave to understand that, but when I think about it, a comfortable, warm and loving relationship is what I crave now, not awkward sex with strangers in filthy pub toilets.

We land without ordeal and move to another queue for a bus into the city. Dave is impatient though. We grab a taxi instead. As we pull away, I'm reminded of the last time we sat in the back of a taxi together, with Kayla and Michelle heading to that 80s night.

It seems like a million years ago now. So much is different. I haven't heard from Kayla in a while, and I'd forgotten that she'd asked me to come out for a drink. I wonder if that offer still stands, or if she's found someone else to entertain her.

Probably a bit late. I'm my worst enemy in these situations. Overthinking until the problem just dissipates on its own into nothingness.

Oh, well. We are deposited outside our hotel and the driver grunts a thank you to the tip Dave offers, a strange Polish note called zloty. Worth about three quid, I think. We changed a load of cash in the airport, probably being royally ripped off in the process.

The hotel is fine. Nothing wonderful, but not terrible by any means. Nicer than the boring ground-floor rooms of the Priory of St Augustine Hotel back in good old England. There's a charm, different from home. My room overlooks an enormous square in the old town. I take a breath and look out at the people milling around outside, each on their own path, unaware of my existence. For all our modern methods of communication, we are still dreadfully disconnected from each other in reality. There's a distance between us, our minds a locked fortress of knowledge, impossible to break into.

A text buzzing in my pocket breaks me from my daydream. Dave 'Bar. 5 mins.'

I chuckle and grab a fresh shirt from my suitcase, spray on a whiff of aftershave, and check myself in the mirror. My daily routine with Riss is showing, I reckon. I'm feeling less lethargic, more able to tackle the world. The headache I've had now forever has faded into the background. Still there, if I go looking, but I can ignore it. The world still has that hazy gauze covering everything, like I'm behind some kind of curtain, looking through at everything from a distance. Nothing seems real. Am I here in Kraków, about to hit every bar in a mile radius? Am I present inside my body? Sometimes I wonder. The dreams I have seem more real than my waking moments. A strange thing to admit.

I shake away the thoughts and grab my phone, wallet and room key and take a deep breath. Let's do this.

"I got you a pint, but this is your tab." Dave wastes no time in draining his drink before I've even got my arse on the stool. "Actually, I don't think this is a pint."

"Probably half a litre." I pick up my beer. Cold condensation beading on the glass, it goes down smoothly and hits the spot. "Another?"

"Thought you'd never ask." Dave grins and I nod to the bartender.

"What's the plan, man?" I turn to Dave once we are settled into our second drinks.

"No proper plan. We'll have this one, then go for a walk and find the next interesting bar. Look around, take in the atmosphere, check for likely candidates to bring some female colour to the evening, and if there's nothing obvious, we move on. Repeat."

"What time is the gig?"

"That's tomorrow evening."

I nod. "Fair enough. Get that down you, then."

· · ·

Dave nips off for a slash and I take a moment to look around the hotel bar before we leave. There's a few people around, but not many. Mostly older folks who probably won't go out into the hedonism surrounding us. Kirsty would be one of them if she was here, content to stay in the fancy hotel bar, rather than explore into the world beyond where danger and excitement may lie. Saying that, she's certainly not averse to exploring the world of relationship danger. 'Throuple' is not a word I'd ever expected Kirsty, of all people, to say, let alone take part in.

Dave asked me, casually, if I was ready for this Kraków trip, hinting at what happened in the Jacuzzi last time… I had to think about it for a moment, but I replied — 'Yeah. I reckon.' Kirsty is a memory, dim and smeared now. It hasn't been that long, really, but the body adapts and time heals, as they say.

Minds change, people grow, I guess you can't expect anything to last forever.

I glance at a couple sitting at a table at the back of the bar. They must be in their sixties, obviously married. He's reading a paper, she's got her nose in a book. They seem content. Lucky.

Sometimes, I resent the animalistic drive in me to couple with someone. Wouldn't life be so much easier if I could just be single, happy and free? Not constantly walking on eggshells, and worrying about offending or upsetting someone because of an absent-minded glance or comment. Then again, do I want to end up alone in my dotage, farting around watching daytime TV with no one to direct my cynical sarcasm at?

Life is complicated. No doubt about that.

"Ready?" Dave gently punches my arm. "You okay?"

I stand up. "Yeah, mate. Ready for the onslaught."

Thankfully, everyone speaks perfect English here, or we'd be totally lost. Dave tried to learn a few words of Polish from an app on his phone, but I don't think he's got the accent for it. When he tried to say 'You are beautiful' in Polish to a girl at one of the many bars we've visited, she looked at him sideways, quizzically, and then walked off shaking her head. I'd imagine the dozen or so beers we've downed didn't help his pronunciation. When I looked at the words spelt out on his phone, I didn't even bother trying to attempt it.

We've walked all around the square and off down a few side streets, climbing down into cool, dimly lit, highly atmospheric bars that stink of generations of drunken disorder. This place is great. The music is lively and loud, the beer is cheap and tasty, the women are indeed gorgeous as Dave is constantly pointing out, but so far, we stand alone.

"We're just getting warmed up, Andy." Dave looks like he's more on the side of shutting down than warming up. He stumbles, unstable, but I nod and chuckle. The booze adds a soft-focus effect on the evening. I look around the bar we've just come to, over on the west end of the old town square, underground, down a brick stairwell that winds around as it dives. The bass thump of music met us twenty steps before the rest of the tune, and as we opened the door into the bar, we were hit with a blast of heat, steam, light, shadow, noise and chaos. Contrasting and confusing.

"This is the place, mate. I can feel it." Dave glides his head around in a smooth semi-circle, slowly taking in the scene and noting down the location of potential targets as he does. The skilled predator reconnoitring the Savannah before he springs into action, cutting down three fawns as he sprints silently across the plains…

At least, that's what he'd normally be doing, but I think this Polish booze, combined with the early start, the travel and the heat in this place has knocked him squarely on the arse. He sits down abruptly on a stool and falls into a heap, head on the bar. I chuckle and wave to get the barman's attention.

"Err, water, please." I point to the slumped pile of Dave next to me. "And one for me." May as well use this opportunity to take a brief break and regroup. We should probably get some dinner to soak up the booze.

"Is your friend okay?"

I turn around to an attractive young woman behind me. She looks genuinely concerned for Dave. Her accent is strong, but her English is good. I assume she heard me ask for the water.

"Oh. Yeah, he'll be fine." I wave a hand and smile. "We haven't even started on the vodka, yet."

She chuckles, "Are you men on vacation?"

"I suppose you could put it that way. We came for a weekend to have a bit of a laugh." I suddenly realise this woman seems to be interested in me. I should act on this instead of letting it slip by, as my previous self would have done. Dave told me once a woman could walk up to me with a T-shirt that said 'I WANT TO SHAG YOU' and I'd still mess it all up... "Can I get you a drink?"

She sits down next to me at the bar. "Sure, vodka and coke, please." The way she says coke sounds a lot like 'cock' and I have to stifle a giggle with a throat clear.

"I'm Andy, by the way." I stick out a hand.

"Agnieszka, but you can call me Aga." She smiles. "I know you don't pronounce that word easily."

"Lovely name, Aga. My Polish is a little... err, non-existent."

"I'm surprised." She laughs.

"He tried to learn a few words." I point to Dave, who seems to be sleeping on the bar. I'll let him rest for a minute. "But I don't think he has the tongue for it."

"And you? Do you have a good tongue?" A coy grin flickers across her face as she sips her drink and eyes me over the rim of the glass. I feel warmth in my cheeks.

"Never had cause for complaint." I laugh. "Your English is excellent, I must say."

"Thank you, I lived in London for four years."

"Ah, right. Nice. You came back?"

"Yes, I missed the homeland." She snorts. "No, I broke up with someone, quit my job and packed my bags…"

"Oh, sorry."

"Pff, no, I'm glad." She waves a hand. "Are you sure he's okay?" She nods towards Dave, who makes a groaning noise.

"I suppose I should get him back to the hotel. Let him sleep it off…"

"Do you need some help?"

I start to say 'No, thanks, I'll be fine' but then I realise she wants to come with me, for reasons that are beyond my understanding, but never look a gift horse, as they say… "Oh, yeah, that would be great." I pause. "I'm getting hungry, do you know any good restaurants around here?" Smooth, Andy, smooth…

She grins. "There's many. What do you like?"

"I'm easy." I chuckle. "I mean, I eat anything."

"Good to know." She flashes that coy smile again.

A combination of dragging, pulling, pushing and coercing, and we manage to get Dave back to the hotel, under duress, but I promised him Kraków would still be here once he was feeling a bit more awake. The booze or something has really knocked him sideways, and once we got his hotel door open by wrangling the key out of his pocket, he fell onto the bed and immediately started snoring. I'm sure he's fine, it must just be the long hours and early starts we've been doing. We're not in our teens or twenties any more. The effort of life is taking its toll.

"Well, that's Dave out for the count." I smile and Aga returns the look. "Thanks for your help."

"No problem. We all need to take it easy sometimes."

"Can I buy you dinner, in return?" The words flow out of me before I realise what I'm saying.

She runs a hand through her dark hair, pausing for a moment, seemingly pondering. "Sure, why not?"

After a short, but awkward walk to one of the many nearby restaurants, I suddenly realised what is going on here; I've asked a woman to dinner after knowing her for all of seventeen minutes.

This must be a record for me, but the realisation stuns me a little and a flood of imposter syndrome feelings wash over me. I'm not a smooth, womanising bloke who can pull interesting conversation out of the air at a moment's notice. I agonise over the most simple things, preparing and rehearsing what I'll say and do. I have no script now, and sitting down opposite a beautiful woman makes me nervous, despite the booze in my system.

I try to remind myself; she approached me, and she's had ample opportunity to walk away if she wanted to. It'll be fine, Andy. Calm down…

"Is this your first time in Poland?"

I look up from the menu. "Yeah, never been this far east before."

She raises an eyebrow. "What do you think?"

I check my watch. "Well, after about four hours, I think I like it."

She laughs. A lilting tone that reminds me of someone… Chloe. The dream-woman who won't leave my thoughts. A pang of guilt kicks me in the stomach. I shouldn't be out with another woman — Chloe is the closest I've felt to a woman in a long time. I loved Kirsty, and maybe I still love the memory of her, but I'm realising that I loved who I thought Kirsty was, but not who she actually was. Her beauty blinded me. I was unable to see past her glamour.

With Chloe, I feel a deep connection. I know her thoughts, feel her sadness or joy as if it is my own. I shouldn't be betraying her.

I can hear Dave's voice in my head, berating me. 'Chloe in't real, you daft twat. Aga is. And she's sat in front of you three feet away, pretty and gagging for it. Don't bugger this up.'

He's right, of course. But why do I have these guilty feelings?

"What do you do, Andy?"

"Oh, I'm very boring. I'm a hardware technical advisor. We do these custom installations for other companies…" I sense the boredom growing in her as I speak. "Err, techie stuff, you know. Computers."

She nods. "Nice, I used to do procurement for a big tech place."

"Cool. And now?"

"Since I came back home, I don't do much. Trying to find my passion, you know?" Her eyes widen.

"Good for you." I smile. "No point in doing something if you don't like it." I'm reminded of the heap of work that we've done for Ron all week. I should practise what I preach. I don't know what my passion is, but I know that comparing the technical and security release notes of network card firmware versions is not it.

A waiter comes to the table. He says something in Polish and Aga responds. He nods and walks away.

"I ordered some beer. Hope you don't mind?" She grins.

"No, not at all. Good call."

Over dinner, Aga tells me something about her life. How she wanted to be an artist when she was little, but that dream was ripped away from her by the reality of having to pay rent and bills. She dabbles with oil and canvas sometimes, but occasional sales to friends online aren't enough to call it a job. I tell her that doesn't matter, and she should pursue her dreams if that's what makes her happy. What else is the point, when you think about it? You only get one chance at life, so you may as well make the most of it.

I get the feeling she's leaving out huge parts of her history. Especially about the ex that she left in London. That's fine, I don't need to know her life history. I'm mostly enjoying listening to her accent.

When she enquires casually about my situation, I try to skirt over the details, but perhaps lubricated by the booze, I blurted out most of the Kirsty story in all the gory detail. She raised her eyebrows when I mentioned the 'throuple' thing. Not nearly as shocked as I was, though.

She waves over the waiter and says something incomprehensible. He smiles and flits away.

"I think we need something fun. Don't you, Andy?"

"Always up for fun, me." I'm probably not if I'm honest. I'm intrigued, though.

"You'll like this. Trust me."

The waiter returns with two small glasses of something. I take a sniff of the liquid. "Wow, that smells strong. What is it?"

"Krupnik. Take a sip."

I do as she suggests and a burn of warmth explodes on my tongue and all through my chest as it goes down. "Holy crap, that's good."

Aga laughs and picks up her glass. "Nasdrowia." I look at her blankly. "It means good health. To fun times ahead."

"I'll drink to that."

Aga downs her Krupnik in one gulp and then bangs her glass down on the table. She looks me directly in the eyes. "Look, Andy. I didn't have sex since I came back to Poland three months ago. I don't want a relationship, I don't want any stress or pain. I'm attracted to you, I think you are attracted to me... I just want to fuck the night away and enjoy myself. Are you okay with that?"

I nearly choke on my drink. "Err, yeah... I mean, sure, whatever, no problem!"

I think I might be in here...

Chapter Twenty-Eight

The incessant drone of a plane always makes me sleepy. My wrist is sore from holding up my chin. I don't want to rest my head on the window, in case the glass bursts out, and I'm sucked through into the freezing, thin air. Unlikely, but better safe than a bloody pancake on someone's roof.

I open my eyes. The little screen on the back of the chair in front of me shows a map and a thin yellow line from where we came, to where we're going. I don't recognise the landmass below our current position. It doesn't seem to be any country I can recall from my geography lessons, and I can't make out what the text says. My eyes won't focus on the letters.

I glance around the plane, dimly lit, and from what I can see all the other passengers are asleep. The window next to me peers out into deep, empty black. I pull down the blind.

I pull out my phone automatically, but then realise I have no signal here, and for reasons that no one understands, you aren't *meant to use cellular phones on planes. I put it away again and delve into the seat pocket in front of me for some distraction.*

There's a selection of sales catalogues, thinly disguised as magazines, a laminated sheet describing what to do if we have to land in the ocean, and someone's notebook. I should hand it in. Maybe they are looking for it? But a quick peek can't hurt?

The cover is cutesy, patterned with hand-drawn flowers. Honeysuckle, I think. I open the page, nervous, glancing around me in case anyone is watching.

I wouldn't normally peek into someone's private thoughts, but the boredom of travel drives you to extreme measures. The front page reads: 'Chloe's Notes' in an ornate calligraphy flourish.

I almost drop it on the floor. Chloe? What are the chances? Maybe it's a different Chloe? But something tells me this is my Chloe. I check myself; My Chloe?

I furtively look around again, but no one near me is awake. The seat next to me is empty.

The plane drones on and I look back down at the notebook in my hands. I turn the page again.

Hypnagogic Hallucinations
Chloe Jessop

I turn the pages and skim over the text. It seems to be a dream journal of sorts. Experiences and memories from her point of view. I read one that seems familiar:

.   .   .

We're sitting on the side of a hill, looking over the countryside laid out like a patchwork quilt below. A little stream runs down the hill, bubbling and gushing. It sounds young and energetic. Excited to flow into the river, growing up and leaving home, packing its bags of smooth pebbles and little fish and moving out. I stand up and walk towards it, bending down and taking a scoop with my hands. A sip of that cool, effervescent water is like a jolt of adrenaline and I run back to where he's lying, flicking spots of water over him from my fingers as he lazes on the ground, looking up at the clouds.

I run off, giggling before he can catch me. Down the hill and through the meadows that stretch empty and calm all around us. We are safe here. No one else knows about this place. A bird flies low above me and seems to call out my name as it flaps into the distance. 'Chloeee, Chloeee, Follow meee.' it announces. So, I do as I'm told.

He catches up and laughs, then I step across the stream as it flattens out into a deeper river. He flinches, watches me from the other side. Seemingly unwilling to follow. I beckon him over, but he stands still, nervous. I hop back over and grab him, jumping across again to where the land draws me. I set off on a run towards the horizon, occasionally looking back to make sure he's still following. I don't know where I'm going, but the destination isn't relevant. The journey is how you learn the rules of the universe. As I run, music plays in my mind. A delicate violin and piano melody. I wonder if he can hear it, too? Who is he? Where did he come from? I don't recall his face from my life. But yet, somehow, I sense that I know him.

Suddenly, a flicker of white catches my eye and I stop, abruptly. There's a creature hidden amongst the grasses. I bend down carefully so as not to frighten it. Then I see it, a tiny white kitten, filthy with grass seeds and buds. He's nervous but lets me pick him up. I stroke his matted fur, and he purrs and snuggles into my hand. Barely bigger than my palm. For want of anywhere better, I stuff him into my shirt where he can see the path ahead, then resume my run.

The man follows behind me, without question. Will he follow me forever?

We travel far, over land that is wild and free. Empty plains, wooded paths. By a river that snakes into the distance, across a sandy beach, then up high into mountainous climbs, but never do we falter our pace. Running with the wind behind us. If I had wings, I would soar high above the land. I sometimes jump, but the ground pulls me back.

Eventually, we slow, stopping where there's an enormous stone shaped like a bench. We sit, and I check on the kitten nestled in my cleavage. He's pure white, perfectly clean and purring like a train. I tickle him under his chin.

I need to leave. The pull of normal life draws me back. I wish I could stay here and run with him forever.

Maybe we'll come back here another night?

I look up from the book and around me once again. The plane is empty now. No other passengers in the seats near me. I stand up, but all the seats stretching into the distance seem to be empty. No sign of a hostess, either. I sit back down and open the window blind. Pitch-black outside. The drone of the engine throbs on.

The map on the screen in front of me now shows our location hovering above the destination point.

Something about that dream diary stirs a memory in me. I remember that day, running across the plains. The kitten, the cool stream water that she flicked on me, the stone in the shape of a bench where we sat... Chloe had the same dream as I did? How is that possible?

I clutch the book to my chest and shuffle out of my seat into the corridor.

Where is Chloe now? How could she have left this notebook here? Was she travelling somewhere on the same plane as me?

Chapter Twenty-Nine

I'm jolted into sobriety by the harsh law of gravity thudding us onto a runway. What goes up, must come down, as they say. A few seconds pass before I realise where I am. No longer in Poland on a weekend away, but back to reality and work in the morning. Good weekend, though.

The plane lights flick on, and people move around me. Dave jumps up the second the seatbelt light goes off and opens up the locker above. Yanking out our bags.

"Come on, sleepyhead. There's an evening still ahead of us if we get a shift on."

"Ha. You can talk, mate. Do you need me to put you to bed tonight, as well?" I cackle. He shoots me a look of daggers.

"I told you, I reckon someone drugged me!" Dave's face flicks into 'victim mode,' his eyes wide.

"Were you, bollocks. You just fell asleep like a baby." I laugh.

"Come to think of it, I left you with my pint when I went for a piss. Maybe you drugged me, so you could have that bird to yourself."

"Yeah, that must be it." I shake my head. "Still, good weekend, eh?"

"Bloody brilliant." He gives me two thumbs up.

We exit the plane, then the airport without incident. Back to Dave's house for a few cans he has ready in the fridge. We slump into the back of a taxi.

The gig was brilliant. I can't remember the name of the band now, it was some unpronounceable Polish name, but they rocked. It didn't matter that we couldn't understand a word of the lyrics. Music is the universal language, and with the aid of some more beer, we let loose. I even managed to move my body in some kind of vague rhythm. Aga came along with us, and thankfully for Dave, she brought a friend, Ewa. They seemed to hit it off, and we drank the night away after the gig.

The night before with Aga was wild. Unhinged. Raw and animalistic. She had some pent-up sexual tension, I reckon, and I was an escape valve. Once we left the restaurant, I suggested we stop in a bar for another nightcap, but Aga dragged me on. We went straight to my room and the moment the door was shut; she pushed me down onto the bed and ripped my clothes off. It was amazing. Exhilarating and visceral. I'm thankful I had the energy to keep up with her demands. My fitness training finally paying off for something useful.

In the morning we had a leisurely breakfast and then went and banged on Dave's door. That's when he claimed someone had drugged him. 'Sure…' I laughed. 'Someone dropped a roofie into your pint because you are normally hard to get.' He woke up when I introduced him to Aga, anyway. She took us for a tour around the old town during the day. Dave unsubtly hinting that she needs to call her friends and sort him out with an escort for the evening. She laughed, but she got the message and Ewa showed up in the evening when we were heading out for the gig.

Our second night of passion was more laid back, but even more sensual. She found some soft music on the hotel TV and danced with the lights off, pulling me up with her, kicking off her shoes and clothes, one by one, until we fell back onto the bed, the wee small hours blurring into the sunrise, and by the time we lay back, sated and sweaty, the morning sun streamed in through the open window.

We said our goodbyes after lunch and Dave and I made our way back to the airport. We didn't get their numbers or even Facebook pages. It was a hedonistic weekend of fun with no ties. The sort of thing every teenager dreams of. I'm left feeling a bit empty now, as we pull up to Dave's place in the cab. Did that just happen? Am I too old to be doing things like this? Irresponsible, dangerous even. The world is different now.

People are still the same, though. Deep down. We all want to be loved and wanted. To release tension and energy. To go mad, every so often.

A thought wiggles its way into my head. A tightness in my throat. A pang of overwhelming guilt.

I shouldn't have slept with Aga… A total stranger in a strange land. But… Why not?

Chloe.

The reason drifts into my mind like a leaf on a breeze. I'm feeling pangs of guilt because of a character in my dreams. This is ridiculous, but try telling my guts that.

.   .   .

"You okay, mate?" Dave taps me on the shoulder as we get out of the cab.

"Yeah, fine." I shrug.

He looks suspicious. "You've gone white as a ghost like you did in Ron's car that day. Remember?"

I do remember. That was when the headaches started. It hit me like a train that morning and hasn't gone away since. I've learned to live with it. I shrug again.

"You aren't thinking about bloody Kirsty again, are you?" He looks at me through a squint.

"No. God. Well over that…" Now he mentions it, truth be told, I realise I have barely even given Kirsty a moment's thought all weekend. When I think about her now, there's a hazy fog over her memories. A distance between us, as though we were never more than acquaintances. I'm surprised at how little I care now. I'm numb. Maybe this is my defence mechanism. My brain has re-calibrated and Kirsty is no longer the main character in my story.

No, now I have someone else haunting my consciousness. Someone who doesn't exist in the real world at all. I can't tell Dave that, though. He'd be taking the piss all evening.

"What is it, then?"

"Nowt." I smile. "Just thinking about the weekend."

Dave seems to relax. "Come on, then. There's a fridge full of beer with our names on it and a massive pizza coming soon."

Somehow, through the dirty murk of three hangovers all merging into one massive throbbing pain, we made it to Ron's nine o'clock Monday meeting on time. I stayed at Dave's last night as it was easier than going back to Rissa's. I'll be staying off the sauce for a little while. My guts have seen better days. That's the price you pay for fun, I suppose.

Big Ron Corbishley, cheery as a man who just found out he's related to Nigerian royalty, slaps his hands together at the front of the room to get attention. Dave and I take our usual places at the back, trying not to be seen.

Ron's screen is already projected on the wall. He must have got here early today and got set up. This doesn't bode well.

"Right, ladies and gentlefolks." Ron pauses for a laugh that doesn't come. "We have some exciting news today."

A few murmurs come from around the room and a lot of shrugging.

"We've only gone and done it. We've hit the target, and we've done it early!" Ron bounces up and down, which is a circus act in its own right and taps a button on his laptop, moving the screen onto his next slide. An animated GIF from the TV show, 'The Office' with Michael Scott spraying Champagne over Erin. I'm sure that Ron expected everyone to jump up and dance or something, but instead, there's a vague cheer from the front and a whole load of nothing from the rest of us. Undeterred, Ron carries on. "And do you know who we've got to thank for that?" He looks around the room for anyone stupid enough to take his bait. Then he points down towards me and Dave. "Gentlemen, please stand up and come forward."

Oh, shit.

Dave turns to me with eyes wide. I shrug, and we tentatively stand up and edge through the sea of chairs to the front.

"These fine chaps have busted their arses to get this deal done on time, and thanks to them, we are ready early, and the customers are gagging for it." He slaps us both on the back. "Round of applause please, for Andy and Dave!"

A pitiful and short clap comes from the twenty-odd folks dotted around the room. I feel a burning in my cheeks. Did not want this attention. Especially today as we nurse the dregs of Kraków's finest beer and women hangover. I guess our haste last week to clean up, so we could skive off, has paid off, and we're well and truly in the good books.

"Well done, chaps. There are two inspire awards in the mail for you now. "

Dave seizes the opportunity. "Thanks, Ron. Pleasure working with you." They shake hands, and he takes an ostentatious bow and the crowd cheers, this time with more gusto. I cringe but follow suit.

Half the people in the room are salaried, like me and Dave, but the other half, presumably the vocal half, are paid on commission. This project readiness is a big ka-ching to them. I can see a few at the front already planning an extra trip to Tunisia this year off the back of the work we did. I smile, hoping it doesn't seem too fake.

We are allowed to sit again, but Ron has provided us with seats of honour at the front. Wonderful.

Ron opens up his eternal PowerPoint of doom for the millionth time this month, and my brain automatically switches off.

My mind wanders as I look up at the projection on the wall. Hardware and software details, but all I see is the green background that Ron has chosen for his slides. A photo taken from some free stock-photo site, meant to inspire creativity or some bollocks. Motivational imagery. It's a shot of rolling hills fading into the distance, with a vast mountain range looming over the countryside. A river snaking through. It triggers a memory.

The dream I had when I fell asleep on the plane coming home. Chloe… She left a notebook in the seat pocket. She had detailed a dream that I have the same memories of. But, that was in my dream?

A dream, of a dream, of a dream…

This is getting insanely recursive now. I'll end up flickering out in a puff of smoke, or up my own arse if I keep this up.

She said she felt like she knew me. I have the same sensation. Could we have some kind of telepathy? A shared consciousness? If this was Star Trek, there would be no question. Obviously, a Vulcan mind-meld has connected us, and now we must share each other's thoughts for the rest of our days, or at least until the episode ends, whichever is the sooner.

But this isn't Star Trek. This is my actual life, and I'm at a loss to explain it. I can't tell Dave about this because he'll chide me for being stupid. 'Chloe is a dream, you twat!' and I reckon he's right. Still, I can't get this out of my head. Chloe is real. Sure, she's in my dreams, but I didn't just invent her. Somewhere, there's a woman who looks just like her, and I have met her. I just can't put my finger on when or where.

Then there's the guilty feeling. I thought it had subsided, washed down with more cans of beer back at Dave's house. But I woke this morning to the sensation of remorse at what I'd done in Kraków. Even though I don't know Chloe in the waking world, somehow I feel like we are 'together' in the dream world, and same as I would never in a million years have cheated on Kirsty in real life, I should never have cheated on Chloe.

This is crazy. I need to get my shit together. Whatever next?

Will I propose to Chloe in my dreams, will we have a dream wedding, dream babies, dream kids and dream school runs?

Maybe Dave is right, and I should forget this whole Chloe thing. Concentrate on my real life and work. Perhaps if Ron does put in all these good words for me, I might get the promotion I've been wanting for years now.

I snap out of my daydream and look over at Ron who is mid-monologue, once again drilling down into the fine details of what everyone already knows and is doing. Micro-manager of the year.

I sigh, internally. It's easy to see why I fall into wild dreams. My actual life is utterly boring and dreary.

Ron gets to the end of his PowerPoint and there's a silent sigh of relief from the room.

"Dave, Andy, John and Sandra. Would you mind staying back for a few minutes?"

Oh, brilliant. I nod and smile.

Once the room is clear, and we four chosen ones are given an extra coffee and special chocolate biscuits that Ron had hidden behind his laptop, he perches on the front of the desk in what he probably thinks is a cool pose, a serious expression on his mug. Haven't seen John from marketing since we went down to the customer last time, and Sandra is a new recruit to the inner sanctum. I think she has something to do with finance. An older lady stuffed into a pale blue business suit. Her hair is three shades of grey, styled with a plastering trowel and enough hairspray to burn another hole in the ozone layer. She smiles as I make eye contact. We are the chosen ones. We now have a forced sense of camaraderie.

"Right, as you know, we've moved mountains and got this all done in record time." There are some nods. Ron shifts his focus to me and Dave. "Mostly because of the sterling work these chaps have put in. I'm recommending you both for promotion at the end of this quarter. Well done."

My ears perk up at that. "Really? Wow, thanks, Ron."

A big smile from Dave. All we had to do to get recognised was triple our normal workload. Who'd a thunk it?

"When you book your rooms for the last trip down to see Eternitive again, at the end of this month. Go wild, executive suites. We've all earned some comfort and pampering."

I'd agree with that statement. We most certainly do. I wouldn't mind a sauna and massage right now to burn out the rest of this booze from my system.

Back at my desk, I log straight onto the hotel website and do my room booking. I like to get these things sorted, so I don't have to worry about it later. Super efficient, me. I choose the same suite as I booked last time.

The memory of that night in the tub comes crashing back. I made a mess of that night with whatshername. Gemma, was it? I wasn't in a great state of mind. Am I any better now?

If I'm honest, not really. I've gone from mourning the loss of my girlfriend to feeling guilty for having sex with a random Polish woman. Why can't I just have a normal, boring, safe and sensible relationship?

Chapter Thirty

"Have you had any luck finding a place?" Riss jogs along beside me. I'm keeping up, but I think she's easing off for me. I got a bit out of practice for a while, and I'm feeling the pain. I still maintain that eight in the morning on a Sunday is not the right time for exercise. Isn't there the rest of the day when we can do that?

Riss insists, but she's always been a morning person… Annoying.

"No, not really." I shrug. I did do some online searching for a flat or house in the area, but all I came up with was places I don't want to live. Estates full of dangerous packs of kids, or flats above shops in the high street. I don't fancy either. I sort of forgot about the need, with everything going on at work and the whole lads' weekend away. Now, a pulse of anxiety courses through me. I told Riss this would be a temporary thing.

"No rush, just curious." She smiles.

"I'll get looking again, maybe need to go out of town further where it's cheaper. Oh, and I'll be away for almost a week at the end of the month for that work thing. Give you a bit of space. Ron insisted we stay in the executive suites this time."

She nods. "Well, I might have some longer-term news…" She trails off.

I stop running, and Riss laughs, then stops ahead of me. "What news?"

She walks back over to me. "Well, don't tell anyone, especially Mum… But…" She pauses for dramatic effect. "I might be pregnant!" She squeals in excitement.

"Oh, my god. Rissa!" I throw my arms around her and squeeze, then realise I shouldn't do that and back off. "When, what, how?"

"Well, it's early yet. I need to do a load more tests to be sure. Seriously, don't tell anyone yet in case it… You know, doesn't work out."

"Right. Sure. Wow." A thousand thoughts burst into my head, all vying for attention. "I wonder if I'll be an Uncle or an Aunt?"

Riss smirks. "An Uncle, Andy. Always an Uncle. Unless you have something going on that I don't know about?"

I laugh. "I'm so happy for you, sis. This is HUGE!"

"Thanks, Andy." She smiles and we hug again.

"Is Nick happy?"

"Err, well, he should be. But… I haven't told him yet. Just in case."

"Oh, right. Okay."

"Don't mention it at home. A few more days and I'll do another test, to be a hundred percent sure, you know. We've tried for so long now. There's been some false positives before. But I have a good feeling, this time."

"Mum's the word. No pun intended." I chuckle. "Sure, no

problem. I'll be careful." I look at Clarissa, her cheeks red, but I can't tell if that's from the jog or the news. "You'll be a wonderful mum, Riss."

She smiles. "Thanks, brother dearest. Come on then, we still have two miles to cover."

"Take it easy. Look after that little bean-creature in your belly."

"I'm fine for a while, yet." She zips off at full speed, as if to prove a point.

When we get back, I shower and change, but then start looking for a flat urgently. If I get the promotion I deserve and need, then it could make flat searching easier. A couple of hundred a month extra could make all the difference. I'm used to the posher side of town now, and while it might make me seem obnoxious, I prefer not to have my car nicked and my neighbours screaming and yelling at all hours. Riss said there's no rush. That I can stay as long as I need to, but I know her. She's itching to decorate my room as a nursery. I bet her Amazon basket is full of cute baby stuff already. Even if she's not decorating, there'll soon be a proliferation of women bringing strange gifts and advice. Gender reveal parties, baby showers, pushchairs, car seats, bottles, not to mention the weird breast pump devices and sterilisation units. It'll turn from comfy house to a hospital laboratory in no time. The complications of procreation have always confused me. I'm not ready for it yet.

After her revelation, I told her all about our trip to Kraków. I'd told her the basics already, but I left out the part about Aga. It just didn't seem important before. Now, I'm not sure why, but I told Riss my guilty feelings about the event. She said it was most likely because I acted like a dumb teenager, and sometimes you just need to get that stuff out of your system. That isn't it, though. I'm used to acting like a fool. This was different. I told her I felt guilty for betraying Chloe. She looked at me strangely, but she didn't judge. She thought about it for a moment, then told me maybe I should apologise to Chloe in my dream world. Explain what happened. Perhaps that would set my mind at ease?

Maybe. But I haven't had another dream since the one on the plane, at least not that I can remember. I've slept long and soundly.

I know I'm being ridiculous, but I can't get rid of the feelings. I need a distraction, and looking for somewhere to live is likely to be a good one.

Riss said she'd help if I wanted. Come along to look at places with me, so I get the woman's intuition point of view. I said I only need somewhere that doesn't stink and has relatively quiet neighbours. I don't care about fancy curtains and pot plants. Still, I appreciate the help.

I've marked a couple of places as potential, and I'll see about a viewing soon.

I have also pondered asking Dave if I could rent his spare room for a while. However, it still seems like a bad idea, living and working with him, drinking almost every night. I'd quickly fall out of my fitness routine that Riss has got me into, and I'd swap it for a lifestyle of beer, TV and pizza. At least I don't have to leave the room to fart at Dave's house. Then again, I suppose that's why his house has that bachelor stink to it. Farts, dirty laundry and sex. I'll keep looking.

Work has been stressful this week, despite us being ready for the big customer deal, Ron has already lined us up with future deals. Since we worked well together, he's now requested that Dave and I are always assigned to his projects. He's even on about creating a new dedicated A-Team, as he calls it. I'm torn between wanting to puke at the mention of 'A-Team' and wanting the money that a promotion would bring. I have to play the game, I guess. Until I've got something better as an option, I'm stuck with Big Ron and his deals. Beats the dole queue, I suppose.

As usual, like a video game or something, the reward for hard work is more work. You clear a level, then you get another, tougher level with an even more angry boss to deal with.

Now I know why many people slack off and do the absolute bare-minimum required. If you do anything on top, they swamp you with more and more stress. I suppose that's just life in our culture. This is what we work all our lives for. More hassle to get a little extra money for someone else to get rich.

Is it all worth it? I've sort of bumbled along in my career to this point. Never really had a plan apart from work, make money, spend money, repeat. I was lucky at the time to get this job. Funny how you go from grateful for the money, to resenting almost every second you spend in the bloody place, over the course of six months. Eight years later, I'm still doing the same thing. Should I look around for something different?

I think back to the advice I gave to Aga in Kraków. Follow your dreams if that makes you happy.

Then I think about my dreams. They mostly involve a strange but beautiful woman who leads me through wonderful places and crazy scenarios. We've been to other planets, laid in a bath cut into rocks, run across plains and mountains, had the most amazing sex I've ever experienced, and most of all, when I'm with her I feel safe and comfortable. Chloe makes sense to me. Chloe makes me happy, and she's a dream I want to follow. I just don't know how or even where to start.

Then there's that other chap who shows up in my dreams. Thomas. I think he's also the monk that was so frightening earlier. I don't know how I know this, I just do.

A monk, in a hotel called the 'Priory of St Augustine.' There has to be some connection? Something about the bar. Lodestone Bar. A strange name, and Thomas mentioned 'the stones' a few times. Dreams and images. Hypnogogic hallucinations, as that notebook said. What do they mean? I have no bloody idea.

I reach for my phone, a bit of X-Box and beer sounds like a good plan now for some escapism. Dave might be up for a good slaying by my twin-flaming, double-sword wielding, scantily clad Elven rogue.

Before I can type out the message, my phone buzzes in my hand and I look up at the sender's name, startled.

'Hello, stranger.'

From Kayla…

"Hadn't heard from you in a while. Thought we should catch up."

Kayla, pretty in jeans and a low-cut blouse, with a denim jacket on top, far from her goth Siouxsie outfit I remember her in, invited me out for a drink, and this time, I accepted immediately. I smile and take a swig of beer. Kayla has a vodka and coke and I chuckled at that. Same drink as Aga had in Kraków.

"Lovely to see you again, Kayla. How have you been?" I try my smooth, sophisticated persona, hoping it doesn't appear creepy.

"Yeah, not bad." She looks me up and down. "You look great, Andy." A smile creeps onto her lips.

"Thanks. My sister has been forcing me to run with her. She's very strict on the fitness regime."

"It definitely shows." I recognise a sultry look in her eyes. Oh, boy.

I smile, blushing a little. "What you been up to?"

"This and that, you know." She curls a strand of hair in her fingers. "Saw someone for a bit, broke up with him… Got back again, broke up again." She sighs.

"Ah, right." I nod. "People are complicated, aren't they?"

"You got that right." She pauses. "Speaking of which, how are 'things' with you?" She makes air quotes and sits back on the bench seat. Eyes wide.

I exhale. "Well… How long you got?" I laugh.

"Like that?"

"Isn't it always?" I pause. Where do I start? Kayla is a nice girl. I could see us having 'something' together, but if I go down this road, am I going to spark up the guilty feelings again? A thought occurs to me. "You know about dreams and whatnot, don't you? Spiritual stuff, moments of clarity and all that malarkey?"

"I dabble, yes." She sits forward, intrigued. "What's on your mind?"

I ponder for a moment, wondering if I should say anything at all, but Kayla is easy to talk to, and she doesn't judge or tell me I'm mad. I want to talk to someone about all this, someone who isn't Clarissa or Dave, or even Chloe. I need to bounce it all off someone. Maybe explaining everything will allow me to understand it all, get it out of my system, whatever it is.

"Well, if you are sure you want to know?" She nods. "I think we'll need another drink, first."

I tell Kayla about the trip me and Dave took to Kraków, how I met a woman and had wild, unrestrained passionate sex and then left the country. She rolled her eyes. But I assured her, that's what Aga wanted. But then I told her about the guilty feelings I've had since then.

"Do you have a girlfriend?" Kayla sits forward.

"Err, no. Not as such." She raises an eyebrow. "Remember, I said about the dream I had where I shouted out a name. Chloe?"

"Oh, yeah."

I shuffle, awkward in my seat. "I think I'm in love with her." As I say the words, they sound utterly ridiculous.

"Sorry, you're in love with whom?" Kayla tilts her head.

I knew I shouldn't have said anything. She thinks I'm a nut job now, and I've just totally crushed any chance I had of getting anywhere with Kayla. Why am I such an idiot? I can hear Dave chiding me in my head. 'You bloody twat, Andy.'

"Dream woman, Chloe. I know it sounds mad, but…" I shrug.

"Interesting." Kayla leans back again and takes a sip of her drink.

"Now I say it, I realise it seems wild, but… How else do you explain it?"

"Well, I'm not certain. Did you ever find out if you know this Chloe person in real life?"

"Not that I know of."

"These must be bloody good dreams, Andy." She laughs.

"They are. I've been keeping a journal, on and off." I hesitate. "Would you like to see?"

"Damn right!" Her eyes widen again.

"Some are a bit… Um, personal, if you know what I mean." I feel warmth in my cheeks again.

"Think of me as your therapist." She chuckles. "I won't tell anyone. Promise." She mimes closing a zip over her lips.

I must be mad, but I open up the dream journal app on my phone, pick a dream that isn't too explicit and hand the phone to Kayla. I know this is against all rules of modern society, but to be honest, it feels like a relief to get this off my chest, properly. Maybe this is what it takes to reset my brain. Reboot myself and purge all the caches.

I stand up to go to the toilet.

"I trust you. Be right back."

When I get back, Kayla is still engrossed in my phone screen. I sit back down and watch her as she smiles, then eyes wide, seems to be shocked. Occasional giggles.

Finally, she puts the phone down on the table in front of me.

"Thank you, Andy." She stands up. "My turn for the ladies' room. Be right back. Get another one in?"

I do as she suggests and get myself a whisky chaser this time; I think I need it to calm my nerves.

Kayla comes back and sits down. She smiles.

"You are quite the romantic, aren't you, Andy?"

I shrug. "I mean. If you reckon?"

"That was lovely." She nods towards my phone. "You are much more than meets the eye. That Kirsty didn't deserve you."

"Dave said the same. So did my sister. I'm starting to believe that was true."

Kayla nods. "It is. Mark my words." She pauses. "Now then. Chloe…" Her eyes widen, and she picks up her new drink. "Oh, and who's the bloke, Thomas?"

"I don't know, to be honest. He's a bit of an anomaly as well. I can imagine dreaming up Chloe. She's literally my dream woman." I feel a quiver in my voice as I say those words, but I cough to cover it. "But, Thomas… Who knows where he came from."

"What's a Lodestone?"

"A naturally magnetic rock. Lodestone is the common name for magnetite. It's the only variety that possesses the north-south magnetic polarity." Kayla raises an eyebrow again. "I've been googling." I chuckle. "Ancient philosophers thought the stones had souls, or something, because of the way they attracted iron. They had no other way to explain it. Eventually, people figured out you could use it as a compass."

"Interesting indeed."

"Well, now you know all my darkest secrets, Kayla. What do you think I should do?"

She ponders for a moment. Swirling the drink around in her

glass. "You've got two choices, Andy."

"Yeah?"

"Yeah. One; you just forget this whole dream thing, and you get on with your life." She smiles, and I'm sure I notice a 'look,' again in her eyes. "Or, two; you go find this Chloe woman because unless you are the type of bloke who secretly reads chick-lit romances, I think there's more going on here than you know about."

"How do you mean?"

"Well, before all this started, did you ever have dreams like that," she motions again to my phone. "Some of that stuff is beautiful, I'm amazed, Andy."

"Well, no. Now you come to mention it. I mostly just dreamed the usual stupid crap, you know, endlessly looking for a toilet to go for a piss. Old school memories, stuff like that."

"Have you ever heard of the collective unconsciousness?"

"Nope."

"Jung coined the term. His explanation for how people have a baseline understanding of things, a bit like instinct, but more detailed. He said in dreams, these primordial images can surface, and they may have no connection to your personal experiences."

"Err, that's… What?"

"Well, on top of that, I've seen reference to what they call 'mutual dreams'. Where two people are connected in the dream state, and they experience the same things, at the same time."

I sit forward. "Sorry, are you saying Chloe is real, and we may be sharing dreams? This isn't all in my head, but it's in her head, as well?"

"I've never known it happen to someone before, especially this detailed. But, yeah, I mean, it could be possible." She shrugs.

I sit back, suddenly hot and sweating. "Bloody hell."

Chapter Thirty-One

I've looked at seven apartments, four lofts, three bungalows, a town-house... Oh, and I saw a tent in a field behind the park where a couple of tramps are cohabiting.

I think the tramp-tent was the best of the lot. Bring your own shovel.

I'm trying to be open-minded, but mildew, damp, odd stains, nosey and noisy neighbours, no parking spaces, shared laundry facilities, lichens — on the inside, toilets that you have to know a secret hand move to get to flush, and one place that had a delightful view over what I'm fairly sure is a brothel. All these things add up to why I'm still living at my sister's house.

The estate agent visibly enjoyed telling me that within my price range, these were the best available at the moment. She said the words 'price range' as if they were filthy, and she didn't want to touch them. Anyone who has such a thing should be grateful they aren't sharing an outside toilet with twelve other families.

I give up. I'll just share the room at Rissa's house with the baby. Or I'll sleep under the dining table. Anything has to be better than the dumps I've seen.

The experience has made me yearn for the good old days, back in my previous house with Kirsty, but there's no way I can stretch my salary to afford something like it alone.

I open up the home-finder app once again and scan through the available options. Nothing strikes me as interesting, and the thought of looking at more dumps today brings a tightness to my throat.

I get out of bed and quietly slip downstairs to make a coffee. Still early, I'm up before Rissa for a change. I can't sleep much lately, and when I do sleep, there are no dreams, at least that I can remember. Nothing as vivid and lucid as I had before.

I checked in my journal. It's been two weeks now since I had the last dream; Chloe's notebook on the plane. Since then, nothing.

I'm not sure why, or what changed. I'm doing more or less the same things every day. Work, run, eat, sleep. Repeat. Work is still busy; Ron is still annoying.

Maybe this is like the ear-worm head-songs? A tune gets stuck in your head on repeat until you can push it out by actually listening to the song. Perhaps my dreams were some fantasy I had pushed to the limits in my unconscious imagination, and now I've played it out, by actually having some fun in my real life. The fantasy is over; the dreams stop.

I miss them, to be honest. They were so raw and real.

And when I think about it, which I do rather a lot, I deeply miss Chloe.

Silly, I know, but there it is. No one ever said love should make sense, did they? I feel the loss in my gut, in my chest. An emptiness. Worse even, than when Kirsty walked out.

Kayla has offered me all manner of strange explanations, from the mutual dreams, my stress levels, my mental state, all the way down to something I ate. I want to believe, but with every day that passes and no more dreams arrive, the supernatural explanations become ever less likely.

I'm tired. My head pounds with no alcoholic cause.

I peer outside through the blinds. The morning light creeps over the houses across the road. I pull the blinds shut again and sit down at the table, staring into my black coffee.

"You're up early." Riss startles me, coming into the kitchen, flicking on the light. She's in pyjamas and slippers, wrapped around with a fluffy pink dressing gown. Like a giant marshmallow.

"Couldn't sleep." I force a vague smile and lift up the cup of coffee. "Want one?"

"Yeah, cheers. Decaf for me, though."

I nod, get up, and flick the kettle on. "Decaf?"

A smile flickers on her face, and she sits down at the table. "Well, since you are here, bright and early…"

"Dunno about bright. Early, though, for sure."

Riss pulls something out of her pocket. A white plastic stick thingy. She hands it to me and I look down at it. It's one of those pregnancy testers.

"Turn it over." She bites her lip.

I twist the tester around and there's a little screen with the word 'Pregnant'. I look up at Rissa. "Oh, my god!"

"That's the third one in three weeks." She squeals quietly, clenching her fists.

"That must be it then? You really are."

Riss shushes me with a wave of a hand. "Yeah, I'm gonna tell Nick today." A massive grin erupts on her face. I lean down and hug her. "Happy for you, sis-Riss."

"Thanks, brother."

Riss chatters away quietly, mostly to herself, because I know little about midwifery and nappies. A thought occurs to me, I should make myself scarce today, so they can celebrate in private.

"I'm going out after we get back from our run."

"More house viewings?"

"No, not today, thank feck. I don't think I can stomach any more." I pause. "Don't worry, I'll find something soon." I offer a weak smile and Riss nods. "Might go over to Dave's for a few cans, or down the local." I shrug.

"You don't have to go out on our behalf."

"Aye, I do. This is your time." Riss smiles and reaches over to squeeze my hand.

I'm happy for them, genuinely, but there's a part of me that's jealous. She's younger than me, and she has her life together. Decent home and job, now a family on the way. Here I am chasing crazy dreams, nowhere to live, no relationship other than in my head. I've blown my chances with Kayla, and the thought of going out into the world looking for new love overwhelms me with dread, not unlike the house situation.

I thought I had everything sorted, but it vanished in a puff of smoke, lost and forgotten like a dream memory.

I'm what's technically termed as a loser, I reckon. Not good. Where did I go wrong?

"Well, what crazy plan have you got lined up for us next?" I grin at Dave over a beer can, pulled from his re-stocked fridge.

"Haven't given it much thought, now you come to mention it."

"Amsterdam? Prague? Oh, what about a US road trip around a load of states? Start in New York and make our way over to Vegas or something."

"Sounds expensive." Dave flinches.

"Oh… Yeah." The sad realisation that I can't afford a home, let alone a holiday, slaps me on the forehead like a brick.

"You're in a good mood."

"Not really, if I'm honest. I was just thinking that the Kraków trip worked out well, maybe we can do something else… You know?"

"Sounds like a plan. Maybe if Ron comes through with the promotions, we can afford something grand."

I nod. "Hopefully. I need to find somewhere to live first, though."

"There's always my spare room, mate. Told you."

I scratch my chin. "Cheers, Dave. I just, I think we'd end up fighting or something."

"Don't be daft. We aren't kids…" He scoffs. "Or women."

I chuckle. "Yeah, but still." I pause. Maybe this is my best option? "I'll keep looking for a bit, but I may yet take you up on that. I just… I want to settle down with a woman, you know. Not a bachelor pad."

"There'll be plenty of women, Andy, me old mate." He sniggers and crushes an empty can.

"You know what I mean…" I go to the fridge for another

couple of beers. "I've been chatting with that Kayla again, on and off."

"Oh, aye?" Dave grins and winks. "She's a wee minx, that one."

"Nah, not like that. She's been helping me with my… Err, dreams and whatnot."

"Huh?" Dave looks incredulous.

"You know, all that Chloe stuff. I told Kayla about them… She said maybe they were more than just dreams and that it's possible to share a dream with someone…" As I say the words, I realise how crazy it all sounds. I trail off. "… Well, anyway, I think it's all over now. All the dreams and that. They've stopped since we came back from Kraków."

"You told Kayla about your dreams?" Dave's eyes are wide as frying pans.

"Shut up. I just needed someone to talk to." I look up. "Someone who might understand."

Dave shakes his head. "I don't even know where to start."

"Well, never mind. What I'm saying is, I reckon it's all over now. I just needed to get it out of my system. Maybe it was all because of Kirsty and that. I dunno. But talking to Kayla helped, even if she just told me what I wanted to hear. It's made me think about it a bit more rationally, and now I reckon I'm over it."

Dave looks like he's going to say something but then thinks better of it. "Well, that's good then. I suppose."

"Yeah. After Ron's bloody customer thing, we should think about our next adventure. What do you reckon?"

"Sounds like a plan, man."

Chapter Thirty-Two

"That's the last of it. Cheers, mate." Dave takes a box out of my car boot and strides off up the stairs. I grab the bag of takeaway and cans I picked up en route and lock the car.

I weighed up the pros and cons, then ignored the gigantic pile of cons because I wanted to get out of the way for Rissa and Nick. She tried to hide it, but I could tell she was ecstatic that she can finally furnish and decorate her nursery. Uncle Andy will help paint and assemble if needed. I'm a dab hand with an IKEA Allen key.

It won't be forever, I've told myself this over and over. But I mean it. I don't want to wake up in my forties, still living at Dave's, drunk every night, reeking of sweaty socks and cheap aftershave. This is only until I get myself sorted, however that might happen; lottery or miracle…

Dave lives in a semi-decent area, and he has a spare room. It makes sense if you look at it that way.

"You don't have much stuff, do you?" Dave looks around my

new room. Laptop, a few clothes, this and that… Yeah, I haven't got much to show for my life. When I was packing up my clothes, I found the terrible garments that Kirsty bought me, which seems like a lifetime ago now, that she wanted me to wear on our holiday. Lucky escape, I donated them to the charity shop. If any octogenarian golfers happen to swing by, they'll get themselves a bargain.

"Travelling light or something." I scoff. "Kirsty took all the good stuff."

Dave rolls his eyes. "Right, well, let's get stuck into that Chinese and cans. I've got the latest Marvel movie." Dave winks. "Four words: Scarlett Johansson — skintight leather."

"Well, I'm sold."

Yeah, this will work out great.

My phone buzzes in my pocket. I struggle to sit up after the feast of Chicken Kung-Po and all the trimmings we downed. A special occasion, Dave said. The beer hasn't helped either. I have to stand up, in the end, to get the phone out of my jeans. I unlock and double-take. A text message… From Kirsty?

'Andy, can we meet up, tonight if possible?'

"Err, pause the movie for a second, Dave."

Dave looks up, half-asleep on the couch. "Hey, what's up?"

I show him my phone.

"It's a trap, mate, Don't answer it."

I ponder. He could be right. But if I don't find out what she wants, I'll be wondering about it all night, and for the next week, if not a month.

"I'll be careful."

I reply. 'What for?'

'It would be easier to say in person if you don't mind?'

'Right, okay. Shall I come to the restaurant?' It still annoys me that she calls her Starbucks a restaurant.

'No, definitely not. Do you know Hardy's in the town?'

I turn to Dave. "Hardy's?"

He screws his face up. "Bloody poncy wine-bar place."

I nod. Typical. 'Nope. But I'm sure I can find it.'

'Thanks, Andy. Can you make 7?'

'Yeah. See you then.'

I put my phone away. I'm curious now. She was almost friendly for a second. Must want something, but I don't think there's anything left for me to give her. Blood?

"Do you want backup?" Dave sits up.

"Nah, mate. I think I can handle one little girl."

Dave grins. "No, lieutenant, your men are already dead."

As Dave said, Hardy's is indeed a poncy wine-bar. I don't know how these places work. Is it a restaurant or a bar? Do they bring us drinks or do we go up and get them? I peek in briefly and recoil back. I'm not waiting in there to be looked down on by snooty waiters. Sorry, sommeliers.

I stand outside. I'm two minutes early.

On the journey here, on foot, because I've had a few cans, and a whisky for the nerves, I've tried to think of what this impromptu meeting could be about, but aside from some kind of vehicle-related issue, I can't imagine. If it was a bit of paperwork, we could have done that by post and not met in a wine-bar. I guess I'll find out shortly.

I don't have to wait long. Kirsty gets out of a taxi and walks over to me. She's still beautiful, but the effect is dulled now because I know that beauty is only skin deep. Jeans, mid-length red coat, minimal makeup, but immediately from her gait I can tell something isn't right.

"Hi, Andy. Thanks for coming." She's definitely not right. There's none of her usual energy. She makes eye contact for a moment but then looks down.

"Yeah, no problem." I hesitate. "Do you want to go inside?"

"Sorry, yeah."

I open the door for her and follow behind. She walks to the back of the place and finds a table far from anyone else. Dimly lit, plush carpet soaks up the background noise.

She takes off her coat and folds it neatly, placing it on the seat next to her. I slump down opposite. A silence hangs between us. She would normally make some kind of small talk, but today she's blank.

"You okay?"

"Yeah, well, no…"

A waitress comes over to us with complicated menus. Kirsty waves them away. "Rioja, please."

The waitress turns to me. "Don't suppose you have any beer?" She shakes her head.

"Right, same as she's having then, please."

I turn back to Kirsty as the waitress walks off. "What's up?"

Kirsty pauses. She looks me straight in the eye and I can see she's upset. Her eyes are moist, her eyeliner is smeared, she's been crying, probably in the taxi on the way here.

"I'm going back to Hinckley, for a bit at least."

"Hinckley? You mean, to live? At your parents?"

"Yeah…"

"Oh. Right." My mind swirls with possible reasons for this. She hates her parents, she can't be doing this by choice.

"What happened? Err, I mean, if you don't mind me asking."

She sniffs and shrugs. "I don't know who else to talk to…"

I try a sympathetic face, but the memories of how she walked out on me flood back, and it's hard to be sympathetic. Still, I'm not a monster, like she is.

The waitress brings our glasses. Kirsty takes a big gulp.

"Head office is closing my Starbucks." Kirsty looks up to the skies with a sigh. "That's what started it all, I suppose."

"Really? Shit. Sorry, Kirsty. You're out of a job?"

"Yeah, we all are. Town centres aren't prime retail any more. There's another one in the mall outside town, and they've been doing triple our numbers for months. I guess it was inevitable, but…" She sniffs again. "And then, err, Laura, Nathan and I…" She spits their names out as if they are poisonous. "We broke up."

"Oh." Part of me desperately wants to gloat, to say 'I told you so' and laugh, but again, I'm not the monster. "Sorry, Kirsty."

"Thanks." She stifles a tear.

"Dare I ask?"

"Nathan is such a fucking pretentious fop!" She raises her voice. "Sorry. I…"

"No problem." I look around to see if anyone noticed her outburst, but also, so I can hide a smirk. I can't help but agree with her statement.

"And Laura… Well, you think you know someone. Oh, my god."

Kirsty regales me with stories of how petty they both are and how everything had to be 'just so' in their house, and, disturbingly, in their bed.

"I was absolutely mortified, Andy. They sat me down at the dining table with coffee. Nathan had a clipboard. An actual fucking clipboard! They had a list of 'points' to discuss regarding our sex life. It was like a bloody job interview." Kirsty has opened the floodgates now, and I sit back and listen. Shame I don't have popcorn. "Nathan doesn't like kissing. Says it puts him off. Nor does he like when I take the lead." She shudders. "Laura... Well, she doesn't like anything, as far as I can tell. She especially doesn't like her nipples or feet touched." I have to cough to cover a laugh. Trying to keep a straight face is getting harder and harder. "Andy, they made me SIGN THE SHEET, in triplicate!" That does it. I burst out laughing.

"Are you serious? Sorry, Kirsty."

"I have a copy." She shakes her head, motioning to her bag. "I couldn't look them in the eye after that, but we tried again to have 'mutually agreed upon throuple sex'."

"You went back in for more?"

She nods. "Well, what else was I meant to do?" She gulps down her wine and waves the waitress over for another. "I tried, taking all their notes into account, but I accidentally brushed Laura's fucking tit and, well, when she pointed out my mistake I just ran off to the bathroom, locking the door and crying my eyes out."

"Oh, god. Kirsty, that sounds... Horrible."

"I wanted the earth to open up and swallow me. I stayed in there for two hours until Nathan threatened to call the police."

"No way? Wow, that escalated quickly."

"Yeah. So, that's all over. I packed up some stuff, and I'm in the Travelodge until tomorrow. Getting the train home." She slumps back in her seat. Exhausted and drained.

I look over at her, pretty and vulnerable now. She's lost all the bravado and entitlement she once had. Now she's just a scared little girl. They really beat it out of her. I'm in two minds to go over to Nathan and beat the crap out of the nasty little shit, but what's the point. I'd end up the bad guy in jail and he'd thrust the sex contract in the judge's face, absolving him of any responsibility.

"Go on, say it." Kirsty picks up her glass again.

"Say what?"

"Told you so." She sighs. "You have every right."

"Well, I never did tell you so." I shrug.

"I'm sure you thought it, though." She drains her glass. "I fucked up. Sorry, Andy, for mistreating you."

I nearly blurt out the words 'No problem', but I stop myself in time. It was a problem. "Apology accepted."

There's a moment of silence between us. Awkward. A million memories flood my brain, our trip to Bruges, all the fun times we had together. Is there any chance we could start again? When I look at her now, I see the woman I loved, not the heartless bitch who dumped me. But she's there, lurking in the wings, waiting to come out again and take charge.

"What have you been up to?" She feigns a laugh to hide the awkwardness.

"Oh, not much. Work and stuff…" I trail off. I'm not going to mention our trip to Kraków for beer and random sex, nor the weird and wonderful dream-relationship I've had with Chloe, nor the evenings with Kayla… "I moved into Dave's place today."

Kirsty raises an eyebrow. "Oh, nice. The boys' bachelor pad." She sniggers. "I bet that smells delightful."

I shake my head. "It's only temporary, till I get somewhere better."

She nods. "Sorry, I shouldn't judge your life choices."

"I didn't have much of a choice." I hesitate. "I was staying with Riss… But." I shrug. "Well, she's got some stuff going on." Kirsty nods dismissively, but I know she's intrigued. "She's preggers. They've been trying for ages, apparently."

"Oh, wow!" Her eyes are wide. "Give her my congratulations."

"Dunno if I'm meant to tell anyone yet, but I will when it's safe."

"Oh, right." She does the lip-zip mime, then shuffles in her seat. "Are you, err, seeing anyone, now?"

I raise my eyebrows. "No." I shrug. "Still free and single."

"What about that Chloe thing?" Kirsty's knuckles whiten as she grips her glass.

I shake my head. "That was just a dream, Kirsty. I don't know where it came from, but I have never met anyone called Chloe in real life."

"Okay." She pauses, biting her lip. "I better get a taxi. I have to be up early for the train." She pulls out her phone.

"Oh, sure."

"Thanks, Andy, for letting me vent. I can't tell Mum and Dad this stuff."

"Yeah, no problem."

"Dad is coming down with me next week to collect all my furniture and stuff. That'll be a fun day, I'm certain."

I chuckle. "I can imagine." I remember my house being

purged of Kirsty's belongings not so long ago. I stood by and watched my life fall to pieces, helpless.

"Can I drop you at Dave's in the cab? It's on the way, isn't it?"

I'm tempted to get into a cab with Kirsty, tell the driver to go straight to her hotel, snog in the back and then while the night away, making up for lost time, but I resist. My body wants one thing, but a niggle in my head tells me this is a bad idea. "Thanks, but I'll walk. I need to burn off the calories." I chuckle.

"You look great, by the way."

"Cheers. Riss has been very strict with the running."

"It has paid off." She smiles, sweet and pretty. I stand up before I get pulled into her spiderweb, trapped and consumed. I have some thinking to do.

Chapter Thirty-Three

The sign on the door says 'The Lodestone Bar.' I push it open and go in, there are a few people dotted around, but it isn't busy. The plush carpet is soft, the room is quiet and cosy. I'm meeting Ron and Dave for a pint shortly. This week has been mad, getting everything ready and double, triple checking things. I've earned my drink, I reckon. I've earned a month off if I'm honest. Chance would be a fine thing.

I sit down at the bar, look up at my reflection in the mirror behind the glasses and bottles. Smooth down my hair. I'm tired, and my reflection shows it.

Something catches my eye and I turn around, swiftly. A gaunt man lurches behind me. A thud of adrenaline pulses through me.

"Thomas?" He's thin, tall and pale, his skin is dry as parchment. A waft of burnt oily stench passes over me.

"Good evening, Andrew, or should I say, good morning?" He attempts what may be considered a smile, but it instils dread, not joy. I shudder.

"What are you doing here?"

He looks taken aback. "I live and work here. I've been here a very long time, Andrew. A very long time. In fact, I may never leave."

"Oh. Right." I turn back to the bar. Thomas sits down beside me.

"It is I who should be asking you, what are YOU doing here? And while we're at it, that woman friend of yours, Chloe, I believe? What are you two doing here among the stones, and where did you come from?" He raises his eyebrows, waiting for an answer. "Hmm?"

"Chloe?" I sit up. "You know Chloe?"

"Indeed, I know all of this realm. Well, I thought I did…" He tails off.

"Where is she?"

"Ah, now that, I do not know."

There's an awkward silence. Thomas steeples his hands together at his lips. I look away.

"Did someone call me?"

We both turn around in shock. Chloe, delightfully beautiful, delicately coy, stands but a few feet away, pouting.

"Chloe!" I jump off my stool excitedly. She smiles at me, then peers at Thomas.

"I shall leave you two, for now. We will see each other again." I turn to where Thomas sat, but he's gone. A vague hint of black smoke fades into nothing. The bar is now empty, save for Chloe and me.

"What the?"

"*Did you miss me?*" Chloe moves towards me and her honeysuckle scent floods my senses.

I grab her in an embrace, squeezing tight. Her warmth gives me energy, life and joy. I lift her off the ground and spin around.

She giggles. "*I'll take that as a yes.*"

"*Yes! I… I thought… I don't know what I thought, that you were a dream, not real…? That I had imagined you.*"

"*Oh, I'm real.*" She smiles. I put her down and release my grip a little. She stands back a pace and looks around. "*Where are we?*"

"*The Lodestone Bar.*" I raise my eyebrows. "*In that hotel near Berkhamsted.*"

"*Yeah. I thought it seemed familiar.*" She looks around. "*What is a Lodestone, anyway?*"

"*A type of Magnetite. A naturally magnetic rock.*"

"*Strange name for a bar?*"

"*Yeah, I thought that myself. I wonder if that Thomas chap knows what it means?*"

"*Thomas, that man who was here a minute ago?*"

"*Yeah. He's a bit odd, don't you think?*"

"*You could say that. At least he's not trying to kill us or whatever, anymore.*"

I nod. "*That is a plus, indeed. He's the same person as the monk bloke, I reckon. I don't know how I know that, but, I have a feeling.*"

"*Yep.*" She shrugs. "*I had the same feeling…*"

I motion around me. "*I'm coming here for a work thing, tomorrow.*"

"*Really? Me too.*"

"*You… What?*"

She nods. "Yeah. We're recording at the studio over the road again." She points towards the door.

"Oh, wow. I'm meeting our customers in the industrial estate."

She grabs my hands. "Well then, I'll meet you here in the bar, tomorrow evening, Andy." She smiles.

"Yeah, okay…" I pause. "Are we dreaming?"

"Well, we must be because otherwise, you wouldn't be this perfect." She laughs.

"I was going to say the same thing." I chuckle and squeeze her hands. "I suppose I'll see you tomorrow, then, in the Lodestone Bar. It's a date!"

"Good. What shall we do in the meantime?" She pulls me down and plants her lips on mine, soft and warm with a giggle.

"I have some ideas…" I grin.

Chapter Thirty-Four

"I'm meeting that Bethany this evening." Dave rubs his hands together in glee.

"Keep your hands on the wheel, mate!" I wince as he deliberately looks away from the road and rolls his eyes. "Jesus!"

"Keep your hair on, Andy, everything is under control." He chuckles.

Everything is most definitely not under control. I was planning to drive my car this morning to the hotel, but a flat tyre put the kibosh on that plan. Already late, Dave offered, and it is absolutely imperative that I get to the Priory of St Augustine hotel today. Ron would have my balls for bookends if I didn't show up, but never mind him, I have a far more important agenda…

I woke from a dream this morning, drenched in sweat, my mind racing faster than Dave's driving, my senses overwhelmed. Chloe was in my dream again, and not only in it, but she told me very specifically she would meet me in the hotel bar this evening.

I showered away the sweat, tried to make sense of the situation. It was a dream, not reality. How could we have organised a liaison from the dream world? But something very real niggles at me. I need to be in the bar this evening, no matter what.

If nothing comes of it, no matter, I will tell no one. I definitely can't tell Dave what happened. He'd drop me off at the nearest loony bin. Will Chloe be in the bar? How could that be possible?

"Just get us there in one piece, please. You dirty bastard."

"Not a problem." He sniggers.

I check my watch. "Shall we dial into Ron's meeting, or pretend we had no signal?"

Dave sighs. "Better dial-in, otherwise we'll only have to hear his mouth later."

"Right." I grab Dave's phone and tap the screen. We are connected to a conference call on the car speakerphone. Ron, also driving, conducts his meeting via his speakers. This should be good.

"Morning, Ron. Andy and Dave here, on the way down."

"Morning lads. Glad to hear it. I'll see you in the bar later."

Ron starts his monotone drag through the same boring old information. He must have it off by heart now, I certainly hope he isn't reading off his laptop screen whilst driving.

I put the microphone on mute and settle into my thoughts. I'm nervous, truth be told. Even the tiniest chance that somehow Chloe is real, and we are unconsciously connected via shared hypnogogic hallucinations, and that we made a date to meet in real life, tonight, in a hotel bar, is enough to set my heart racing.

My gut is full of butterflies. I could barely sup down a coffee this morning, let alone eat.

What if she is there? Will she know me? Will she be the same as I know her from my dreams?

Ron also wants to meet us in the bar. Last thing I want is to drink with Ron and work people when I have a date with my literal dream-woman. I'll have to figure that out when we get there.

———

We arrive early, and just about in one piece. How Dave isn't banned from driving for the rest of his life is beyond me. I reckon we hit well over a tonne on the motorway at one point. He has an app that shows him the speed camera locations. He only slowed down for those. I get out of the car, shaking. Dave chuckles and pops open the boot.

"See, we're here safe and sound."

"Dunno about that. I think my soul left my body somewhere around Milton Keynes when that truck pulled out in front of us."

"Never pull out, Andy." He laughs. "Sounds like a song, that." He hums a tune. "I left my soul in Milton Keynes." He belts out the words, as if from a ballad, overly dramatic.

"Brilliant. You should be on the telly." I snigger. "That way I could turn you off."

"Come on. Let's get this show on the road."

Too early to check into our rooms, they direct us to wait in the lobby or bar until the chambermaids are finished. Ron is probably still miles away. Naturally, we move to the bar for a quickie before the rest of them arrive.

The Lodestone Bar. I look up at the sign on the door, then push it open. There are a few people dotted around, but it isn't busy. The plush carpet is soft, the room is quiet and cosy. We grab a table near the back and drop our bags down.

"Pint?" Dave moves over to the bar.

"Should we? It's a bit early yet."

Dave checks his watch. "Lunchtime. Perfectly acceptable."

I shrug. "Fair enough. I don't take much convincing."

I sit down, but I make sure I face the door of the bar. I want to be able to see everyone who comes in. Now I'm here, the butterflies in my stomach flutter around like crazy. A pint should douse them down a bit.

"When are you meeting Bethany?" Dave drops two pints on the table.

"I said I'd call over to her pub around seven or eight."

"Right." I rub my chin.

"You trying to get rid of me?" Dave chuckles.

"No, mate." I shrug and shake my head. "Just curious."

"Hello, hello, what's going on here?" Dave grins as wide as a bus. "You got a date lined up? Did you text that Gemma?"

"Gemma? No." I scoff. "I doubt she'd ever talk to me again. Nah, I just thought I'd get an early night. Relax, you know. I'm wrecked."

"Hmm." Dave squints at me over his pint. "Fair enough."

I pull my work laptop out of my bag. "May as well take advantage of the peace and get some emails done."

"Boring fart." Dave chides but also reaches for his laptop.

Anytime the door of the bar pops open, my heart skips a beat. I can feel anxiety flowing in my veins. Anticipation and nervousness. This is mad. I need to get a grip on reality. Chloe won't be in this bar. How could she be? It was a dream. I may have finally lost the plot. Maybe I should be carted off to a nut-house.

I'm here regardless, so can't hurt to pay attention.

Ron, Sandra and John roll in through the door, loud and obnoxious. Ron sees us and waves. I turn to Dave and raise an eyebrow. He rolls his eyes in return but stands up to greet the newcomers.

"You got here early, gents." Ron sticks out a hand for anyone to shake.

"Yeah, I drove this time." Dave points to his chest. "I don't dawdle around like this lad." He points to me.

"I drive at the speed limit, Dave. Exactly at the speed limit."

"That's what I said."

I sigh. But stand up and shake hands with the group.

Ron goes to the bar. "Drinks?"

Dave goes up with him. "Thought you'd never ask."

"This is a nice place." Sandra looks around the bar.

"Yeah, it's not bad." I smile. "The executive rooms are nice. The ground floor is pretty bland though."

"Have you been here before?"

"Yeah, couple of times." I nod. If you count the times I've been here in my dreams, it's many. Why would my brain focus on this place? It's fine, I guess, but there's nothing special about it. A normal boring business hotel in the home counties. No one should get excited about coming here… Unless they have a dream-date waiting for them, of course.

Ron drops a pint in front of me, then flops down in the seat opposite. He's blocking my view of the door now. Shit. I shuffle over, but Sandra is right next to me. I didn't expect to be hemmed in.

"The Priory of St Augustine Hotel." Sandra picks up a beer mat from the table. "Funny name for a hotel?"

"Used to be an Abbey, many years back."

Oh, no. I can sense Ron gearing up for a lengthy soliloquy about boring history. He's never more than a pint away from some monologue. I sigh internally.

"The Augustinian order known as the Friars of the Sack." He chuckles. "It was commissioned by Edmund, the second Earl of Cornwall back in 1283 who was ruling at the time in the castle down the road." Ron looks around the bar, then points towards the doorway. "A Norman castle that had strategic importance, being this close to London."

I'm trapped in a bench seat. Sandra on one side, Dave on the other, Ron in his element. A captive audience. I feel like I'm back at school. I hated history. I look around at Dave, who is enjoying watching me suffer. Bastard.

"There are still a few walls standing in the castle grounds. Fascinating history. Worth a look if you have some time."

Sandra nods, lapping it up.

"Edmund gave the monks, the Fratres Saccati, a phial of the Sacred Blood of Jesus Christ that he had acquired on his travels in Germany. A prized possession. This was an important site." Ron's eyes widen.

"A phial of Jesus's blood?" Sandra enquires. I mentally will her to shut up, Ron thrives on questions. Say nothing.

"That's what they say."

"Blimey!"

"He had plans for this site. Some say powerful, magical plans."

"Oh. That's fun, isn't it? We're staying in a place of history." Sandra chuckles.

Ron has a twinkle in his eye. He'll never stop talking now. I can feel my eyelids closing.

A receptionist lady appears behind him out of nowhere. "Sorry to interrupt, folks, but your rooms are available to check into now."

Saved. Thank feck for that.

Coincidence, but I'm in the same room as last time. The huge Jacuzzi-bath looming, reminding me of what happened before. I shudder. I don't need to dredge up those memories again.

Kirsty and her bloody threesome now dissolved. She'll probably be back at her parents' place by now. I wonder if they've argued yet?

Part of me feels sorry for her. She's right, she made a big mistake. We had a decent life before she made a mess of it all. Too late now. I'm not going back down that road. Kirsty is history, and as previously noted, I hate history.

. . .

I set up my laptop on the desk and unpack some clothes and bathroom stuff. We're here for four nights this time. May as well make myself at home.

A free day to get settled, then customer full-on every day after. I'm dreading it, but at least this is the last time. Ron is of course ecstatic. He stands to make a fortune from this deal. I'll get nothing. He's said nothing more about our potential promotions. I should bring it up again once he's had a few beers.

We've got an hour to get ourselves freshened up, then we're meeting again in the bar for more drinks. I don't want this to turn into a session, not with work folks.

Besides, I have other plans. Don't I?

I lie down on the sumptuous bed. Staring up at the ceiling. What am I doing with my life?

The rhythm of train wheels on tracks clack beneath me. I stare out of the window at the passing countryside. Miles of green fields, dotted with sheep, trees, picturesque villages that butt against the railway. Dirty industrial buildings, a quarry that empties stones from one vehicle to another. The miles tick away effortlessly, and I only need to watch.

I look around the carriage, empty but for me. My bag is on a shelf above me. I always worry it will fall out and whack me on the head. But it seems solid.

A door opens at the far end. I hear the automatic pneumatics sigh in and out. Someone walks along the narrow corridor. A breeze from the door delivers the scent before I can see her, but I know it's her. Honeysuckle on the air. I stand up.

"Oh, hello." She smiles.

"Chloe!"

"That's me." She giggles and I grab her in an embrace. She holds me tightly, then pecks me on the lips.

We sit. She is opposite me, facing forward.

"Where is the train going?" I look around for a display.

"London, Euston."

"Right. And where are you going?"

She smiles. "Not there." She looks me in the eye. "I told you, I'll meet you in the bar later."

"Yes, you did. I'm just… I don't know what to think."

She leans forward, takes my hand. "Don't worry, Andy."

"Right."

"Nearly there. Look." She nods towards the window. The landscape changes and we pass through a station. 'Milton Keynes' flashes by, but we don't stop.

She points. "That's the Grand Union Canal." I look as we pass by the waterway. A brightly painted barge skids along the water like an insect.

I look back at her. She watches through the window, reflected. Both images of her as pretty as a sunrise. She's elegant, made up, hair tied back. Her dark eyes focused into the distance.

"Travel is tiring, isn't it?" She yawns.

"Very."

An alarm rings, loud and violent. It startles me and I stand up. The train around me fades into blackness, Chloe zooms out of focus, I try to grab her hand, but it disappears.

"See you later!" She's gone.

I grab my phone from the nightstand, sliding to answer.

"You okay there, Andy?" Ron's voice, tinny in my ear.

"Yeah. What's up?" I rub my eyes and sit up. I must have fallen asleep.

"There's a pint on the table for you, mate. We've started without you." I can hear the background noise of the bar.

"Oh, right. Sorry, must have dozed off. Be down in a minute."

He chuckles. I disconnect and get up, stumbling into the bathroom. I was dreaming again. Chloe on a train. Coming here?

The team is assembled around the same table we had earlier. Ron is midst a rant about the cost of keeping his Mercedes maintained as I get to the table. He's showing John a photo of the dealer invoice on his phone. "Bloody daylight robbery."

I have little sympathy for his vehicle woes. He'll be able to afford a brand-new Merc when this deal goes through. I roll my eyes and plop down on a seat next to Dave. He nods a hello and points to a pint glass on the table.

"Get stuck in, mate."

"Cheers."

"You okay?"

"Yeah, fine. Just nodded off. Didn't sleep well last night. The beds here are too comfy." I chuckle to lighten the mood.

"Where are we going for dinner tonight?" Sandra pipes up, nursing a glass of what looks like Sherry.

"There's a great Italian place near here. Real authentic stuff."

Ron rubs his hands together. "We'll have these and head off if you are hungry?"

"Starving, now I think about it. I missed lunch." Sandra grins. "Italian sounds lovely."

A horrible thought rings in my head. I'm not leaving this bar now. I need to stay here and wait for… Chloe? I look around, but they are all nodding agreement on heading off soon for the Italian restaurant.

"Dave, could I have a quick word?" I motion over towards the bar.

He looks up. "Yeah, sure."

We get up, and I walk around the other side of the bar. Ron is busy yapping on about the time he got lost in Milan, the others are enthralled. They don't notice us leaving the group.

"What's up?" Dave looks concerned.

"Err, well, this is going to seem weird, but hear me out." Dave tilts his head. "I can't leave this bar this evening. I'm not going to come to the Italian."

"Why not?"

I rub my chin. "Because… I'm meeting someone here. I think I am, anyway."

Dave's face lights up in a grin. "I fucking knew it. You sneaky little twat!" He laughs. "Who is she?" He slaps me on the arm.

"Well, that's the weird part." I look him dead in the eyes. "Chloe."

His face changes. He looks at me incredulously. "Chloe… Your dream woman?"

"Yeah."

"Andy, mate. She in't real, how can you be meeting her here?"

"I have no bloody clue, but I have to wait here, in case it is real."

He looks at me, speechless.

"I've had two dreams where she told me she'd meet me here, tonight. Two. Ron just woke me up from one. She was on a train, said she was coming here."

"Dreams, Andy. These are dreams."

"I'm well aware. But I have to see it through."

Dave sighs. "Well, whatever you think, mate. How you going to get out of this meal then? Ron is big into team bullshit. I'm not looking forward to it myself."

I smile. "That's why my plan is awesome. We both get out of a boring dinner with Ron yapping on about who knows what until the small hours."

"Plan? You have a plan?" He chuckles.

"I do."

I tell Dave what I've come up with, and he nods, smiles, and then grins as wide as the bar.

"Smooth, Andy. Smooth."

We walk back to the table and sit down. I sup down my pint.

Ron is still jabbering to his audience. Seems the conversation has shifted to patio furniture and a special offer that Sandra got on her paving slabs. Thrilling stuff.

"Shall we have another quickie or head off for dinner?" Ron holds up his empty glass. He's getting quite lubricated now, his eyes have that far-away look that a few beers always bring.

"I vote for dinner." Sandra gets up.

"Seconded." John puts down his empty glass.

"Fair enough." Ron looks at Dave and me. "Lads?"

"Yeah, dinner sounds great, Ron." Dave flashes a smile. I nod.

I scratch my chin and look at Dave. He barely twitches an eyebrow in acknowledgement. He stands up and pulls his phone out of his pocket. Opening up the email app.

"Oh, shit!" He feigns shock.

"What's up?" Ron looks nervous.

"Err, bit of a problem, Ron. The Eternitive server has gone down!"

Ron stands up, suddenly animated and sober. "What!"

"It's probably just a glitch." Dave turns to me. "Andy, take a look at this." He hands me his phone.

"Oh, hell. Yeah, I know what that is."

Ron seems to relax a little. "Can you sort it?"

"Yeah, sure. We'll just need to remote in, check some logs and then boot it all up again." I shrug. "We should have it back in about two, three hours."

"Oh, right."

"I've got my laptop set up in my room. Dave, we can get it done now if you like. Save us hassle in the morning."

"Yeah, good plan."

"What about dinner?" Ron seems concerned.

I wave a hand. "You guys go, enjoy it. We'll order some room-service while we work. No problem."

"If you're certain?"

"Yep, I'll feel better knowing this is sorted before the meetings tomorrow." I smile. "Don't worry, I'll send you a text once it's all fixed."

"You lads are stars, seriously. Thanks. I won't forget the dedication you've given this deal."

"Don't worry, Ron. It's in expert hands." Dave winks. "Go have a nice meal. Bring us back a breadstick."

Ron chuckles. "Thanks, lads."

They shuffle off towards the door. As they go, I turn to Dave, a big grin on both of our mugs.

Without a word, I hold up a hand for a high-five. Dave doesn't leave me hanging.

Chapter Thirty-Five

I switched to pints of water. I don't want to be wasted in case… Well, in case my dream-woman should show up in this bar, even if the chances of that happening are somewhere between slim and not-a-fecking-hope.

Dave left me to go meet his barmaid. He tried to drag me along and told me to come to the pub later in case I got 'stood up.' I told him I'd be fine. If no one shows, I will get that early night I intended, maybe with a dip in the tub first to soak away the stress.

I'm even more nervous now. I keep checking the time. Minutes take hours. Seconds draw out. Each one an epic struggle to complete. I moved to a barstool. Scrolling through rubbish online to distract myself.

The trouble with drinking pints of water is I'm constantly up and down to the toilets. At least they are clean, here. The 'Lodestone Washroom' is bright and pristine. I check my reflection again for the millionth time. Splashing my face with water. Smoothing down my hair. I should have shaved this morning. I'll have to do as is.

The guy in the mirror shakes his head at me. "What the hell are you playing at, mate?" He says. "I honestly do not know."

Sober and getting hungry. I wouldn't mind an Italian meal now, but I'm still not sure if my guts can cope with any input.

I'm in a bit of a state, truth be told.

Back at the bar, I order a bag of crisps to tide me over until I give up my lingering and go back to my room. Another water, too, but sparkling this time. For the variety.

Seven-thirty comes around. I wait.

Eight o'clock, and I'm on first-name terms with Stuart behind the bar. He brought me a sandwich, even though the bar doesn't officially serve food. Hotels can't make a simple sandwich; they have to garnish it with orange peel and delicately sliced tomatoes. A small pile of pickled gherkin slices on the corner of a vast, square plate. I didn't need all that fuss.

I did, however, get another beer with it. I figured that counted as a meal. I told Stuart I'm waiting for a colleague who got stuck in traffic.

I've set an alarm on my phone to ring at nine. At that point, I will send Ron a text message to tell him I have fixed the mythical server problem I invented, then pack it all in and go run a huge bath. I feel better now I have a deadline.

Toilet break number seventy-three. I'm getting quite acquainted with the row of porcelain. I think I favour stall three. No particular reason, but now I've stared down into the water that much, I feel we have a connection.

I go back to my perch at the bar. "One more beer, cheers, Stu." He nods and goes to the tap. This is it. I'm insane, losing it. One can of beans short of a boy-scout camping trip. Of course I didn't have a date tonight. I dreamt it all up. I take a deep gulp of the beer that's placed in front of me.

Head in hands, I look down at my phone screen. 8:55pm. I switch off the alarm. There's no point in waiting five more minutes. I down the rest of my drink and stand up, waving goodbye to Stuart. I sigh, but now I guess I can safely say, Chloe isn't real. This was all hallucinations.

I pause. There's a whiff of something familiar. I look around me, my heart suddenly thumping in my chest. Honeysuckle. I take a deep sniff of the air. Definitely honeysuckle. I walk across the bar to where it seems to come from. Someone is sitting at a table near the back. A woman. She faces away from me. She checks her watch and stands up, smoothing down her skirt. I walk over to her, sniffing the air. The perfume must come from her; no one else around.

As I approach, every footstep is like a thunderclap ringing in my head. My heart in my throat now, pounding, throbbing, my body is on autopilot. I can feel every breath filling my lungs.

I stop as she picks up her bag and turns around. Her dark eyes meet mine and we both freeze for an eternity. My body floods with an electrical jolt of pure adrenaline, my breath petrified in place.

. . .

"Chloe?" My voice barely a whisper.

"Andy!"

Her cheeks flush red, her knees buckle, and she flops back down into her seat.

"I… Err. Chloe? You are REAL?"

"I was going to say the same thing!"

"But, how, who, what?"

"Yeah, I was also going to say that."

I motion to the seat opposite her. "May I?"

"Oh, yes. Please do."

I flop down. "Sorry, just to be clear, you are Chloe, the woman who I've been dreaming about for months?"

"Well, yes. And, equally, you must be Andy, the man who I've been dreaming about for…" She counts on her fingers. "Months, yes."

"I suppose that would be me, indeed."

"Have we met before?"

I pause and look at her properly, for the first time. I know her face intimately, but not from the waking world. "No, I don't reckon."

"Then, how…?" She trails off.

"I don't know."

"I was just about to leave, I thought this was ridiculous to begin with, that of course, you wouldn't be here in the bar, that I was just convincing myself of crazy things. My friend told me I was being utterly insane, and she was moments away from dragging me to the nearest asylum and locking me up…" She laughs, sweetly, exactly how I remember her.

"Err, yeah. My mate, Dave, thinks I'm bat shit crazy. Oh, man, wait till I tell him."

Chloe reaches over and grabs my hand. "Andy, this is

definitely bat shit crazy. But, WOW. You are really real!" She smiles and there's a moistness in her eyes. My heart pounds in my chest again. I squeeze her hand. I want to tell her I love her, but... I met her less than five minutes ago.

"I was about to leave as well, for the same reasons. How long were you waiting here?"

"About an hour and a half."

"Really? Good grief. I've been sat at the bar all day."

"Oh, no. Sorry. I walked around when I came in, but I didn't see you."

"Nerves and pints. I've been in and out of the loo all evening. Must have missed you come in."

"Imagine if we had both left..."

"No, I don't want to think about that. Chloe... I... Sorry, I'm just sort of overwhelmed. Can I get you a drink?"

She nods. "Please."

I pause. "Jack Daniels and Coke?"

"Yeah. How did you... Oh." She laughs. "Well, this is going to take some getting used to."

I stand up to go to the bar. But I pause. "Do me a favour, pinch me, hard." I hold out my arm. "What if this is still a dream?" She does as I ask. "Ow! Okay, probably not dreaming." She laughs.

At the bar, I look back over at Chloe. She's pulled her phone out of her bag and is frantically typing a message. I should send Dave a text, but instead, I remember I have to tell Ron my lie. I tap out the message and hit send. He replies immediately. 'You're a star, mate. Much appreciated.'

· · ·

I place down Chloe's drink in front of her and sit down. I decided to go for whisky. I think my nerves need it.

"Sorry, Andy, but my friend Chrystal wants a photo of you." She giggles, waving her phone.

"Oh, yes. Right. Shall I come over there?"

She nods. I sit down next to Chloe, and she puts her arm around me, holding her phone up and snapping a selfie of us. She chuckles and sends it to her friend.

"Sorry. She didn't believe me."

"I guess that's to be expected, given our situation."

"Indeed." She takes a sip of her drink. "Well. I don't know what to say now. This is by far the strangest date I've ever been on."

"Yeah? I meet my dream women every week in bars all over the country." I chuckle. "Kidding. I know what you mean, this is VERY strange. But… Amazing."

Chloe's phone buzzes on the table. She swipes it open and guffaws, holding a hand in front of her mouth. She shows me the phone. It's an entire screen full of emoji, the same one over and over. 'Surprised face'.

"Well, yeah. I think that's the same reaction I had."

She pauses. "Andy… What's your second name?"

"Clarke. Andrew Clarke. But everyone calls me Andy, apart from that Thomas chap."

"Oh, yeah. Thomas. What the hell is his problem?"

"Not a clue. But I'm glad he's not joining in our date." I chuckle. "And you are… Chloe Jessop?"

"Yes! How did you know that? I never use my real name online or anywhere…"

"I think I found your notebook in the back of a plane seat. In a dream, mind you."

"My notebook?"

"Dream journal, flowers on the cover."

She rummages in her bag and pulls out the exact notebook as I remember, patterned with hand-drawn honeysuckle flowers.

"Yes. That's it."

"Oh, my god." Her jaw hangs open.

"Weird, huh?"

"I just got back from California. I was writing in this on the plane." She holds up the journal. "We were there recording for almost three weeks."

"Oh, nice. Wait... California? Like, eight hours behind?" She nods. "Well, that explains it."

"What?"

"Why I didn't see you for ages. We were asleep at different times."

Her eyes widen. "Good thinking, Batman."

"I thought you were... A figment of my imagination. A hypnogogic hallucination." I nod down at her notebook.

"You read my dream journal?"

"Yes, sorry." A pang of guilt hits me. "But, they were also my dreams."

"I suppose." She blushes a little.

I change the subject. "You said you were recording?"

"Yeah, I'm a producer. Music. I've been babysitting a band to stardom." She chuckles. "Well, that's what they think."

"Brilliant. Do you play?"

"I do. Don't you remember?"

I smile and nod. I do remember the concert she put on for me. "You are incredible."

She blushes. "I do the occasional cover set. Never done a gig like that before, though."

"I'd love to see you play in real life someday."

"I'd like that." She smiles. "Well, Mr Clarke, what do you do, then?"

"I'm a technical hardware advisor. We have a massive customer deal going on here. That's why I'm up and down to this place. Ron, the big boss man on this project, is hyped up about it. Biggest deal ever, or something." I laugh. "Boring stuff."

"Sounds cool. You are a computer chap?"

"Big nerd, yeah." She laughs.

"That's good to know. Lot of tech involved in music, these days."

"I'd be happy to help you with anything." I pause. "Chloe, I err, I feel like we have a connection. I don't want to seem forward, but can I get your number? You know, so we can communicate outside of the dream world."

She chuckles. "Of course. I'll send you the selfie." She starts a message and hands me the phone. "Type in your number."

My phone buzzes. I save the contact and photo. 'Chloe Jessop' It feels utterly mad. But there it is. Real living proof.

"Thanks."

My phone buzzes again. Ron this time. 'We're headed back to the hotel bar if you are still around? Drinks on me.'

"Oh, shit."

"What's up?"

"Ron and the work lot. Coming back here. I don't want to see them now." I look into her eyes again. She smiles. "Would you like to come up to my room?"

Her eyes widen, and she picks up her drink. "I thought you'd never ask."

Chapter Thirty-Six

We watched the sunrise permeate the night sky over the canal and distant forest from the bed. A memory from a dream flickered back to me. Something Thomas said: 'The beauty of creation never ceases to amaze, no matter if you witness it a hundred or a hundred thousand times. Don't you think?'

He's right. The vista is peaceful and calm, even this close to the bustle of London.

Then I turned back to gaze at Chloe. Another beautiful vista. My dream-woman, literally, right here in bed with me. No need to sleep when your dreams are a reality.

Actually, I'm going to pay for the lack of sleep today, no doubt. Ron will be bursting with energy when we go to the customer site. I can feel it already, I'll be struggling to stay awake. Worth it, though.

Chloe, as wild and raw as in my dreams, lies still, her eyes closed, her breast slowly rising and falling. Bathed in soft light and a sheen of sweat. Tangled in the white hotel sheets. She's wonderful.

We talked for hours, filling in each other's blanks. She lives around an hours' drive from me, in a quiet area outside the town, next to a forest. I knew that part. I saw her house once when we took to the air in our dreams. She showed me the location on Google Maps satellite view. It was uncannily like my memories. She owns the property outright, with no mortgage. Paid for when one of her bands went super-popular for a brief period a few years ago. Lucky.

She has a white cat called Buddy, who showed up outside her home one day as a tiny kitten, covered in Goosegrass buds. Her best friend, Chrystal, takes care of him when she's travelling.

We moved to the hot-tub. Well, it was right there, why not? She told me about her life, her family, her travels working with various bands. She's an interesting and talented woman. A year younger than me, but much more mature. Interestingly, we have the same birthday.

Then we strayed to relationships. She has never married, but she broke up with someone a few months ago, she didn't go into details. I didn't probe. I told her about Kirsty leaving, and how my life has been turned upside down since then. I didn't mention that it was her, from my dreams, who started that process.

We lay together in the bath, lights dimmed, quietly watching the water swirl around, and we remembered a dream we'd had together, in a strange cave next to a beach, a pond cut into the rocks, a complicated mesh of copper pipes heating the water from a fire. Chloe told me she visited a cave on a beach like that once as a child, somewhere in Wales, she thought. But there was no heated pool inside. Weird how the mind works.

What remains a mystery is how we come to have this apparently telepathic link, that only seems to function while we're both asleep.

I check the time on my phone on the nightstand. Seven-fifteen. We have a little time yet. I'm extremely glad that Dave convinced Ron that we don't need a breakfast meeting today.

I lie back down next to Chloe, nuzzling close. Running my hand along her skin. She mumbles something, quietly, then grabs my hand, squeezing.

I could stay like this forever. Her honeysuckle scent now imprinted on my memory. I never want to let her go.

There was something deep and meaningful between us when we made love. This was no throwaway one-night-stand. We were connected, physically and something more and intense. I knew what she was feeling on an emotional level. I've never experienced anything like it. I must have burned out a month's supply of endorphins.

My wake-up alarm rings. The motion to reach and silence the phone takes almost more energy than I can muster. Ugh. Shower.

I reluctantly leave Chloe, quietly shuffling out of bed and into the bathroom. She seems to be asleep. Lucky her.

I flick on the light and the harsh reflection in the mirror shows a man who desperately needs to sleep the day away. He won't be allowed. Work and meetings, customers and technical details await. The only way Ron would let me off this is if I was actually dead.

I twist on the shower and wait for life to flow into my veins.

I can't face breakfast, but I absolutely need a bucket of coffee. I slip into clothes, grabbing my laptop, wallet and phone into my bag, then tiptoe over to Chloe, still slumbering with a wall of pillows and sheets all around her, the morning light softly warming her skin. She's like a renaissance painting of Aphrodite.

I stroke her arm. "Chloe, I have to go to work now. You can stay here if you want?"

She makes a soft moaning sound, then reaches for my hand, pulling me down and kissing.

"You aren't making it easy."

A smile appears on her lips. "Go, Andy. Go do your work."

"I really, really don't want to… But, you know."

She opens one eye a little. "It's okay." She reaches for a bottle of water on the nightstand. "Thanks for letting me stay. I don't have to work until later." She sits up a little and smiles. "Musicians don't do mornings."

"I'm jealous." I chuckle.

"Late nights, instead."

"Ah, true… Oh, I forgot to ask, how long are you staying here?"

"All week. Maybe longer if things don't go well recording. You?"

"'Till Friday."

"Good. See you later, then?"

"Yes. Definitely. I mean, sure." I try to act casual. Not smooth, Andy.

She chuckles. "That was… Amazing, last night. I'm… I don't even know what I am, but I'm definitely something."

"It was rather wonderful, I must say."

She lingers her gaze at me for a moment, an endless and silent exchange. But I know what she's thinking. I feel it. "No, we have to work. See you later." She pulls me in for another long kiss, and then closes her eyes again, nestling into the pillows. I chuckle, looking back and wondering what god or devil I must have pleased that he made my dreams come true?

I can hear Ron jabbering on even before I get to the breakfast-room door. As predicted, he's gushing with enthusiasm. Hyped up.

My phone buzzes in my pocket. A text from Chloe. 'Miss you already.'

My heart jumps in my chest. I reply. 'Same… I could say I'm not feeling good. Take a day off sick?'

'LOL, no, it's okay. I have to get up soon, anyway. See you this evening. xxx'

I sneak around the edge of the breakfast room, grabbing a mug of coffee from the waitress before I go anywhere near the work team table. I take a sip and the hot nectar revives me a little. But I'll need a gallon before I'm anywhere near properly awake.

I take a deep breath and head over to the war-zone.

"Here he is. The man of the moment." Ron stands up and slaps me on the back.

"Err, morning, all."

"We were just about to send a search party for you." Ron

chuckles. "Just wanted to say thanks, again for sorting that problem last night. Dave says everything is running like Swiss clockwork this morning."

"Oh, yeah." I had completely forgotten about the ruse we came up with. "No worries, Ron."

I look over at Dave, who flashes me a grin and a nod. I imagine he's interested in what happened to me last night. He'll have to wait. I raise an eyebrow in return.

"Take a seat, mate. Do you want some food before we head off?"

"Nah, thanks, Ron. Coffee will do me this morning. Feeling a little nervy, to be honest." I tap my tummy.

"We'll slay them, Andy. Don't you worry." Ron gives me a wink. "All your hard work will pay off. You'll see."

I sit down next to Sandra who is tapping on her phone. Dave, opposite, gives me a look. I grin. It'll be fun to make him squirm for a while.

We take two cars to the customer's office. Ron in his Merc with John and Sandra, and I unenthusiastically get back in Dave's death-mobile.

He drives out of the hotel car-park but then turns to me.

"Well?"

"Well, what?"

"What happened to you last night, you sneaky sod?" Dave grins, knowingly. "You haven't slept, have you?"

I glance at him, showered, shaved and gelled, but he's got a tiredness about him. "Well, neither have you."

"Aye, but that's a given, in't it?"

"I suppose."

"Spill the beans, then, mate."

I smile. I don't even know where to start. "We don't have time to get into it now. We're nearly at the office."

"Andy, you little prick, did you meet a woman last night or not?"

"I did." I can't stop the grin erupting on my face.

Dave turns to me, incredulous, as we pull into the car-park. Almost slamming into Ron's Merc.

"Take it easy!"

"Shit!"

Dave cautiously parks and then turns back to me. "Well?"

"I think it'd be easier if we just meet in the bar later."

Dave shakes his head. "Fuck's sake, Andy. I'm putting your rent up."

"I'll tell you later. Trust me, it's going to take some explaining, and we don't have time now."

"Hmm. Fine." He humphs.

We get out of the car and merge at the doorway with Ron and the team. I've never seen Ron so energetic. He must have smoked a kilogram of speed.

"Let's do this!"

I roll my eyes and follow him in.

Despite Ron's gushing over-enthusiasm, I'm wishing I had a bit of what he's on right now. Staying awake is a chore in itself. Paying attention to the meetings is killing me. Thankfully, they have a pot of coffee on the table, and I'm throwing down the paper-cups like a man possessed.

Sandra is midst a monologue about finances and warranty

services. I'm losing the will to live.

I excuse myself to the toilet, no one will miss me for a minute. The technical stuff comes later.

I lock myself into a cubicle and pull my phone out of my pocket. I felt a buzz a moment ago, but Ron would kill me if I was texting during his customer meeting. A message from Chloe: 'What if we're soul mates?'

My guts flutter as I read the message. Soul mates? Is that a real thing? Are souls even real things?

I reply: 'I'm not sure what that means, exactly?'

'Me either. LOL. Hope you are having a good day at work?'

'To be honest, I'm about to pass out from a mixture of boredom and tiredness.'

'Sorry. Did I wear you out? :)'

'Yes, but it was worth every second.'

A thought occurs to me. 'Hey, when did you start having the dreams?'

'Oh, yeah, I was going to ask you the same. For me, I think it was about two or three months ago.'

'Yeah, same. Interesting…'

What happened to both of us about three months ago?

'I better get back to the meeting, but my mate Dave is itching to know what happened to me last night. I haven't told him yet. I'm enjoying torturing him.'

'Oh, you are evil. I didn't know that about you. Lol. Have a good day, Andy. I'm off to the studio now. xxx,'

Speaking of evil, I know someone else who will be intrigued by the turn of events. I send my sister the selfie that Chloe took of us last night in the bar. Captioned: Me and Chloe…

As I look at the photo again, I still can't believe what has happened. Chloe from my dreams, beautiful, amazing, talented and funny, is now in my real life. I'm not sure if this has sunk in yet.

I chuckle as I put the phone on silent and back into my pocket. I'll let that nugget of information simmer with Riss for a few hours.

We break for lunch, but rather than go to the canteen, or out somewhere for food, they have organised a working lunch in the conference room. I'm itching to escape and check my phone, but the tech guy from Eternitive has cornered me and Dave to discuss his concerns about the implementation. A bit late now, mate. This is all being rolled out next week. We aren't going to change anything at this stage. He's sated by the spiel Dave gives him, and I back it up with nods and the hardcore details I know about. Mostly, we do this by guesswork and hope. It's served us well so far.

You think people in industry must know what they are doing and have a plan, but we're living proof that's not the case. We all fumble and grope around in the dark, hoping that we find the light switch in a coal mine full of bear traps. It makes me paranoid about the world. I've seen backstage.

The afternoon drags on endlessly. I've watched the sun arc across the sky outside the window all day, dropping into the horizon, I'm yearning to leave this place, if only for some fresh air. I'm ready to drop, and we're expected to meet again in the bar this evening, no doubt dragged along for dinner. I can't face it, but as I skipped on the meal last night, I'll never get away with going AWOL again. Finally, Ron slaps his hands together and stands up. Our cue that the torture is ending, at least for today. I vaguely gathered that tomorrow we'll be given a tour of their manufacturing lines. Thrilling stuff. Can't wait.

"Pint?" Dave tips his head towards the bar as we get back to the hotel. He was quiet on the ride back. I reckon he's as tired as me. But curiosity knows no sleep.

"I was gonna lie down for a bit, but fair enough. A quick one."

We escaped before Ron. He got caught on the way out of the building by a group of customer high-ups. Don't turn back. Keep moving. We made it out into the daylight, safe.

I push open that now-familiar door into the Lodestone Bar and head towards the stools. Stuart nods me a greeting. Dave flops down next to me.

"Two pints, please, Stu."

"No worries. Oh, your friend came in a moment ago. She's at the back." He points to the back of the bar where I sat last night with Chloe.

"Oh, cheers."

I turn around and see her sitting at the same table. I look around at Dave. "Follow me."

Chloe jumps up as I tap her on the shoulder. She's typing something into her phone. "Andy! I was just texting you."

"Hiya." I smile, then turn to Dave. "Dave, this is Chloe."

He looks at me, raising his eyebrows. I nod. He turns and stares at her, his mouth dropping open. For a long time, he doesn't move.

"You all right, mate?" I chuckle.

He shakes his head. "Sorry, err. Hi, Chloe. A pleasure to meet you." He sticks out a hand and flashes me a quizzical look. "I've heard a lot about you…" He trails off. Chloe stands up and shakes his hand with a grin.

"All good, I hope." She chuckles.

Dave nods. "Yeah, but… Hang on here a minute." He scratches his head. "How, what, who, where?"

"We don't know either, mate." I laugh and go to grab our pints.

Chloe smiles as I sit down next to her. "I just got here. We had to end the session early today due to 'artistic differences'" She rolls her eyes and chuckles, making air quotes, then stifles a yawn. "I wasn't going to argue, though. I'm wrecked today." She flashes me a look.

"Chloe is a music producer." I look at Dave who sat down opposite, still staring, mouth open. "She just got back from California, and now she's working with a band here." I can't help but boast about my dream-woman.

"Oh, cool. A band I might know?" He perks up.

"They haven't made it yet. Huge potential, though."

He nods. "Let me get this straight." He clears his throat. "You two met in a dream, well, many dreams, then you planned to meet here in this bar last night, which you did?"

"That's about right, yeah."

Chloe nods.

"And you've never met before, or even online or something?"

"Nope. Never." I shake my head. Chloe does the same.

"Bloody hell." Dave scratches his head. "That's incredible. Weird. You should tell a paper or something."

"God, no. I don't want my personal life all over the tabloids." Chloe makes a face.

"Yeah. No way. Can you imagine the fruit loops who'd contact us?"

"Good point, yeah." Dave concedes. "It's… Unusual, though. I mean, happy for you, both."

"Cheers, mate."

Chloe grabs my hand under the table. Squeezing gently. Her smile is enough to melt my heart.

"I was thinking, Andy. It was soon after I stayed here in this hotel a few months ago when the dreams started." She looks around the bar. "First weird one I can remember was in this bar. The Lodestone Bar. I wondered where it was at the time, but then it came back to me. This hotel…"

"Now you come to mention it, that's about when I started having the dreams." I think back to the first time we came down to meet the customer. Then when I got back home, my sleep-talking got me into trouble.

"Is it something to do with this place, then?" Chloe, wide-eyed, turns to me.

"I mean, maybe?"

"What was that Ron said yesterday? This place has some ancient history to it. Some bloke called Edmund built an Abbey here…." Dave pipes up. "And he said he had plans for this site. Powerful, magical plans."

"Magical plans?" I scoff. "What was he, the Derren Brown of the thirteenth century?"

"They did all kinds of stuff back then, didn't they? Witches and whatnot." Dave shrugs. "How else do you explain it?"

"Well, you have a point." I rub my chin. "How did Ron know all that stuff, anyway?"

"God knows. He seems to know everything…"

"Did I hear my name? Know what stuff?" Ron suddenly appears, bounding across the bar.

"Oh, hey, Ron." I stand up. Ron has a grin as wide as a bus on his mug. He notices Chloe. "Err, this is a friend of mine, Chloe Jessop."

"Charmed." He reaches down to shake hands then turns back to me. "We just got back, I thought I'd find you guys in here. Good day, wasn't it?"

"Yeah, went very well." Dave nods.

Ron is still hyped up. Where does he find the energy? "What stuff do I know?" He smiles.

I can't believe I'm going to do this, but needs must. "About the history of this hotel. You seemed to know a lot about it."

"Yeah. Fascinating place, isn't it? They built the old Abbey over seven hundred years ago." He sniffs. "There's a leaflet on the desk in the bedroom. Tells you all about it."

"Really?"

"Yeah. Edmund, the Abbey, the Fratres Saccati." He chuckles. "I always read the brochures they leave out in places like this. Get to know the world around you." He taps his nose.

"Good thinking."

The Priory of St Augustine Hotel.

Rich in history and intrigue, the castle in nearby Berkhamsted was built in 1066 to obtain control over a key route from London to the Midlands during the Norman conquest of England in the

11th century. Robert of Mortain, William the Conqueror's half-brother, was responsible for managing the castle's construction and became the castle's owner.

By 1283, Edmund, 2nd Earl of Cornwall inhabited the castle, and after travelling through Europe, he commissioned the construction of an Abbey on this site, near to the castle grounds. An Augustinian order known as the Friars of the Sack (Fratres Saccati) was established in the Abbey. Edmund donated the order a phial of the Sacred Blood of Jesus Christ that he had gained while travelling in Germany.

The Abbot of the Priory, Thomas Bonnhomme, was well known to be eccentric in his beliefs and practices. He instructed the Abbey to be built on a foundation of, exotic for the time, gems and stones. He claimed they had magical powers that would benefit the Earl.

Lodestone, a rare but naturally magnetic magnetite, once thought to be a living entity by ancient philosophers, was placed throughout the building. Each stone carefully aligned and paired with a gem of green Peridot for its protection and rejuvenation qualities. We can find such gems in Egypt, sought after by the ancient Pharaohs seeking their protective energies.

The Abbot passed away sometime in the early 1300s, taking the mystery and secret of his 'potentiam lapis' (stones of power) with him, and he was laid to rest in a small cemetery close to the Abbey.

Now, the Priory of St Augustine Hotel proudly invites you to visit the Lodestone Bar, in memory of Thomas and Edmund. Enjoy a fine wine surrounded by a wealth of history and mystery before relaxing in our five-star restaurant, The Priory Grill, where our world-class chefs will prepare you a sumptuous meal fit for Kings and Earls.

Chapter Thirty-Seven

"Remember, you asked me once if I'd ever had a moment of clarity?" I twist my head on the pillow. Chloe next to me, two inches from my face. I have to shuffle back, so I can focus on her eyes.

"I do. I think." She scrunches up her nose. "Hard to remember, sometimes."

"I think I had one."

She props herself up on one elbow. Looking down at me, wide-eyed. "Yeah?"

I nod. "There was this overwhelming feeling of, err, everything, all at once." I struggle to find words. "Warmth, safety, love, calm and peace. A flood of happiness and belonging. I was home, and I knew that nothing else mattered. I found my purpose."

"That's lovely." She smiles. "When did it happen?"

I pause, biting my lip. "When I met you."

Her cheeks flush red, her eyes become moist, but she doesn't look away. Instead, she leans down and kisses me on the forehead. Soft, with pure love. "I felt it, too."

I reach for her hand, but I can't find it, I look down and Chloe slowly melts away in front of me. Her body fades into a pale mist, I jump back, my heart thudding in my chest. She's gone.

I sit up, the room spinning around me. Adrenaline courses through my veins and a smell of burning oil chokes my throat. I get up and try to hold on to a solid object. The bed canopy melts away as I grab at it. The walls all fall to the ground and splash into silent steam. I'm left in a dark room, damp and cold. The only light comes from a single candle on a table. I approach it, but I'm suddenly doubled over with a terrible pain in my gut. I fall backwards. Shadows paint the walls with darkness. My chest is pounding in fear. The walls seem to close in, moist and cold, clammy with sweat. I'm paralysed, pushed into a corner, overwhelmed with terror that has no cause. The candle flame dances a slow waltz. I focus on the flame, and gradually the fear subsides. Function returns to my limbs. I stand and shuffle towards the candle again.

"You'd be wise not to go that way." A voice from nowhere, I look around. "At least, wait a moment."

I turn all the way around, even looking up, but it isn't until I turn once more that I see him. Thomas, lurking in a doorway that wasn't there a moment ago. He flicks a switch on the wall. "There, should be better now." He flicks another switch, and it bathes the room in light from a single bulb, hanging naked from the middle of the ceiling. The doorway leads to steps going up. The floor is rough. There's a dankness that only comes from being underground. We're in a cellar.

"What's going on?"

"Just a precaution. No need for concern."

"What are you doing here? Where's Chloe?"

He shakes his head. "The latter, I can't answer. The former, well, I already told you." He tuts. "The modern predilection for ignoring the obvious will never cease to amaze me."

I stare open-mouthed. "What?"

"I live here, Andrew. Do pay attention." He furrows his brows. "And so do you, now."

"Can I ask a question?"

He nods.

"Do you ever make any sense?"

He cackles a dry, heaving, dusty roar. "This place isn't good for logic." He steeples his fingers to his lips, then points directly at me. "Find me in the waking world. It will be easier for you." He waves a hand. "You are close. Open your eyes, Andrew. Look with your eyes."

He snaps his fingers and where he stood, a plume of black smoke hangs in the air, fading quickly to nothing. A thud surges through my body and the room blinks out of existence.

"Chloe!" I jolt awake with panic throbbing through me. She's not here. "Chloe!"

"You called?" She appears from out of the bathroom, carrying the kettle. "Fancy a cuppa?"

"Oh, my god. I had a nightmare." I sit up and rub my eyes. "What time is it?"

Chloe puts the kettle on the little stand and flicks it on. "Are you okay? It's about seven, I think. I fell asleep. Just woke up."

"Err, yeah. Shit. Ron will want to go for dinner."

"Do you need to go?" Chloe sits down on the edge of the bed. I grab her hand.

"Chloe, I met Thomas in my dream, just now."

"Oh, really? What happened?"

"It was horrible. There was this gut-wrenching feeling of panic and dread. I was paralysed, freaked out. Then he appeared, and the panic faded away. He turned the light on, and we were in a cellar or something. Musty smelling and dank." The memories begin to fade. "He said I should find him in the waking world. That it would be easier."

"Easier than what?" She gets up and pours water into two tiny cups for tea.

"I don't know." I stand up and walk over to Chloe, throwing my arms around her. She squeezes back. "That's better." I feel her warmth calming my mind. I notice she's wearing my T-shirt.

"Find him in the waking world?" I look down at Chloe.

"Well, maybe we should go find him?"

"Yeah, but how?" I pause for a moment. "He said he lived here. I think he meant this hotel?"

"That's a start."

Dressed and sneaking down into the hotel reception, so we don't bump into the work team, I sent Dave a text. 'Cover for me, got stuff to sort.' He sent me back a thumbs up. My phone is riddled with questions from Rissa, but I'll have to come back to her.

Chloe walks up to the reception, I follow. She beams a grin at the lady behind the desk. "Hi, I was hoping you could help me?"

"Of course, Madam." The receptionist is the poster woman for friendly customer service.

"We're looking for an older man called Thomas, he works here at the hotel."

"Thomas the groundskeeper?"

Chloe flashes me a look, I shrug and nod. "Yes, that's him. Do you know if he's around?"

"I'm sure he is. He's always around somewhere." She smiles.

"That's great. Thank you. Do you know where we can find him?"

"Well, the groundskeeping lodge is at the rear of the property. If you go through the bar, there's a back door that leads across a courtyard, then go through the walled garden and the lodge is right there. You can't miss it."

"Excellent. Thank you so much."

I'm sure the receptionist is wondering why we want to see Thomas, but she doesn't mention it.

Chloe grabs my hand and leads the way.

As we get to the door of the bar, I stop. "Ron and all might still be in there. I don't want to get caught up with them now."

She nods and goes through, cautiously. She comes back. "Coast is clear." She sniggers. "This is fun, isn't it? All very clandestine."

"If you put it that way, I suppose. A bit of adventure."

"Come on." She pulls me through into the bar, and then to the back where the door is. Outside is a nice little courtyard. A beer garden. They probably do weddings and things here. We traverse the space into the walled garden through a rusty gate. There's a herb patch and a sprawl of nasturtiums growing all along the wall. Then at the back, the lodge as mentioned. You can't miss it.

"What now?" I turn to Chloe. Suddenly nervous.

"Well, I guess we knock at the door?" She laughs.

"But what do we say? Hello, are you Thomas, the weird bloke in our dreams?"

She chuckles. "We'll wing it." She steps forward and knocks on the door. My heart thuds in my chest.

Presently, the door creaks open and a dark figure appears in the doorway. He steps forward, and there's no doubt. He's Thomas, but not as imposing. An old gent, maybe in his late seventies, stooping with the gravity of ages. He fumbles for a pair of glasses which are on a chain around his neck. "Yes?"

Chloe takes the lead. "Hello, are you by any chance, Thomas?"

He looks up, now wearing his glasses. "Ah, yes. I have been expecting you." He grins. "Come, come. My old bones feel the cold."

He motions for us to follow him inside. I turn to Chloe. She shrugs and goes through the door.

Inside is a pleasant room, pot-plants everywhere, knick-knacks on every shelf. Figurines, carvings. A smell of oldness. The room is dim, but a fire blazes in a hearth. Thomas slowly creaks down into a beaten old armchair that sits in front of the fireplace. "Sit." He nods towards an equally beaten old couch opposite. We do as we're told.

"You've been expecting us?" Chloe asks. I'm glad she's taking the lead. I don't even know where to start. "Do you know who we are?"

"Yes, of course. You are the delightful Chloe, and your quiet friend here is Andrew… Andy." I look up. He seems like a friendly old chap. Not at all as I remember him from the dreams.

"You know what's going on?" Chloe asks.

"I do."

"Well, thank heaven someone does." I sit forward. "Thomas, would you mind telling us what on earth is going on with our dreams?"

He smiles. "To do that, I must tell you the history, first." He looks at us, wide-eyed. Oh, boy. I should tell Ron to come and listen… "In seven hundred years, you are the first to join me here."

I turn to Chloe. She looks at me with a shrug.

"Edmund, second Earl of Cornwall, an obnoxious man. He caused this." He spreads his arms out wide. "All this was his doing." He chuckles. "With my knowledge, of course." He shakes his head.

He looks over at us. "I should start at the beginning."

Thomas tells us the same tale as is printed in the hotel brochure. But he adds some nuance that Edmund was not a pleasant chap, and had a strong desire that he should live forever, never meeting death in battle or age. He commissioned the building on this site as a monastery, where he hoped eternal life would be granted him through the research that the monks would be working on. Thomas tells the tale as if he was there.

"My work was blasphemous. I should never have studied the stones." He shakes his head. "And now God has forever forsaken me."

"The stones?"

"You must know by now? The lodestones. The soul stones. They trap you inside their shell."

"I think that's the part we aren't clear on." Chloe offers a smile.

"Placed under the old abbey are twenty stones, sourced from all over the world as we knew it then… I spent my life collecting, honing, testing and refining. But eventually, I had a method." He breaks into a fit of coughing. I move to stand up and help, but he waves me down. He grabs a glass of water from a small table next to his chair and takes a sip. Pausing for a moment. "I am not as young as I once was." He grins. "Corporis libero animum." He chants the words and gazes up to the ceiling. "Free the soul from the body. It seemed obvious, then." He shakes his head, then looks at us directly. "Your souls are trapped inside the stones. As is mine. We share our dreams because we are together under the building. In a soul bank, if you will." His eyes wide.

"Sorry, our souls are trapped inside the stones?"

"I imagine it was the storms that did it, the dynge struck and caught you fast." He shrugs. "I'm uncertain. But here you are."

I glance at Chloe. "Thomas, may I ask, how old are you?"

He laughs. "This body, I guess around eighty, eighty-two."

"But you talk as if you were the one who laid these stones, seven-hundred years ago?"

"It was I, yes." He grins. "My soul has passed through many stones. Eighteen, I believe, at last count. Each stone a body I stole. Each life displaced into nothing."

"But, how?"

"The method is simple. A suitable donor is found and coaxed, by fair means or foul, to the room below. The night must be stormy, but this valley attracts lightning. We chose this location well. A rod of iron directs the strikes to the cellar. Then, we wait. I place the new stone on the donor's body as he lies incapacitated. The thunder takes care of the rest. I wake in my comfortable new body and carry on my long life. The previous stone is spent, the energy is gone."

"Incapacitated?" Chloe tilts her head.

"Yes, it used to be a messy business, much easier now I have the device."

"If I may summarise?" I stand up. "Are you saying that you are the same soul as built this 'soul bank' seven-hundred years ago?"

"I am."

"And you have passed your soul through eighteen different people's bodies over those years, by lightning strikes and magnetite stones?"

"Now you have it. Vitam aeternam. Eternal life." He taps his nose and looks up at me.

"But we didn't do any of that?" Chloe looks a bit worried now. I sit back down next to her.

"No, but you must have stayed here during a storm? They were doing some maintenance on the building recently. I'd wager that the electrical work has changed the direction of the flow. You were unlucky. Dragged into this realm to join me."

An awkward silence lingers for a moment while we all seem to soak in what he's said.

"What about Edmund?" I sit forward. "Wasn't this soul bank for him?"

"The fool died before I could carry out the process on his soul. He became ill and withered. I used the stones myself." He shrugs.

"Right." I ponder for a moment. "You say there were twenty stones, and you have passed through eighteen of them, leaving two for," I nod towards Chloe. "us?"

"Quite correct, child. We have come to the end of our adventure."

"What happens when we die, then?" Chloe seems scared.

"Your bodies will rot, your souls will stay in the stones, as long as they are protected. Each lodestone is paired with peridot to ward away evil."

"Oh." She leans forward. "I'm not sure if I like the idea of that."

"I don't doubt it. After this long, I despise the idea myself." He shrugs. "My soul is damned. I went against God's will."

"May I ask, Thomas, why did you do this?"

"I was young and foolish. It was a different time, then. I wished to prove my worth to the Earl." He steeples his fingers to his lips. "And since then, the world has changed. I knew the end was coming soon, and you two have merely shortened my time a little. No matter, I am ready to face God's wrath."

"Err, is there anything we can do?" I look around at Chloe. "To get our souls out of the bank and back into our bodies? Make a withdrawal, as it were?" She nods.

"There may be a way. I can't say for sure, but since you arrived by alternative means, perhaps your transfer wasn't complete." He ponders. "If only a fragment left your bodies, then perhaps, when released, the fragment would be drawn back."

"And how would we release them?"

Thomas stands up and walks to a huge old dresser that's in the corner of the room. He opens a drawer and rummages inside, pulling out a big hammer.

"We break the stones."

Thomas leads us through the Lodestone Bar, into a storeroom behind, then down a set of steps. The building rapidly changes from modern to ancient. The steps are worn smooth from ages. There's a musty smell, but also the stench of burning oil. He gets to the bottom and pauses. "Do not enter yet. I must deactivate the device."

He pulls a huge old key from his pocket; I recognise it from my dreams. The smooth metal key was in my gown. He turns it in the door and pushes it open. Inside is pitch dark, but he steps through. He fumbles on the wall and flicks on a switch. The room is bathed in light. Then he bends down, slowly, and picks up a long wooden stick from the floor and pokes it towards a plug that has an old twisted cable snaking off towards the back. He yanks out the plug and stands back up.

"It is safe to enter now."

"What was that?" I try to follow where the cable went, but it vanishes into the wall.

"It brings panic and fear. An infrasound generator." He chuckles. "One of my previous hosts had invented it by chance. It makes a low-frequency sound that vibrates the very cockles of the body, causing the sensations. Dread and terror keep any unwanted visitors out of the cellar. The burning of oil is a similar deterrent."

I look over at Thomas. "Is that what happened, in my dreams?" He nods. "Jesus."

"He had nothing to do with it." He grins. "Fear and terror are man-made emotions."

"Right."

"Deeper inside, we will find the stones." He moves onward.

The cellar narrows into a passage. Thomas flicks on more lights as we negotiate our way through the tunnel. It seems to lead on deep under the bowels of the hotel. Eventually, it expands into a circular room. Low ceilinged, I stoop down to enter. The only light is an ancient-looking rusty lamp on the floor. A cable runs along the wall to it, low to the ground.

"Here we are." Thomas chuckles. "The Soul Bank." He motions to the wall and spins slowly around. In the wall there are several small cubbyholes chipped into the stonework. In each one there is a green gemstone and a crumpled pile of dust and rock. On a small table near the lamp is a book. Ancient looking. Three words in elegant calligraphy on the cover. 'Corporis Libero Animum'.

"These are ours." He turns again and points to three holes in a triangle formation. The stones in these three are whole.

"Which is which?" I peer into the holes, using the torch on my phone to get a better look. A rough and dusty nook, a green gemstone and a dark grey lump of rock. The magnetite is filthy with specs of something covering the surface. Iron flecks, I guess. In the middle of the low ceiling, there's a spike protruding down, rusty and sharp. Dangerous looking. The muddy ceiling around it is blackened, and a complicated mess of copper pipes leads away from the centre to each of the nooks.

Thomas picks up one stone from the bottom left of the triangle. "This is me. I'm afraid I don't know which you reside in."

I turn to Chloe. She is quiet, looking around at the walls and their dusty nooks. She shivers. "Doesn't matter." She pulls one of the other stones out. "This is me. I reckon." She shrugs, then hands me the stone. "Smash it, Andy."

Thomas hands me the hammer. I was expecting it to be something ancient and worn, like the key, but this has a black plastic handle and a label on it that says £10.99, from B&Q.

"Are you sure this will work?" I turn to Thomas.

"No, not at all." He shrugs. "But it might."

"Great." I look at Chloe. "Yeah?"

"Do it." She shudders. "I don't want my soul trapped in here forever. It gives me the creeps."

"Okay, then. Cover your eyes." I put the stone down on the ground and kneel next to it. Raising the hammer and bringing it down with all my force. A crack forms in the stone. I do it again and again and the lodestone is turned to rubble. I pick up a small piece and rub my finger along the surface. The iron flecks rub loose.

I look up at Chloe. "Anything?"

She shrugs. "I don't feel different."

I stand and grab the other stone from the nook, repeating the process. Smashing it into the ground. I didn't feel anything either.

"Okay, now what?"

Thomas grips the stone in his hand. He bends down and hands it to me. "Break my stone, Andrew. My time has come."

"Are you sure? What will that do to you?"

"No, I am not sure. But I feel the need. Whatever happens, happens."

I look up at Chloe. She nods. "Fair enough." I lay Thomas' stone down and whack it with the hammer into smithereens.

"It is done. Now we can sleep, perchance to dream alone."

Thomas goes back to his lodge, after setting his infrasound trap again in the cellar and locking the door. He said we shouldn't have the dreams anymore if our soul fragments have left the stones now. His stone acted as a plug, stopping his soul from leaving the body it currently inhabits. Now he expects that when he passes, his soul will be judged and damned for all eternity for his crimes. I'm not convinced if I believe that, but to be honest, I'm not convinced I believe any of what happened this evening. Soul stones in a soul bank? Breaking them to release the souls back into our bodies? It seems ridiculous.

Chloe is quiet. I think she's a bit shaken by the experience.

I open the door to the back of the Lodestone Bar for her. "Well, that was smashing! Fancy a pint?"

Chapter Thirty-Eight

Bleary-eyed, I mash at the wake-up alarm ringing on my phone. I think I need a holiday soon. A proper one. Two weeks of peace and nothing. No agenda, no hangovers. My body is rebelling. I slept like the dead last night.

I feel a stroke at my back and jump. I turn around. Chloe, lying beside me, serene and messy with bed-head hair. She's beautiful. I lean down and peck her on the cheek.

"Work. Bleh."

I shuffle out of the bed, but Chloe grabs my arm.

"Did you dream?" She doesn't open her eyes, her face pressed into the pillow. The words come out squished. I chuckle.

"No. Not that I remember."

"Me either." She peeks open one eye. "Do you think it worked?"

"What, the stone smashing?" I raise an eyebrow.

"Yeah, all that malarkey." She sits up.

"I mean, I find it very hard to believe any of that stuff."

"Yeah, but…" She points to her head and then to me. "We were linked."

"You have a point." I hesitate. "Do you believe in souls and whatnot?"

"I don't know. Some days I do, some I don't."

"Today?"

"Today, I do."

I nod. "And Thomas. Do you think his soul is seven-hundred years old, or is he just a nutty old man who's read a load of history?"

"I believe him." Her black eyes are wide. "Andy, he knew us. He knew our dreams."

"Yeah." I rub my chin. "Just, when you've slept on something, you tend to find the logic." I chuckle. "I mean, stones in a soul bank? Does it make any rational sense?"

"Does anything?" She laughs. "We're monkeys that spin around a star on a ball of rock and water. What the hell do we know?"

"Fair enough." I smile. "You know what? Sod it. I'll believe Thomas. For want of any better explanation."

She smiles and squeezes my hand. "Yeah, me too."

"I have to shower and go to work." I make a sad face, but an idea pops into my head. "Care to join me? At least for that first thing…" I raise an eyebrow.

"Oooh, don't mind if I do." She sniggers, coy.

I grab a coffee and a piece of toast in the breakfast-room. I'm feeling a bit more alive, today. The solid night's sleep did me a world of good.

Ron is holding court at the breakfast table, telling a tale about a project he was working on years back for a customer in Ireland. I've heard this one many times. They wanted a server farm, on a farm, and the bloke's name was Mike Wazowski, like that green monster from the Pixar movie. Hilarious. I roll my eyes.

I sit down opposite Dave. "Morning, mate."

"Hey, you okay?"

"Yeah, not bad. Not bad at all." I smile. "Tell you all about it later."

"Someone's in a good mood, today." He grins. "Nice one, mate."

I am feeling good, now I think about it. Something is different. No headache. No dull thump, no gauze over the world. I'm not tired, not sluggish.

I suppose that means the smashing did work, and I have Thomas to thank for my new found vitality. Maybe we'll visit him later, see if anything has changed for him.

Ron notices me at the table. "Hey, morning, Andy."

"Ron. Lads." I nod to John and Sandra.

"Missed you again at dinner last night."

"Oh, yeah. Sorry."

"Andy had some family business to take care of." Dave butts in.

"Right." I clear my throat. "Don't worry, all taken care of, now." I flash a disarming smile. "Looking forward to dinner, tonight. Where are we going?"

Ron is appeased. "There's a great Indian round the corner if you like a bit of curry?"

"Sounds great." I rub my hands together. "Love a good curry."

"Champion."

. . .

Not to miss the thrilling events of today; the Eternitive Medi factory tour, Ron commands us to get up off our arses and head for the car-park. Dave rolls his eyes at me. I shake my head. Can't wait.

I let team Ron go out first and hold back with Dave for a moment.

"You dirty bastard. You got lucky with that Chloe lass. Tasty." He slaps me on the back.

"She's wonderful." I grin. "I mean, unbelievable."

Dave laughs. "Fair play to you, mate. You've earned a good'un."

"Cheers." I sigh. "Come on, then. Let's go look at a boring factory."

Outside, there's a bit of commotion. An ambulance and a police car, a few people standing around gawping. Ron included. We walk over to him.

"What happened?"

"Someone died." Ron looks sombre.

"Oh, no. A guest in the hotel?"

"No, they said it was the groundskeeper." Ron nods towards a group of the hotel staff. One lady, a chambermaid, I think, is crying.

"The groundskeeper, Thomas?" I feel a shiver run through me.

"Yeah, how did you know?"

"Err, I met him last evening. He knows… Knew all the

history of this hotel..." I tail off. Thomas died. Shit. All the blood freezes in my veins.

I pull out my phone and send a text message to Chloe. 'Thomas died! There's an ambulance outside here.'

The reply comes immediately. 'OMG!'

I notice the receptionist we spoke to yesterday among the group of staff. I wander over to her. "I'm so sorry for your loss."

She looks up. "Thank you. Thomas was part of the furniture here. He's been around for as long as anyone can remember. He'll be greatly missed."

"We met him yesterday evening. A lovely chap. A wealth of knowledge about the history of this place."

"Oh, yes. You found the lodge, okay, then?" Her reception instincts take over for a moment.

"Yes, thank you. He told us tales of Edmund and the monastery here. Fascinating stuff."

"He was a big history buff." She smiles. "Shocking." She shakes her head towards the ambulance.

"Do you know what happened, if you don't mind me asking?"

"Annabelle took him his breakfast this morning, but there was no answer." She motions to the lady who is still in tears, being consoled by another chambermaid. "Well, once they got the door open, they found him in his chair. He passed in his sleep, it seems."

"That's awful, I'm sorry."

She nods. "I only saw him last night. He seemed fine. He'd always wander by and say hello after he had his glass of red wine before bed." She stares at the back of the ambulance. "Goodbye, Thomas Bonham." She wipes away a tear.

.   .   .

"Andy!" Chloe comes over to me, grabbing my hand.

"Hey." I look down at her. Eyes moist. "It's okay. He passed in his sleep, they say."

"Poor man." She squeezes my hand tight.

I lead her away from the crowd, back inside the hotel. "Do you think it was the stone?"

"Well, it must be?"

"He was ancient, and he was coughing up a lung."

"Still. Bit of a coincidence, isn't it?"

"Yeah." I pause. "I feel horrible. I smashed the stone…"

"He told you to."

"I know, but…"

"He said it was his time." She flashes a sympathy smile. "He did live eighteen lives, over seven-hundred-years."

"Right, I guess he had a good innings."

"Now his soul really is free of the body. Corporis Libero Animum." She looks up to the heavens.

"True." I pause. "I wonder what's in that book?"

"Ancient spells, no doubt. Or his transference method, or the names of all the people he possessed. Who knows?"

"I bet it stays there, untouched until they eventually bulldoze this place. The soul bank and all."

Chloe nods, then wraps her arms around me, squeezing tight.

"Good thing I took these souvenirs, isn't it?" She lets go of me and fumbles in her jeans pocket, pulling something out.

"What's that?"

She opens her hand. I look down at two small, green peridot gems, and two broken lumps of magnetite. My mouth drops open. "You robbed the soul bank?"

"I believe these belong to us, Andy." She smiles and hands

me one pair. "Don't lose them. We may still be in there, somehow. Soul-stone mates."

"Thank you, Chloe." I smile and pocket the geology, then kiss her on the forehead.

I laugh. "It brings a whole new meaning to soul-sucking business trips, doesn't it?"

She rolls her eyes, but chuckles and squeezes me once again. "I'm glad we found each other, Andy."

"Me too!" I feel her body pressing against me, and her soul entwined with mine. "I guess dreams really can come true…"

Do me a favour?

I genuinely hope you enjoyed this story and I'd love to hear about it. So would other readers. I would be eternally grateful if you would leave a review on Amazon for me.

I don't have a big-name publisher or agent, or any marketing help. I rely on the kind words of readers to spread the word and help others find my books.

In a world of constant rating requests from everything you buy, I know it's a pain, but it does make a huge difference and it encourages me to keep writing.

Thanks!
Adam.

www.AdamEcclesBooks.com

Also by Adam Eccles

In order of publication:

Time, For a Change

The Twin Flame Game

Who Needs Love, Anyway?

Need a Little Time

facebook.com/AdamEcclesWrites

twitter.com/AdamEcclesBooks

Need a Little Time, unabridged audiobook.
Narrated by Mark Rice-Oxley

Get it now on Audible, Amazon or Apple Books.

Printed in Poland
by Amazon Fulfillment
Poland Sp. z o.o., Wrocław
09 August 2021

23495848-e8e2-4a9a-b050-53975f0ef57dR01